FIRST KISS

"What are ye doin' here?" a familiar voice asked.

Braden. She breathed out her held breath and a thousand excuses raced through her mind.

"I was . . . looking for you," she tried.

"Yer lyin'. Ye were stealin' my horse."

She gazed up at him, hoping her face was covered with a look of innocence. "You are the police. Have you not told us we must not steal?"

"Somehow I'm thinkin' those words were lost on ye, lass. Now tell me the truth."

Dancing Bird focused her attention on his hands gripping her arms and how wonderfully warm they were against her skin, how firm and tender they would be if clasped around her waist. His breath ruffled her hair, engulfing her with the smell of him, an unusual scent composed of horse, prairie grass, and something else . . . something sweet.

"You cannot prove I was trying to steal your horse. I have my own." She nodded toward Wind, now grazing peacefully a few feet away. "Sioux women do not steal horses."

"I'm thinkin' yer not like most Sioux women."

Dancing Bird moved toward him, emboldened by the power she sensed she held over him at this moment. She was lured to him by some invisible force against which she seemed to have no defense.

"What are ye about, lass?" he asked, alarm edging into his voice as she raised up on tiptoe. She stared into his eyes and saw first fear, then something else flit through his expression. Then, with her eyes closed, she touched her lips to his.

She was temptation personified in the silvery light. The toes of her soft moccasins nudged against the toes of his dusty black boots. She raised her face to look up at him and he knew, for the second time in his life, that he was lost.

Dear Romance Reader,

Last year, we launched the Ballad line with four new series, and each month we'll present both new and continuing stories set everywhere from medieval England to the American West—the kind of passionate, romantic stories you love best, written by the most gifted authors. At the back of each book, we'll tell you when you can find subsequent books in the series that have captured your heart.

This month a group of very talented authors introduces a breathtaking new series called *Hope Chest,* beginning with Pam McCutcheon's **Enchantment.** As five people unearth an abandoned hotel's century-old hope chest, each will be transported back to a bygone age—and transformed by the timeless power of true love. Kathryn Fox presents the next installment of *The Mounties.* In **The Second Vow,** a transplanted Irishman who must escort the Sioux across the U.S. border meets a woman whose loyalty to her people is as fierce as the desire that flames between them.

In the third book of the charming *Happily Ever After Co.* series, Kate Donovan offers **Meant To Be.** The free-spirited daughter of a successful matchmaker is determined to avoid matrimony—unless a rugged sharpshooter can persuade her that their union is no accident of fate . . . but a romance for all time. Finally, rising star Tammy Hilz concludes the passionate *Jewels of the Sea* trilogy with **Once an Angel,** as a woman sailing toward an uncertain future—and an arranged marriage—is taken captive by a man who will risk anything to save her from a life without the love only he can offer.

Kate Duffy
Editorial Director

The Mounties

THE SECOND VOW

Kathryn Fox

ZEBRA BOOKS
Kensington Publishing Corp.
http://www.zebrabooks.com

ZEBRA BOOKS are published by

Kensington Publishing Corp.
850 Third Avenue
New York, NY 10022

All Kensington titles, imprints, and distributed lines are available at special quantity discounts for bulk purchases for sales promotions, premiums, fund-raising, educational or institutional use.

Special book excerpts or customized printings can also be created to fit specific needs. For details, write or phone the office of the Kensington Special Sales Manager: Kensington Publishing Corp., 850 Third Avenue, New York, NY 10022. Attn: Special Sales Department, Phone: 1-800-221-2647.

First Printing: June 2001
10 9 8 7 6 5 4 3 2 1

Printed in the United States of America

One

Little Bighorn River
June 1876

The soft whirr of a dragonfly's wings fanned cool eddies of air across Dancing Bird's face as she lay on her stomach, watching the slender insect bob and dip above the surface of the stream. Cold spring runoff had swollen the Greasy Grass into a greedy beast that chewed at its banks and threw cold splatters of water at all who dared approach.

She rolled over onto her back in the soft grass and closed her eyes, letting the song of the stream wind through her thoughts. The leaves of the gnarled cotton-wood trees quivered in a warm, midday breeze, casting patterns of sun and shadow she could see even behind her closed eyelids. The united tribes of Cheyenne, Ogala, Brule, Sans Arc, Miniconjou, Blackfeet, and Hunkpapa, her own people, had defeated Three Stars and his blue soldiers in a battle that had pitted warriors against a force twice their size. So angered was he by Three Stars's unrelenting pursuit, Sitting Bull himself had ridden with his young men into battle despite arms tortured and swollen from his flesh sacrifices at his sun dance days before. Now, a thousand lodges camped together along the banks of the Greasy Grass at Sitting Bull's urging.

Many nights, Dancing Bird had crept away from her mother's sharp eye and lain on her stomach in the cool grass behind Sitting Bull's tipi, listening as the men discussed—and worried over—the blue soldiers who swarmed over their land and a man named Long Hair. Long Hair, so named for his long, golden-red hair, was crazy, they said, even for a *wašíchu.* He did things no good leader would do. He divided his men into small groups, left his extra ammunition far behind, attacked villages where women and children slept.

Three Stars they could figure out and understand. He was a warrior, albeit a relentless one, seemingly bent on the destruction of the Sioux. But he fought with bravery and fairness . . . and he had lost magnificently. A sense of unity and victory now swelled hearts long filled only with fear and sorrow.

Feasting and celebrating had continued long into the summer night. Stories of coups and bravery were told again and again by the light of roaring fires, related by warriors who had charged fearlessly into the midst of confused, frightened men in blue.

The white men wanted the wandering bands to leave their land and live on reservations, to give up hunting the buffalo and scratch at the hard ground to grow their food. Dancing Bird laughed, startling the curious dragonfly that had perched on the fringed top of her dress. What silly people these white men must be. *Wakantanka* provided the plants they needed, placing them in the right places for the People to find. How would they know what to plant and where to plant it?

The sharp whine of a bullet tore through the afternoon stillness and rained pieces of cottonwood leaves onto her face. Another split a limb off a tree overhead. She rolled to her side to avoid the plunging branch.

"They are charging, the chargers are coming! Where the tipi is, they say the chargers are coming!" Red Moon's soft alto voice carried through the now-shattered afternoon stillness, fulfilling her role as herald for the Hunkpapa circle of tipis.

Dancing Bird scrambled to her feet and ran toward the cluster of lodges that dotted the newly green river banks.

"Where are the soldiers?" she asked as she reached Red Moon and grabbed her elbow.

Red Moon dragged her gaze away from the southern horizon to stare down into Dancing Bird's face. Fear filled her rich brown eyes, which only last night had danced with laughter. "They are at the place where the burial tipi is, where the warriors fought Three Stars eight suns ago."

Dancing Bird quickly calculated the distance the huge group of people had traveled in the past eight days while herding horses and dragging travois laden with household goods. The soldiers would be in their village any moment now.

"It is fulfillment of Sitting Bull's sun dance vision. Soldiers upside down, falling into the village. They will all be killed." Red Moon's eyes had glazed over—whether from fear or some vision of her own, Dancing Bird couldn't decide.

Another bullet split a lodgepole on her right, zinging and whizzing its way through the trees. Tipis tumbled into pools of jutting poles and soft skins as women yanked the structures down, rolled them up and stowed them quickly on readied travois. Children cried and searched for their mothers in the carefully orchestrated retreat.

Dancing Bird dashed through the Hunkpapa camp, weaving her way toward her own family's lodge. Her mother, Moving-Robe-Woman, hurriedly rolled up the tipi's skin and her sister pulled down the long, bare saplings that served as lodgepoles.

"Where is Father?" Dancing Bird asked as she helped her mother fold the bulky cover and stuff it onto a travois already hitched to a black and white pony.

Her mother paused and glanced around. "He is there, taking women and children up to the trees." She pointed to the far southern edge of the camp. Dancing Bird looked where she gestured and recognized her father's shirt. His long dark hair was loose about his shoulders, a sign he'd only recently awakened. Seated behind him on the bare rump of his plunging black pony was a child, its tiny arms wound around his waist. He was hauling a woman up in front of him even as his pony lunged into a gallop for the tree line in the distance.

As she watched him ride away, Dancing Bird felt a surge of pride. Even though he'd seen almost forty summers, he could still beat the young men in the swing kicking game. But he was a man with responsibilities, and he would stay behind to defend the women and children while the young warriors rode out to meet the blue soldiers.

"Come and help your sister." Her mother gave a last yank on the carefully wrapped package that had been their home, her voice steady and even.

Absorbing her mother's calmness into her fluttering

heart, Dancing Bird tried to concentrate on packing the household belongings strewn about on the ground.

The cries started at the edge of camp nearest the river. Women screamed and children wailed. The sharp pop of rifles split the air and a thin cloud of dust crawled through the village, casting a pallor of disbelief over the growing confusion. Men ran to get their war paint, their clothes half on. Ponies ran free through the camp. Over the tumult rose the wail of death songs and the warbling tremolo the women made to encourage their men.

To the south, dusty images in blue bore down on the village. One Bull, Sitting Bull's nephew, and Gray Eagle, his brother-in-law, galloped through the fray, leading a string of horses recently reclaimed from the bench of flat land on the other side of the river. One Bull stopped at Sitting Bull's tipi and pulled his mother up behind him. Sitting Bull claimed another of the ponies and did the same for his mother and his other sister. Then the two galloped for the hills, leaving the rest of the family to pack belongings while they dropped the women in the safety of the trees and returned.

•

A child's scream tore through the stillness, ripping apart the peaceful Sunday afternoon. Another shriek joined the first, then pandemonium broke loose. Tiny feet pummeled the newly laid board floor and tiny bodies scattered in all directions. A huge bear lunged with a lumbering gait, one furry paw swiping at legs and feet as the pursued scrambled to safety atop tables and chairs.

Then one little boy climbed down to challenge the

beast. He moved with the silent steps of a warrior, the elaborate fringe on the hem of his shirt swinging against his legs with a soft whoosh. When he stood at the head of the great bear, he shoved aside shiny black bangs and stared at the beast with huge, brown eyes. With a trembling hand, he snatched away the bearskin and grinned down into Braden Flynn's dancing blue eyes.

"Uncle Braden, you ain't no bear." Relief quivered on the child's voice flavored with the throaty accent of the Blackfeet, but he quickly quelled any sign of fear on his face, turning proudly to his companions still perched high above the bear's reach. "See, I told you it wasn't a bear," he announced.

" 'Tis a brave lad ye are, Little Elk." Braden rolled from his position on all fours to sit cross-legged on the floor of the Fort McLeod dining hall. His assumed position was an invitation, and soon his lap was full of children. "But ye see, the bear is a crafty beast who thinks like a man and acts like an animal. He'll attack without warning." Quickly, Braden swept Little Elk's knees with a stiff upper arm and the child tumbled into his lap as well.

A chorus of giggles erupted as the children squirmed for position, then snatched off Braden's hat and took turns trying it on. They examined his bright brass buttons, rubbed the palms of their hands across the rough grain of his scarlet serge jacket, and examined his ears.

A broad, bulky shadow fell across their play and they all looked toward the open doorway.

"I've told you you need a few a'them yoreself." Maggie Fraser stood in the doorway, her protruding belly casting an odd shadow across the floor. Sunlight haloed her head, hiding her face, and for a fleeting moment,

Braden saw his Anise as she would have been had she lived to become his wife.

Maggie stepped into the mess hall and absently rubbed the tight skin of her abdomen. She and Colin were expecting their first child any minute, a fact that had Fort McLeod betting pools flush and eager. And as with every time he looked at Maggie and the happiness that shone from her face, Braden envied Constable Colin Fraser with every fiber of his being.

Colin Fraser had found the pot of gold at the end of the rainbow in his wife Maggie. The daughter of a whiskey trader, she had fallen in love with Constable Fraser, caused him to break every rule of the Mounted Police, then married him and was about to present him with a child. Was a man more blessed than he who found a woman to warm both his heart and his bed? And Colin Fraser had both, indeed.

"I happen to know"—Maggie rocked back on her heels, teetered for a moment but then regained her balance—"that there's a group of young ladies out for a walk on this fine afternoon," she finished with a twinkle in her eye. "And they ain't a-walkin' fer their health, if you get my meaning."

"Scat, ye rascals." Braden dismissed his lap full, then scrambled up off the floor, brushing dirt and dust from his buff-colored pants. Children scattered out the door in a dozen directions.

Maggie swiveled to watch them go, then turned back to Braden, a hand on her stomach. "Ain't it a wonder they can grow so fast?"

"Aye. 'Tis a wonder they live ta grow at all, the scamps. They'll wear a man out, they will."

"You ain't a-foolin' me, Braden Flynn. There ain't a man on this post loves young'uns more'n you."

"I love 'em as long as they're somebody else's." Braden swept his hat from the floor and plopped it onto his head.

"And I suppose this here bear pelt waddled over and draped itself across yore back?" She toed the discarded pelt and narrowed her beautiful blue eyes at him.

He'd once been in love with Maggie Hayes—before she was Colin's wife, of course. But she'd never known, never even suspected.

Then again, maybe love wasn't exactly the right word. He admired and respected her honesty and courage. He was infatuated with her kind heart and fascinated with the depth of her devotion to Colin. Maybe what he wanted was someone just like her.

Or did he want no one at all? Perhaps that was the source of his attraction to the rough and tumble mule-skinner who'd won his best friend's heart. Bestowing his affections on Maggie was safe. She'd never know, nor would Colin. Braden would never act on his feelings, and he could justify closing off his heart to all others.

The intensity of her gaze brought his attention back to her face. These days she reminded him of a cat who had the run of the storeroom—smug, happy, and the master of her domain. Colin looked pretty smug and happy himself these days. All in all, Braden figured he was possessed with a healthy dose of envy, yet reluctant to pursue the same situation for himself.

"It's time you found yoreself a wife, Braden," she said, her voice dropping to the low alto that meant she was deadly serious.

Maggie's simple solution to all the world's problems—love.

Enough love would cure anything.

But no amount of love would bring back Anise. Or his parents. Or half the population of Ireland.

He shook his head and Maggie stabbed him with a look that said he was in for an argument. Braden stepped forward and cupped her shoulders with his hands. "Marryin's just not in my plans, Maggie dear." He watched her face, hating to say the next words. He'd told Colin his plans only this morning. "Steven and I are transferring to Fort Walsh."

Huge tears welled up in her blue eyes. "Fort Walsh. Oh, Braden, why? Colin'll miss both of you." She blinked and the tears rolled down her cheeks. "You won't be here when the baby's born. Colin won't have nobody to brag to."

Always her thoughts were of Colin. "Sure, the whole post is bettin' on the date and time. He'll not be lackin' in braggin' rights."

"You know it won't be the same if yore not here."

Braden let his hands slide off her shoulders. "If yer an obedient lass, ye'll have the babe tonight so I can win."

She waddled away to the window with a rollicking gait that both amused him and made him marvel at the stamina of women. "Why Fort Walsh? Why now?" She looked out the window onto the porch, where burgeoning spring leaves made a leafy pattern of sun and shadow on the newly milled boards.

" 'Tis the place to be, lass. McLeod thinks the American Sioux may try and cross into Canada somewhere near there. The American government is grabbin' up their land, herdin' 'em like cattle onto reservations, expectin' 'em to stop bein' hunters and farm for a livin'."

"I feel sorry for 'em," Maggie said, still staring out at the sunny spring day. "I never did like nobody a-tellin' me what to do on my own place. Can't imagine they do, neither."

"Can't imagine they do."

Maggie turned to face him. "Promise me you and Steven'll come visit us."

Braden smiled, even though the tears glistening in her eyes stabbed a sharp blade into his heart. "I promise."

"And that you'll come see the baby."

"I'll come."

"He loves you like a brother, Braden. I reckon you already know that."

Braden nodded, remembering the almost indistinguishable disappointment that had flickered across Colin's face when Braden told him his plans. "I know."

Maggie hesitated as if she wanted to say more, then suddenly turned and shuffled away. Braden watched as she met Colin halfway across the parade ground that was surrounded by barracks and other cottonwood log structures. He leaned down and she stretched upwards until their noses almost touched. Words were exchanged. Then they both smiled, nodded, and parted without a touch. He couldn't have done that, Braden thought, couldn't have taken leave of the woman carrying his child, even for the briefest of times, without touching her. Life was too unpredictable and death too swift.

Colin stepped onto the porch and strode through the open mess hall door. He glanced at the discarded bear pelt and smiled. "Caught you, did she?"

Braden chuckled. "Aye, she did."

Colin laughed, and Braden envied the flash of tenderness that always passed through his friend's eyes at the mention of Maggie's name.

"McLeod wants to see you." Colin jerked his head in the direction of the assistant commissioner's office.

Together they crossed the broad parade ground and entered the low log dwelling James McLeod called both home and office. Beloved by his men, McLeod had built Fort McLeod on a gentle bend of the Old Man's River and established law in lawless western Canada in a few short months. Now he served as one of three justices of the peace for the Territories. Rumor had it he would be appointed commissioner when Commissioner George French resigned, but McLeod waved away all speculation and kept the daily activities focused on the huge territory for which he was responsible.

McLeod looked up from reading a three-month-old Ottawa paper. Dark-haired, he wore well the handsome ruggedness of his Scottish ancestry.

"Constable Fraser, any news yet?" he asked over slim, gold-rimmed glasses.

Colin smiled. "No, sir. Not yet."

McLeod picked up a piece of paper from his desk, squinted, and held it at arm's length. "Two-thirty tomorrow morning. That was my choice for the time of birth." He looked back at Colin. "See what you can do about it, hmm?"

"I'll speak with her, sir." Colin grinned.

"Although I'm sure my opinion will be of as little value to your wife as it ever was," McLeod said, a twinkle in his eye.

Braden hid a smile at the pink flush that crept up the back of Colin's neck. "I should be getting back to her," Colin said, and McLeod nodded his dismissal.

Maggie and Colin had caused McLeod more than one headache during their courtship, an event Braden knew their commander was not eager to repeat in light of the Force's negative stand on its members marrying.

McLeod shifted his gaze to Braden. "Constable Flynn. I'd like you to be prepared to leave for Fort Walsh as soon as possible. A detachment of men is coming from Swan Lake and going on to Fort Walsh. I'd like you to ride with them."

"Have ye heard any news regarding the American Sioux?"

McLeod shook his head. "No, only what I related to you before. I suspect they will cross into Canada somewhere along the Montana border, most likely near Fort Walsh. It is my belief they will ask for sanctuary here to escape Crook's forces, who are pursuing them as we speak."

"And are we goin' to give 'em that sanctuary, sir?" Braden asked.

"That is a matter to be determined if and when the request comes."

McLeod was never a man to tip his hand too early, and Braden knew that was all he would get out of his commander on the matter.

"And when do ye think the men from Swan Lake will arrive, sir?"

"They should be here tomorrow, Constable."

Braden felt the first wave of loss as McLeod's words sank into his thoughts. Fort McLeod had become the first home he'd known since leaving a devastated Ireland; he'd miss the familiarity he had grown to value.

"Inspector James Walsh is a fair man, capable of overcoming any problems thrown in front of him. I expect him to handle the Sioux situation in the manner most equitable to all involved." McLeod took off his glasses and folded his hands over the newspaper. "May I ask why you requested to be reassigned to Fort Walsh?"

Braden swallowed and wondered how much of that question McLeod's sharp perception had already answered. " 'Tis new adventures I'm seekin', new sights. Fort McLeod's become too civilized for a lusty Irishman like meself, sir."

McLeod harrumphed deep in his throat. "The Cypress Hills don't offer much in the way of entertainment, Constable Flynn, and the only new sight you're likely to see is a different herd of buffalo."

"I'm interested in the Sioux and their situation, sir. And if they should cross into Canada, to have somethin' to do with easin' their pain . . ." Braden let his words drift off, at a loss to explain the connection he felt for people hungry, pursued, and driven to desperation without delving into his own pain.

"Do you find you have something in common with their plight?" Again, McLeod's piercing stare read his thoughts.

"Yes, sir, I feel I do."

McLeod paused until Braden began to squirm under his assessment. "Fairness and consistency to all involved is of utmost importance here. If the Sioux ask for sanctuary, they are pitting us against the United

States government in granting that sanctuary. We must tread lightly on all egos."

Braden nodded.

McLeod drummed his fingers on his desk and studied the tiny black print of the newspaper without his glasses. "Make sure, Constable Flynn, that you're running toward something—and not away."

Dancing Bird peeped over the hill's edge at the cloud of dust that had marked the battle. She and the other women were hidden among rolling hills and thickets of trees from which they could observe the fighting. Men and horses appeared, then disappeared like specters in the billowing smoke. Rifles popped and warriors' shouts and tremolos filled the tree-dotted draw where yesterday meadowlarks had bid good-bye to the day.

Then the sounds of battle tapered off to an occasional shot from a carbine and an odd victory cry. Slowly the cloud of dust and smoke lifted and drifted to the south. Warriors wandered the battlefield leading their horses or else were on foot. Bodies clad in dusty blue littered the ground like dead branches culled from trees in a winter storm.

"The attack is over," Dancing Bird cried and lunged forward, eager to participate in the celebration of victory.

Her mother's firm grip stopped her. "Shush," her mother breathed out in disgust. "Stay here where you are safe. Let the men come home and bring their stories when they are ready."

Dancing Bird flopped down and propped her chin on her crossed hands. The boys had all the fun. She'd realized that at a young age when she'd found that scraping the huge buffalo hide across her lap was really work, while her brother was permitted to play war games undisturbed. From that moment on, the inequity had burned within her. She longed for the adventure her brother enjoyed, yearned for the freedom to ride off with friends and explore new places without a parent to remind her of the dos and don'ts of life.

But such a fine life was not to be. As a Lakota woman, she was expected to adhere to certain standards: to learn her chores well so she might be able to supply a family with the things they would need, to guard her reputation and never be caught in a compromising position with a young warrior. Such a mistake might prevent a good marriage. All these rules made her head ache.

"You wish you were out there, with the warriors?"

Her father's slim form slid into place beside her and he nodded in the direction of the battlefield. He, like many other men with families, had stayed behind to protect the women and children while the young, unmarried men fought the battle.

"Tonight they will bring home stories of coups and bravery and everyone will lean forward to listen when they speak at the celebration."

She turned to look into her father's face. In the last few years, silver strands had grown into his long black hair. *No doubt put there by me,* Dancing Bird thought with a flush of guilt. He was more attentive to her than any of the other fathers were to their daughters, nearly to the point of breaking tradition. Fathers usually left the raising of daughters to mothers and grandmothers, but as far back as she could remember, her father had been her playmate and her teacher. Perhaps she got her rebellious streak from him.

Dancing Bird smiled, and he smiled back. "The boys have all the fun," she said with as much annoyance as she could muster in the face of his sly smile.

"Not all the fun. Women have babies."

"Babies aren't fun. They're a lot of trouble and they smell and make noise."

He searched her face for a moment, then stood, grabbed her hand, and pulled her to her feet. "Come," he said and started forward, pulling her behind him.

"Wolf," her mother began, then bit back her words.

"She should know," he said simply. The rest of the explanation passed between them in the silent language of looks they often exchanged.

Wolf and Dancing Bird crossed the Greasy Grass and climbed the bluffs until they stood in the middle of the battlefield. Women and children moved among the dead, stripping them of weapons and clothes. The naked white bodies seemed to glow beneath the dying sun, and Dancing Bird tightened her grip on her father's hand.

They stepped over mangled bodies, both white and red, until they stood beside Sitting Bull. He stood without war paraphernalia or weapons, having given them to his nephew at the beginning of the battle. Looking slightly dazed, he watched the ransacking of the bodies.

"My vision said we were not to rob the bodies of the dead. The Lakota should not set their hearts or their heads on anything the *wašíchu* have or it will be a curse to them." He shook his head sadly and his shoulders sagged. "For their failure to obey, they will always want the *wašíchu's* belongings."

The words were more murmured than said, but as his voice filled her head and shut out the visions of battle, Dancing Bird suddenly wondered if what she'd over-heard behind the council tipi was true. Was she witness-ing the last peaceful days of her people?

Two

Pinto Horse Buttes, Canada
May, 1877

A wide path of crushed grass marred the newly greened carpet stretching across the flats into the deeply rolling hills beyond. Pinto Horse Buttes thrust west from the flank of Wood Mountain in the distance, its ragged outline barely visible in the early light. Dawn had tucked pockets of shadow between the hills and cast doubts on the men's feelings of security. Piles of horse dung and deep parallel gouges of travois gave away the presence of thousands of Sioux Indians.

Braden shifted in his saddle, suddenly aware of the openness of the terrain. A red and white pennon popped in an unexpected breeze, and Braden's horse flinched beneath him. He looked up at the pointed red and white fabric that flew from the long lance securely lodged in his stirrup and wondered at the wisdom of traipsing about the prairie so bright and bold in their scarlet jackets and fluttering banners. After all, the tracks before them surely belonged to the elusive people whose arrival had been much debated and anticipated by the Northwest Mounted Police.

Sitting Bull and his band.

Since the Battle of the Little Bighorn in June of last year, where General George Armstrong Custer and his Seventh Cavalry had been annihilated, the United States cavalry had been in pursuit of the last free bands of Sioux, intending to take them by force and drive them onto reservations. Knowing their days of freedom were nearing an end, the Sioux, Sans Arc, and some Cheyenne had begun a slow surge north, following the buffalo and dreams of a peaceful return to their nomadic life, with General "Three Stars" Crook nipping at their heels.

Fighting down a shiver of fear and excitement, Braden glanced at Superintendent James Walsh, commander of Fort Walsh, and wondered what he was thinking of the evidence before them.

A gentle man, reasonable and steady, Walsh was a lover of words and justice, and dedicated to the oath he had taken upon joining the Northwest Mounted Police. Appointed to lead Fort Walsh after the successful deployment of the Northwest Mounted Police in 1874, Walsh took his responsibilities for this potential crisis seriously and bravely. And like their beloved Commissioner James McLeod, Walsh's men would gleefully follow him through the gates of hell.

Braden turned his attention back to the wide swatch of churned turf before them. Here in the tortured grass was evidence of their destiny. Here were the footprints of the feared chief Sitting Bull. And now their tiny patrol of seven had been sent to intercept and confront thousands of terrified, hungry, desperate Sioux.

Walsh shifted in his saddle and scanned the horizon, his hand shielding his eyes against the early morning glare. Occasionally he bent his head to confer with Louis Levéille or Gabriel Solomon, the two scouts who had accompanied them.

"This is the trail of Sitting Bull's band," Walsh said, turning his horse around to face the rest of his patrol. "No doubt about it. They're headed for the border. We should catch up to them in a few hours, if Louis here is any judge of horse dung."

The famed scout smiled slowly and Braden had no doubt that he was indeed a fine judge of just about everything involving the prairies and Indians.

"Do you think there'll be a skirmish?" Constable Steven Gravel asked, voicing the question on every mind.

Braden glanced at Steven, a man who clowned freely for the Blackfoot children who sometimes accompanied their parents to Fort Walsh, yet yielded his smile rarely for anyone else.

"No," Walsh shot back, his voice carrying no hint of doubt. "We're here to explain the laws of Canada to them. I have every reason to believe Sitting Bull to be a reasonable man."

"Maybe somebody shoulda told that to Custer's men."

Braden chafed at the sarcasm that dripped off Marion Quinn's words. An able constable and mounted policeman, Quinn had a blind spot where the Sioux were concerned. Reared along the United States border, he saw his family killed in a Sioux uprising when he was a child. He'd never forgotten nor forgiven the incident, and Braden wondered if Walsh had assigned Quinn to this patrol for that reason.

"General Custer was a foolish man," Walsh countered

without hesitation. "He violated every rule of engagement and abandoned every concern for his men. He orchestrated his own defeat before Sitting Bull's warriors arrived."

Quinn seemed about to comment further, but he nodded briefly, then remained quiet.

They rode down from their vantage point on the hills and converged with the Indian trail. Hundreds of tracks of unshod ponies churned the dark soil, and anticipation prickled the hair on the back of Braden's neck. Sitting Bull's reputation was far flung and varied. Some said he was a kind but stern man, interested primarily in the welfare of his people. Others said he was the very devil himself, a coldhearted murderer who cut out and ate the hearts of his victims. Braden supposed the truth lay somewhere in between. He and the six other men now riding in Sitting Bull's tracks would be the first to know.

Ahead, Walsh held up a white-gloved hand. Braden's gaze flitted over the surrounding landscape as his heart thudded against his ribs. Several warriors stood on a hill ahead of them. Long hair flowed around their shoulders, teased into flight by a breeze.

"Keep moving," Walsh said softly. "Make no move toward your weapons. Understand?"

More figures appeared on the surrounding hills now beside and behind them as well as ahead. As they rode deeper into Indian Territory, the silhouettes of clutched rifles became evident. Despite their threatening appearance, not one Indian approached them. They seemed to be waiting for something.

The party entered a deep valley between two ridges of rolling hills, an excellent location for an ambush. Sentries watched them, weapons cradled in their arms.

Walsh and his men were close enough to discern that their clothes were tattered and dirty, their faces gaunt and drawn.

Braden glanced over at Quinn. His clenched jaw drew the skin taut across his face, and a fine sheen of sweat glistened there in the early morning light. His eyes darted from ridge to ridge, and his hand inched closer to the revolver on his hip.

"Quinn . . ." Braden began, his heart leaping into a staccato beat.

Quinn turned his face toward him, his eyes dark with fear.

"Walsh knows what he's doing."

Quinn nodded and eased his hand back to grip his reins.

They rode over a small hill at the head of the valley. When they reached the summit, Walsh suddenly drew his horse to a stop. Spread before them was an immense, deceptively peaceful Indian village. Conical tipis dotted the flats below them like small white mushrooms, and horses grazed peacefully along White Mud Creek.

Walsh led his party down the embankment to the very edge of the village, where he signaled a halt and dismounted.

"We'll set up camp here," he announced, brushing at a streak of mud on his buff-colored riding breeches.

"Is he out of his mind?" Quinn asked, his eyes wide. "Camping right on the doorstep of the filthy savages?"

" 'Tis all a game of bluff, Quinn," Braden replied, smiling. "Sure and I'd trust the Inspector to pull it off."

With the sun rising in the summer sky, they pitched their tents and set up tripods to cook their meal. A small knot of Sioux men gathered at the outskirts of the village, their heads leaned together in counsel. Then they began to walk toward the Mountie camp, shoulder to shoulder.

They halted only feet away from the still-saddled horses, their eyes darting left and right, as if expecting a mounted contingent to come pouring over the hill in the background. Walsh calmly finished tying down his tent, then straightened and gave his attention to the men standing before him.

"I am Spotted Eagle, chief of the Sans Arc." The leader spoke in his language and the translation was muttered softly by Louis Levéille. Spotted Eagle was a tall man with a square, handsome face. Long, dark braids encased in leather wraps fell over his shoulders and lay on his broad chest. Long fringe dangled from a finely beaded shirt crisscrossed with colorful patterns.

"You are in the village of Sitting Bull, chief of the Hunkpapas. Never has a white man dared come so close, as if Sitting Bull did not exist," spoke Spotted Eagle.

"I am Inspector James Walsh, messenger of the Great White Mother. She has sent me to speak with Sitting Bull."

Spotted Eagle looked over the rest of the patrol. Fear rolled off Quinn in waves, evident in the way his gaze darted from man to man. Steven looked mildly interested, and Solomon and Levéille looked alert, but at ease. Braden could feel sweat dampening the palms of his hands, but he was amazed that he felt no fear, only excitement and wonder. Here before them, speaking a beautiful language that seemed perfectly at home on the rolling prairies, were men to whom stories of untold horror had been attributed.

Walsh extended his hand. Spotted Eagle stared at his outstretched hand for a moment, then clasped it with his own. Walsh smiled. Spotted Eagle smiled back. When Walsh moved his arm up and down in a handshake, Spotted Eagle followed suit, his grin broadening.

Braden looked beyond the small group of leaders to the edge of the Sioux village, where a crowd had gathered to watch. A young woman stood apart from the others. Dark hair slid in a silky curtain across her shoulders as she bent to touch two dark-eyed children entwined around her legs. Her clothes were ragged and worn, but there was no defeat in her eyes. Instead, bold defiance, tempered by compassion, molded her expression and unexpectedly touched Braden's heart.

Their eyes met across the gathering of men, and an amazing intimacy flowed between them, two people separated by distance, language, and culture. Maintaining the contact between them, she lifted her chin a bit, and information passed between them on the conduit of human intuition. She was brave and loyal, as smart as she was beautiful—a woman well suited to life in a land that could be as brutal as it was desolate.

Seconds passed, and he knew he should look away for fear she would interpret his admiration as rudeness, but fascination held his gaze fixed. She seemed as reluctant as he to end the silent conversation between them.

"I would like to meet Sitting Bull as soon as possible and tell him the Great White Mother's message," Walsh was saying, causing Braden to break the connection and glance at Walsh. When he looked back, she smiled softly and turned away, one hand on the back of each of the children, who now trotted at her side.

She moved with a gentle sway of hips and fringe, pausing once to glance back over her shoulder and smile slyly as she tossed her dark hair over her shoulder. Braden sensed the movement was done deliberately for him. A dismissal? An invitation?

Suddenly, he yearned for the touch of a soft hand, a gentle caress to glide down his arm and slim fingers to entwine with his. The unannounced reappearance of desire disturbed him with both its timing and intensity. He hadn't thought of another woman in quite that way since Anise's death, years ago.

"You will see Sitting Bull now. He and his chiefs wait in his lodge." Spotted Eagle pivoted and pointed in the direction of the large village.

Walsh removed his long white gloves from where they were tucked into his belt and pulled them onto his hands. "Follow me," he said to his men, then stepped confidently into the Sioux's midst.

The curious crowd increased in number, and the Mounties had to push their way toward Sitting Bull's lodge, a huge, tattered tipi situated strategically at the end of the village. Hands reached out to touch the brilliant scarlet serge of their jackets. Quinn, safely sandwiched between Steven and Braden, recoiled in fear and disgust from the groping hands, but Braden enjoyed the contact, smiling down into broad faces that, except for color, could just as easily have been seen on some street in Ottawa, dressed in the latest English fashion.

He searched the crowd for another glimpse of the young woman and her two charges, but she was nowhere to be seen. Other young women met his gaze, but their eyes were fearful and timid, and their gazes quickly slid down to stare submissively at their feet.

A small cluster of men waited for them in front of the large tipi, their feathered headdresses cascading down their backs to tickle the ground in the gentle breeze. Like the others, their faces were gaunt and their eyes sunken in both fatigue and hunger. As Walsh extended his hand in greeting, distrust flickered through their expressions, but he held his hand steady and met their eyes evenly. One of the men stepped forward, his skin wrinkled and swarthy with age, and grasped Walsh's hand.

"That's old Sittin' Bull himself," Braden heard Levéille mutter to Walsh.

The feared chief narrowed wise eyes and swept Walsh from head to foot, pausing at the gleaming white helmet on his head. *Itúhu ska."*

"Seems you got a name, Cap'n," Levéille said. "White Forehead."

Walsh smiled, nodded, and reached up to touch the smooth helmet. "Seems the name fits, wouldn't you say?"

Sitting Bull watched Walsh's reaction carefully, then smiled and nodded. He stepped back, opened the tipi flap and waited expectantly.

Walsh ducked inside first and Braden followed, every sense alert. His eyes adjusted quickly to the darkness as the scent of grease and wood smoke assailed his nose. The outside size of the tipi hid a spacious interior, albeit bare compared to some of the Blackfoot lodges he'd been inside during his years at Fort McLeod.

No rolls of pelts lay stacked against the outside walls waiting to be traded. No bows and arrows or lances hung from the lodgepoles with rawhide thongs. No dried plants or herbs dangled from carefully fashioned baskets.

Two buffalo robes had been spread before a small firepit, but the rest of the floor was bare. Piles of freshly pulled grass completed the circle of offered seats. Sweetgrass smoldered on a small altar near the fire, its bittersweet odor quickly filling the tipi.

The Sioux leaders filed in quietly, sat down around the firepit, and turned expectant eyes toward Sitting Bull. Braden crossed his legs and sat down beside Steven, his heartbeat hammering in his ears.

"My people and I were once children of the Great White Mother," Sitting Bull began. "Many years ago a chief of the Great White Father told our forefathers that if we did not like the *wašíchu,* we could move north. We do not understand why the *Shaganosh* gave our land and us to the Americans." He fingered an elaborate medal hung around his neck on a rawhide thong.

As Levéille interpreted, Braden frowned, trying to make sense of the words.

"He's referring to the American War of 1812," Walsh said softly to his men. "They claim they were once British citizens who fought against the Americans. Nice strategy." Walsh smiled and nodded. "I recognize the medallion. It was issued by King George himself and meant to honor the Indians who fought on the British side."

"My people have suffered much hardship because of the blue soldiers. First, they want to take away *Paha Sapa* because of the yellow metal in the ground. Then they want the rest of our land to keep for themselves. They kill our buffalo and make our women cry."

As he listened to Levéille's soft voice translate,

Braden studied the faces of the men sitting across the firepit. They bore no expression, no hint as to their thoughts as Sitting Bull related in detail the injustices they'd suffered in the last year.

They'd been driven like horses after the death of Long Hair, he said, leaving them no time to hunt or prepare food, only time to flee for their lives. They'd faced a brutal winter with no food stores, no new tipis, no clothes. And still the blue soldiers had followed them into the wilderness. Those who had survived the winter had nearly drowned in a flood only a few weeks before. He raised his hands and motioned to the empty insides of the tipi. Those who had escaped had done so with only their lives.

As Sitting Bull spoke, pictures formed in Braden's mind, horrible haunting pictures of hunger and hopelessness. He closed his eyes against the invasion of images.

Women fleeing, long hair streaming out behind them.

Children crying, clinging to their mothers' leather skirts.

And suddenly, in his mind's eye, the brown grass of the prairies shifted to the lush green of Ireland. Soft leather dresses became colorful skirts and blouses. But the gaunt faces that told of horrible, nagging hunger remained the same and merged in his mind. The sharp edge of old pain resurfaced, cutting as deeply as it had the first time.

"The Great White Mother has instructed me to give you her laws," Walsh said when Sitting Bull finished. "If you obey her laws, you will be welcome here above the Medicine Line. If you break her laws, you will have to leave and return to the United States."

Levéille translated and Sitting Bull's face remained impassive. Walsh then recited the same conditions he'd given Four Horns, Black Moon, and Medicine Bear, all Sioux chiefs, when they, too, crossed into Canada weeks before.

No one would be permitted to steal from or lie about anyone.

No man, woman, or child must be injured.

Horses, oxen, wagons, lodges, guns, robes and other belongings would not be injured, destroyed or removed except by their owner.

No woman would be violated.

"We need ammunition for our rifles . . . so we can hunt the buffalo," Sitting Bull said hesitantly.

"We will give you ammunition to hunt, but you must not go back and use the ammunition against the Long Knives. If you do, you may not live on British soil and must return to your homes. Will you obey these laws the White Mother has laid down?" Walsh waited for Sitting Bull's answer.

Sitting Bull showed the first sign of emotion as he smiled, relief softening his eyes. "I buried my weapons before I came to the country of the White Mother. Before that, I was fighting only because I had to. My heart is good except when I face the Long Knives."

He went on to say that he held deep affection for the red-coated officers, that they were unlike any *wašichu* he had ever met, and that neither he nor his people would do wrong while in the country of the White Mother.

Spotted Eagle, the Sans Arc chief who had first approached them, watched Sitting Bull intently, almost protectively, as the chief poured out his gratitude. Then he leaned forward, revealing a wicked-looking three-bladed knife tucked into his waistband.

Braden swallowed and concentrated on the weight of his sidearm resting against his hip. The vulnerability of their situation suddenly became very real.

"You will spend the night here in our camp," Sitting Bull announced when every chief had in turn spoken his admiration for the Mounted Police. "We will share our food with you as you are sharing your land with us."

The chief swung his gaze to Braden. "You will sleep here, in my lodge with my family. My people will see that I trust the red-coated soldiers, and they will not be afraid."

His heart firmly lodged in his throat as Levéille struggled to relate the rapid flow of language. Braden glanced at Walsh, who nodded almost imperceptibly, never taking his eyes off the chief.

"I'd be honored to share yer home," Braden answered with as much conviction as he could muster.

The Sioux men glanced at each other, murmured softly, then looked at Braden.

"What tongue is this you speak?" Sitting Bull asked, and Levéille translated with a chuckle.

"Tell 'im it's the Irish tongue, spoken in the finest land on earth," Braden said, watching Sitting Bull's face as Levéille relayed the words.

After a studied pause, Sitting Bull spoke directly to Levéille in short, quick bursts. Levéille replied, then leaned toward Walsh. "He says he wants another interpreter."

"Who?" Walsh asked.

Levéille shrugged as a young boy sidled around the

edge of the tipi, then ducked outside. A few minutes later he returned, the young woman with the dark, haunting eyes close behind him.

Sitting Bull looked up at her with obvious affection and spoke softly. She gazed down at him until he finished, then she turned toward Braden.

"He says to tell you that I am his . . . *toján.*" She thought a second. "His . . . niece, Dancing Bird. He wants to know where is this Ire-land," she said in perfect but halting English.

Her voice was rich and smooth, like the finest Irish whiskey, sliding over his skin with the warmth and softness of a summer morning, playing his nerve endings like a well-kept fiddle.

"I'm waitin' to see you explain this one, Flynn," Levéille said with a smirk.

Again, his eyes met and held her gaze. She stared at him unblinkingly, and suddenly he wanted her to know something about him, to leave behind a small piece of himself in her thoughts. Braden paused, closed his eyes, and let his memories out for a run. When he reopened them, Sitting Bull studied his face, his brows pushed together in a frown.

Braden turned toward Dancing Bird, shutting out everyone else in the room, concentrating solely on her. A tiny scar marred the perfect line of her upper lip. One beautiful brown eye tilted at more of an angle than its twin. Beneath the smooth brown of her skin, a layer of freckles lay across the bridge of her nose. In an instant, all these things became indelible in his memory. He would never forget this moment.

"Ireland is a green land with fine, soft grass stretchin' as far as the eye can see. When I was a lad, I would sneak out of me house at night and run down to the great water that surrounds the land. The moon would rise out of the still, gray water and hang there, her belly full with light. And as she rose, she'd sprinkle the world with a magical, sparklin' powder."

Walsh and the other men stared at him as if he'd taken leave of his senses, and he wondered for a moment if he had as he watched her emotionless face stare back at him. Then she turned and translated for her uncle. The same language that Louis Levéille had ground out in guttural syllables flowed from her lips like a love song.

Sitting Bull listened, his eyes soft on her face. Then he spoke, and Dancing Bird turned back to Braden. "My uncle says that you must have loved Ire-land very much. He says that your words make him see your home. He hopes someday he will be able to tell you of *Paha Sapa,* his home."

The world narrowed and politics faded into obscurity as Braden looked into Sitting Bull's faded brown eyes. Here was a man who well understood the pain of losing all one had and all one was.

Dancing Bird turned to Walsh and the other Mounties. "My uncle wishes you to make your camp inside the Hunkpapa circle. My brother will take you there." She nodded toward the young man who'd fetched her earlier.

His eyes darting nervously from side to side, the young warrior held open the tipi flap and waited. The Mounties rose and stepped outside into the golden afternoon light.

"Constable Gravel, go with Solomon and Quinn and pack up our camp. Bring our belongings and horses where this young man indicates." The three men strode away as a curious crowd parted before them.

Sitting Bull and his chiefs emerged, making quite a performance of shaking the hands of the Mounted Police, and the tension on the faces of the surrounding people began to melt away.

" 'Tis a sly old fox, he is," Braden muttered beneath his breath.

"Our people have been afraid long enough," Dancing Bird said, her voice disturbingly close to his ear. She stood by his side, also watching her uncle.

"Where did ye learn to speak English?" Braden asked.

"Black shirts came to live among us when I was small. My father wanted me to learn their talk. He said that the *wašíchu's* talk would be important one day."

A tiny strand of hair blew across her face and teased her lips. How he longed to brush it away, a ready excuse to touch her skin.

"Your father was right."

"My father was always right." As she said the words, her eyes filled with pain. "The blue soldiers killed him after we killed Long Hair." She made the admission flatly and without emotion in her voice, as if such denial was long practiced.

"I'm sorry."

"I am sorry, too." She turned for a moment and gave him a twitch of a smile. "What is your name?"

"Braden Flynn," he answered, suddenly realizing he had not introduced himself.

"Bradenflynn? What does this name mean?"

"It's two names, a first name and a last name. Most people call me Braden."

She smiled then, completing the image of her he was committing to memory. Her mask of indifference disappeared and mischief danced in her eyes.

"I will see you again, Bradenflynn." Then, with a sassy sway of her hips, she disappeared into the crowd before Braden could form a response, dragging his heart behind her in the fine prairie dust.

Three

The soft glow of a full moon and the frantic wavering of a campfire blended to create an eerie reality as Braden sat cross-legged and watched the dancers before him. Heads dipped, bearing the weight of the immense carved buffalo masks, they stepped and leaped, acting out the details of a successful hunt and giving thanks for the souls of the great beasts they had killed.

The buffalo had led them north, they said, after the battle of the Little Big Horn. And in the days that followed, when Crook's army pursued them with a relentless vengeance, they had doggedly followed the great beast, putting their faith in the promises of Buffalo Woman and the distant Medicine Line, where they might find peace in the White Mother's Land.

The dancers, fervent in their tattered clothes and new masks, paused and pretended to kill a buffalo with powerful lances and spears. Then they mimicked the removal of the liver and offered their thanks to him who had provided the meal and the beast who had sacrificed his life so they might live.

Moved by the simplicity of the gratitude demonstrated, Braden swallowed a lump in his throat and looked to his right where Walsh sat with Levéille close at his side. Ever unflappable, Walsh watched the ceremony with aplomb, leaning slightly to the side to receive Levéille's constant stream of translation.

Across the fire, Steven sat amid a crowd of young and old, their entranced eyes watching him deftly roll three small blue balls between his fingers. Smiling his enigmatic smile, Steven made the balls alternately disappear and reappear, widening his smile when a chorus of delight rose above the beat of the drums.

Constable Quinn sat in his own pool of terror. An ancient, bent old woman seemed to have befriended him and sat at his elbow, carrying on a one-sided conversation in a high, screechy voice. And yet Quinn seemed to be in control of his fear, focusing his unseeing eyes on the flames and the dancers.

Braden searched the throbbing crowd for Dancing Bird without luck, and a thread of disappointment worked its way into the flood of emotions coursing through him, along with a sharp pinch of caution as his scarred heart protested even the hint of loving again.

"He's a wily old fox and not to be underestimated," Walsh said, his words muffled by the *thump thump* of drums. "I can see why the Americans fear him so. They're in danger of being badly outwitted."

Braden followed Walsh's nod to the other side of the fire, where Sitting Bull smiled up at one of his wives as she handed him a buffalo rib.

They'd all heard the horror stories that had drifted north of the border in the last few years, tales of massacres and bloody scalps hung from lodgepoles, of torture and inhuman acts. "Custer's Last Stand," as the battle had been glorified, had occupied the front pages of papers for months afterward, and now rumors of impending slaughter had surfaced again once the fact that Sioux were moving into Canada had become well known. But now, sitting among his family, laughing, with a child on his knee, Sitting Bull resembled nothing more than a father and husband pushed to the brink to defend his people and his home.

"What will become of 'em?" Braden asked, more to himself than to Walsh as he watched the ceremony and wondered how many more times they would have reason to celebrate.

"They'll live peacefully among us for a time. Then the dwindling food supply will drive them back home, where they'll live out their lives on reservations." Walsh stared across the fire, his gaze focused on something far away. "We're seeing the last days of a proud people, Constable Flynn. Mark this well, because one day your grandchildren will ask you of this, and only those of us who are here will be able to attest to the true nature of Sitting Bull's Sioux."

Walsh was a man of few words, and often those words waxed poetic, but tonight Braden knew his commander spoke the truth. They were the guardians of the truth. Even as the willow logs were consumed by the fire, so time was consuming the way of life of these simple people.

"Maybe they'll stay here on British soil," Braden offered hopefully, somehow anxious to grab at a shred of hope that these people's anguish had finally come to an end and that he might have some small part in ending their misery.

Walsh shook his head. "The buffalo are already dwindling in numbers. With this many additional people, the population will never feed them all. Soon the Blackfeet will begin to complain and tensions will rise." Walsh turned to face him. "That's where our job grows difficult. Perhaps if they stay long enough, the sting of the thrashing they gave the American troops will dull and when they return home they will be treated fairly and peacefully."

"So we're buyin' 'em time, you say."

Walsh smiled sadly. "That's right. That's the best we can do for them."

A sudden shadow fell across them, and they both started and looked up. Sitting Bull stood over them. He jerked his fingers, motioning Walsh to rise and follow him. Laying aside his helmet, Walsh stood and stepped into the churned path of the dancing circle.

Bending low, Sitting Bull carefully traced the steps of the dance, then straightened and looked at Walsh, the gnawed rib bone in his hand. Without a moment's hesitation, Walsh repeated the steps perfectly. The chief grinned broadly and clapped him on the back.

A soft swish of air fanned Braden's ear, and he was aware of her before she slipped into his line of vision. She flopped down in a cross-legged position and tucked an elaborate buckskin dress between her legs. Even as he turned toward her, intimately aware of the small distance between them, she pretended disinterest, her eyes fixed on Sitting Bull and Walsh, a smile playing across her lips. From the corner of his eye, Braden saw her glance at him, then back to the dancers now gathering around Walsh, touching and fingering his scarlet jacket.

He sensed she was curious about them all, but she was also cautious, well-schooled in the careful, calculating reasoning that characterized a people who both ruled and nurtured the vast prairies.

Before he could finish that thought, she turned toward him and ran a leisurely gaze over his face and body in a manner so intimate and bold that his every nerve ending sprang to life and his sleeping desire fully awakened. An urge long forgotten surged through him, shaking him. She affected him as no other woman had in a very long time. Guilt instantly dimmed his joy at discovering he was still a man.

"Why didn't you try the dance?" she asked, nodding toward Walsh and his group of tutors.

Braden struggled to put two words together in some semblance of intelligence. "I wasn't invited."

She shook her head slowly, sending her hair into a sensuous dance across her shoulders. "I cannot show you. Women are not permitted." She wrinkled her nose in a manner that said she was not pleased with this stipulation. "If you watch, you will learn. The steps aren't hard, especially if the men can learn." Mischief twinkled in the deep brown of her eyes.

An intriguing woman, he thought, stifling a laugh. "Your uncle is a good dancer," Braden offered, hoping to find out more about her.

"He has hunted *tatánka* and danced for many years."

"Do women go on the buffalo hunts?"

Her eyes brightened and she wiggled. "The whole village goes, even the children. It is easier to skin the *tatánka* when it falls than to carry the heavy body back to the village."

A practical woman, too. "Do you enjoy the hunts?"

She raised her shoulders, then lowered them in a childlike display of impatience as if she were thinking of the next hunt. "It is very exciting. The men ride along with the *tatánka*. There's much dust and noise. If we have ammunition, then we shoot them. If not, the men shoot bows and sometimes the bulls run away with arrows sticking out of them. They look like big porcupines."

Her laugh was smooth and deep and rippled across Braden's now sensitive body. "Sure and I'd like to see a buffalo hunt sometime."

"We'll go soon. I will ask my uncle if you can come."

"You speak my tongue very well."

She turned away and watched the dance, now in full swing again with Walsh standing on the sidelines, his arms folded across his chest. "I have not talked it in a long time, but Father Michaux said I should remember the white man's talk, so I did." She slid her hands underneath her, palms down, and continued to stare at the dancers, seemingly unaware of the feat she'd accomplished.

She had to concentrate all her efforts on watching the dancers to keep from staring at him outright. His hair was unlike any she'd seen on a man before, curling out from underneath his helmet, one strand falling across his forehead to tease his eyebrow.

And the color! She'd never seen hair the color of his. It was a soft red, the color of the soil in the sacred land of *Paha Sapa*.

The soft wisps invited her to touch them, so much so that she'd used an old childhood trick to keep her hands off things she shouldn't touch. She sat on them. The suggestion had been her mother's when she'd despaired of keeping Dancing Bird from poking her fingers into the bright orange flames of the campfire when she was small.

Temptation had been strong then, but it was almost irresistible now. The white hat on his head looked uncomfortable and heavy, and she longed to remove it and hear his sigh of relief. But she knew better. A good woman never let a man know she thought of him at all—at least not until he invited her to stand in the blanket.

She cut her eyes in his direction and bit her bottom lip. His shirt was the brightest red she'd ever seen, brighter than the sun's path just before nighttime, redder than fresh blood from a buffalo.

He was strong and would be a good provider. His shoulders were broad and his voice carried a confidence every young girl learned to listen for. The best warriors brought home the most horses, and his family would be well-to-do.

But there was something about him that reached out to her beyond the list of qualifications she'd been taught long ago. He was gentle and kind, a quality young brides hoped for but never mentioned. Such intimate knowledge was shared only between a man and a woman in the privacy of their lodge. Only there could a man reveal things to his woman he'd not dare reveal to a fellow warrior.

She curled her toes in her ragged moccasins. Such thoughts sent her heart racing. She was old enough this year to be courted and explore the mystery of man and woman. Her mother had explained in uncomfortable detail the act between a man and his wife that brought babies, but that held no fascination for her. She'd watched the village dogs couple all her life and the prospect of putting herself in that position was less than appealing. But the circumstances that made a man and woman decide to spend their lives with only each other . . . now *that* warranted investigation.

With sudden swiftness, she felt again the loss of her father. His gentle advice and tolerance would have been her guide throughout these swirling emotions. He would have been able to explain to her this breathlessness she now felt every time she looked at the man called Braden. Was this how a woman felt when sweet flute music filled her ears and a young man wrapped them both in a blanket? Should her head spin and her limbs feel heavy, or had she just eaten too much?

She looked for her mother, but she was not with the celebrating crowd. Moving-Robe-Woman rarely attended any celebration anymore, the death of her husband a constant, sharp pain. With his death and the deaths of so many others, Dancing Bird and her brother and sister had become part of her uncle's family, living in his crowded tipi until they could accumulate enough buffalo hides to make their own, and that was a far distant possibility. Her father had left no brothers to take her mother as a second wife. Her brother was too young to hunt a buffalo on his own. Perhaps she'd hunt for them herself. Surely her uncle would understand.

Braden ran a finger around the collar of his coat and his face was an odd shade of red. He must be hot in that shirt buttoned up to his chin on a night as balmy and warm as this one.

A warm breeze caught her hair and swirled it around her head, and improper thoughts of relieving him of that shirt entered her mind. She knew the breeze had been an evil spirit sent to lure her into trouble. She'd been thinking of swimming naked in a cold stream with the warm night air to dry her and only the light of the moon to give away her secret. She could almost feel the water slip over her body. Then, in her daydream, Braden would be there, as naked as she, his skin warm against hers, his eyes dark, demanding.

She snapped open her eyes and felt her cheeks flame. How long had she sat there with her eyes closed? Had he noticed? The visions had been so vivid, so real. She could almost feel his body pressing against the length of hers, his legs entwining with hers underneath the water, his hands finding the soft, sensitive areas of her body.

She glanced at him again. He squirmed beside her and a fine sheen of sweat glistened on his forehead.

"Take off your shirt," she said before she thought.

He swiveled his head around, amazement written across his face. "Beggin' yer pardon?"

Realizing her words had held a double meaning, she tried to hide her embarrassment. "You are hot?"

"Ah, ye want me to take off me coat." He shook his head with a smile. "Can't do. Walsh'd have me hide."

Confused, Dancing Bird pursued. "Does the . . . coat protect you from weapons?"

He laughed, a loud peal that seemed to come from his stomach. "No, lass. I'm on duty. I can't take off me uniform when I'm on duty."

"Duty?"

"Workin'."

Without understanding completely, Dancing Bird surmised that he wasn't supposed to take off his coat, that the presence of it meant something special. But instead of quenching her curiosity, his comments only fired her imagination. Did he have a woman of his own? A family? Remembering his beautiful, poignant words in the lodge, she wondered at his devotion to this land he called home.

"Tell me about Ire-land."

He threw her a quick, startled glance, accompanied by an upturned eyebrow, an expression that was already haunting her naughty thoughts, a disarming glance into his soul. He looked away to gaze into the fire, putting up an invisible wall between them.

"Ireland was my home," he said, a slight vulnerability in his voice that hadn't been there before. He paused and Dancing Bird waited, sensing he wanted to say more. "The grass is a deep emerald green, painted by the hand of God, it was. And when the moon is full, like it is tonight, she lays a fine and glitterin' path across the water right up to the shore."

His words were strange, but his meaning was clear. Ireland was a place he loved . . . and he hadn't wanted to leave. A thread of kinship grew between them. She hadn't wanted to leave the sanctity of *Paha Sapa,* with its shifting shades of red and its deep violet shadows.

"Why did you leave Ire-land?"

His expression hardened with such swiftness that Dancing Bird recoiled.

"We depended on a plant for most of our food, a plant that grew under the ground called a potato. A disease, a sickness killed most of the potatoes and we had nothin' to eat."

Dancing Bird watched him for a moment. "Is potato like the buffalo?"

He searched her face, his gaze warm against her cheeks. "Aye, 'tis, in a strange way. When it was gone, we starved."

Starvation was something she could understand . . .

and the sorrow it brought with it. She closed her eyes briefly, remembering frigid mornings digging in the forest for roots to feed her family when the blue soldiers had forced them to leave behind their winter stores of food.

"There are no buffalo in Ireland?"

His painful smile started an ache deep in her heart. "No, there are no buffalo in Ireland."

"If you had had buffalo, your people would not have starved. There are plenty of buffalo."

He turned his face away from her and stared into the fire. Wondering what she had done to offend him, she changed direction with her questions. "You left your Ireland like we left *Paha Sapa?"*

He paused in his answer, continuing to stare into the flames. Then he turned his face back toward hers. "I left Ireland when my mother and the woman I was to marry died. There was nothin' left for me there."

The sharpness of his tone, the look in his eye said he had not yet finished mourning for his mother and his woman, that their deaths were still a raw scar on his heart.

"No one made you leave?"

"No. At least there was that."

She reached out a tentative hand and touched the sleeve of his coat. Tiny rows of ridges on the fabric tickled the tips of her fingers. The material was soft, yet felt sturdy. Good choice, she calculated in her mind, trained to make the best use of what was available. But his warmth through the fabric shoved all reasonable thoughts away. His fingers flinched slightly as she pressed her hand against his arm in unspoken sympathy.

He quickly covered her hand with his before she

could jerk away, closing his fingers around hers in a way that evoked the evil spirit that had tried to possess her before. More unmaidenly thoughts cavorted into her mind. His hands were warm and hard, comfortingly rough and firm.

"Thank you," he said, giving her hand a gentle squeeze.

She allowed his hand to remain on hers, alarmed at her own boldness. To touch a Sioux man in this manner would surely set tongues to wagging and alarm parents. But as she looked down at the fine, dark hairs that covered his hand, she concentrated on enjoying the forbidden thrill that ran through her.

The drums ceased, and suddenly the night was filled with silence. Families got to their feet and moved away, herding sleepy children before them. The dancers removed their masks and laughed and talked as they stood in a tight knot before the dying campfire.

"It's time to sleep," Dancing Bird said, raising her eyes. Her heart was pounding against her temples as she allowed a fantasy to uncurl like smoke from an early morning fire.

Married men and women went to their lodges together and closed the flap behind them at the end of the day. From that point, she'd heard many different stories, some horrifying, spoken by wrinkled old women, some wonderful and worthy of whispering, told by brides still in the throes of young love.

But Dancing Bird wanted to know for herself the things that went on between men and women. What strange force made perfectly sensible girls want to leave the safety of their parents' protection and agree to scrape hides and bear children for a man? Were they suddenly possessed by an evil spirit, like the one that had teased her tonight? Were they following some commandment from *Wakantanka* she had yet to hear?

This madness seemed to start when a young warrior and a girl stood wrapped together in a blanket outside her parents' lodge. Whispered words and love songs on a carved flute contributed to this spell, and soon they were walking to their own lodge together. Once they went inside, from then on she seemed to surrender her life to this man. Did every man have this power over women? Did Braden?

He was watching her with kind blue eyes, eyes that rivaled the color of a summer sky and crinkled at the corners. A man who smiles often, her mother would say. But there was something else in his smile, something that made the pit of her stomach feel like it was about to drop out onto the ground.

He stood, then extended a hand to her. She looked at his upturned palm, then put her hand into his. He pulled her to her feet, inches away from his chest. Quickly she turned away and started for her uncle's lodge, aware that he followed closely behind her.

The sides of the tipi had been rolled halfway up to allow ventilation on the warm summer night. Some of her family were already stretched out on sleeping robes. Cousin Elk and her new husband slept in each other's arms. Her mother lay on her side facing away from the firepit, her sleeping robe now wide enough for only one.

"I've laid a robe for you," Dancing Bird said, pointing to a spot near the door. "It is cooler here."

Braden unbuttoned his coat and heaved a sigh of relief when the front finally sagged open. He pulled it off, revealing a soft, white shirt underneath, now soaked with sweat. Beneath the damp material, dark hair curled in an enticing shadow. "Where do you sleep?" he asked, shrugging off the red coat.

"Over there, by the back." She pointed across the tipi to where a rolled up grass mat waited.

He plopped down and pulled off his boots, seemingly oblivious to the people who walked past and looked down quizzically. He stretched out his legs and wiggled his toes. "Nothin' better that takin' off these infernal boots."

Dancing Bird laughed at the picture he made, sitting there like a child, admiring his own feet. He seemed not at all afraid, even though her uncle was much feared among the white men. Braden seemed completely unaffected as he smiled and nodded to her sleepy relatives.

Sitting Bull ducked to enter the tipi and glanced down at Braden, who regarded him with the same nonchalance as the others.

"You are satisfied with this robe?" her uncle asked, waving his hand to indicate the spot where Braden sat.

Dancing Bird repeated in English.

"Yes. Thank you."

"You are guest. Night breeze blows cooler near door before it passes over sleeping people." He indicated his prone family, some now snoring. Sitting Bull squatted down until he was on eye level with Braden. "I sleep over there near back. This is the place of chiefs, but I would rather sleep near the door." His eyes twinkled as he spoke in spotty English of defying tradition.

Startled, Braden caught the thread of humor and laughed. So the wily old fox knew some English after all. An effective method of eavesdropping.

"It is time to sleep," her uncle said, putting his hand on Dancing Bird's arm.

Obediently, she rose and went to her spot at the back of the lodge without a backward look.

Braden lay down on the soft robe and locked his fingers behind his head. Weariness set in quickly and he closed his eyes and listened to the sleepy village preparing for bed. Somewhere a baby cried and a mother's voice comforted him into a soft whimper. In the distance, a dog barked. Nearer, an *akicita's* horse pulled up mouthfuls of grass with quiet ripping noises. A policeman, or sentinel, the *akicita* would sleep lightly, constantly alert for trouble through the night, Levéille had said in his nearly constant stream of information since they'd arrived. But even as he tried to concentrate on replaying the day's events in his mind, Braden's thoughts returned to Dancing Bird and her mischievous smile.

He sat up and looked in the direction she'd indicated, but the rows of sleeping bodies concealed her. With a sigh, he lay back down and closed his eyes. And as the early morning hours descended and the moon hung low in the sky, the camp had the feel of his village in Ireland. Peace reigned and family necessities ruled.

His eyelids drooped, and he wondered if his companions were as at ease as he or were spending a fretful and anxious night. He doubted Walsh was disturbed. Unflappable was the term he'd apply to his commander, able to deal with whatever he was handed. Gravel, the same—a silent man who met life with a crooked smile and a sense of humor.

Quinn was a different matter. An adequate and capable officer, he nonetheless carried a deep, unhealed wound inside him that threatened to open up and ooze disaster at any time. Fate had been cruel to Quinn and had thrust him into the position of facing his worst nightmare on a daily basis. Maybe there was a reason for everything.

Soft snores punctuated the quiet of the night. The tipi was packed with bodies, a mixture of families who no longer had homes of their own. But they'd banded together, and no one seemed to be complaining, at least not out loud. And somewhere near the back was Dancing Bird. She flitted through his thoughts like the image her name evoked.

She was a rebel and probably gave her parents nightmares with her questions and curiosity. There was something wistful and sorrowful about her, but also strong and resilient. As sleep claimed him, he dreamed of her standing on the prairie, the sun shooting blue highlights into her dark hair. She was smiling at him, holding out her hand. For the first time in years, his heart lifted and hope crept back in.

Four

Pounding hooves and excited voices filtered through pleasant dreams of warm hands and sweet lips. Braden turned over and then swiped at his face, where the stiff buffalo fur tickled his nose. Instantly alert, he sat up and reached for his boots. From beneath the edge of the rolled-up tipi, he saw a party of warriors ride into the village leading five horses.

Early dawn light gilded everything with a gentle golden glow, but not even the dawn could soften the features of the man who led the group. Long dark hair streamed over his shoulders, checked only by the three coup feathers secured at the crown of his head. Angular and pitted with scars, his face was gaunt and severe.

Braden yanked on his boots and shrugged into his jacket as he hurried from the tipi, stumbling as people rushed past him.

Walsh was already in the front of the crowd, lending his calm demeanor to an uncertain situation. The women's warbles of greeting reverberated off the tipis and the hills around the village. Scouts Gabriel Solomon and Levéille were already at Walsh's side when Braden joined them.

"Them's South Assiniboins," Solomon said softly to Walsh. "Looks to be White Dog."

Walsh glanced quickly at Levéille who nodded affirmation of the other scout's words.

"Sitting Bull offered him 100 horses last year to help him fight the Americans. He weren't of a mind to fight 'em then. Can't say about now," he finished solemnly.

Women and men crowded around the well-fed horses, who obviously had not suffered a prairie winter on their own. Most likely they were stolen, Braden thought, an edge of alarm gathering within him.

Solomon stepped forward and ran a hand down the nearest horse's neck while the three warriors jumped down from their mounts, casting suspicious glances at the men in red.

Sitting Bull pushed his way to the front of the crowd. *"Hau,"* he greeted the men. They replied in kind.

As they spoke, Solomon worked his way through the group of five horses, running his hands down their necks and out across their withers. Finally, he ambled back to Walsh's side.

"Three of them five's stolen. I seen 'em with Father De Corby last month."

Walsh's face remained impassive. "Are you sure?"

"Yep. Sure as I can be. That black there's got a knot on her foreleg. Me and the Father talked about it."

"What do you think, Louis?" Walsh asked the other scout and Levéille, also, examined the horses.

"Yep," he said. "They're the Father's. Look to be in too good a shape to be Indian ponies."

Walsh watched the crowd mill around the newcomers while Levéille translated the numerous murmured comments that swirled around them.

"Constable Flynn, confront White Dog about these horses. If they are stolen, arrest him. Take Constable Gravel and Constable Quinn with you," Walsh instructed.

Braden hid his surprise and surveyed the crowd of warriors before him. He pulled on his long white gloves and adjusted his white helmet. From the corner of his eye he saw Dancing Bird watching from the doorway of Sitting Bull's tipi. The same people who last night had offered them hospitality could now murder them, and no one would be the wiser for weeks. "Constable Gravel, Constable Quinn. Let's go."

Sensing the other two men at his elbows, Braden moved into the crowd that parted to allow him to work his way to White Dog. Voices hushed as they passed by. When he met the warrior face-to-face, the village was quiet. White Dog raised his chin as if expecting a confrontation.

"I am Constable Flynn of the Northwest Mounted Police. You are now in the land of the Great White Mother, and you must obey her laws. Sitting Bull and all his people have agreed to obey these laws, and I expect you to do the same."

Louis Levéille murmured a translation softly at his side, but White Dog never took his eyes off Braden's face.

When Levéille finished, White Dog grinned and laughed, looking out over the gathered crowd. "I am White Dog, and I answer to no white man's law. Is that not what we have fought and died for?"

The crowd was strangely quiet and a moment of indecision passed through his dark eyes before he returned his gaze to Braden's face.

"These horses are stolen from Father De Corby, and I demand that you release them to me. If you do not, I will arrest you."

Braden's heart fluttered in his throat as the crowd's voice swelled into one loud grumble. He felt Steven's arm against his elbow and knew that his friend was watching his back, but Quinn shrank back. Turning his head slightly, Braden saw fear and budding panic in Quinn's eyes. If they had to fight, he and Steven would be hard pressed to stand their ground alone.

"These horses are mine. I will not give them up." White Dog smiled. "No white man will take away my freedom or arrest me." Confidence dripped off his words, and his intentions were clear as he threw a gaze over the heads of the assembled crowd he counted as allies.

The crowd's voice swelled again. Braden glanced down at Levéille. He frowned, trying to catch the words to tell if the crowd was merely surprised or pledging their support for White Dog.

"The white man is stupid and slow. I crush him under my feet like the ants." White Dog ground a moccasined foot into the fine, dusty soil.

Braden felt his temper rising. He'd met many a personality like this in a pub on a Saturday night. He'd formed a response to shoot back when he felt a hand on his shoulder. Walsh stepped into his line of vision and met White Dog's eyes.

"White Dog, you say you will neither be arrested nor surrender these horses?" Walsh moved his hand from Braden's shoulder to White Dog's. "I arrest you for theft."

The camp fell silent, then exploded in a volley of

voices. Gabriel Solomon had disappeared and now stood at the rear of the crowd with the horses in hand.

"Take their guns and knives," Walsh said softly to Braden, who stepped forward and wrenched White Dog's carbine from his hand. Before they could react, he'd taken the rifles from the other two Indians, and Steven had relieved them of their knives.

White Dog's face was blank and his jaw hung slack.

"Constable Gravel, bring me those leg irons from my horse," Walsh ordered, without looking away from White Dog's face.

Steven returned in a few minutes, the iron cuffs dangling from his hands. Walsh took them and held them in front of White Dog's face. "White Dog, tell me where you got those horses, how you got them, and what you intend doing with them, or I shall put these irons upon you and take you to Fort Walsh."

White Dog's eyes flitted from Walsh's face to the evil-looking irons to the crowd that now numbered in the hundreds. But the Sioux showed no signs of coming to his defense. They merely gathered in curiosity.

He paused a moment, then said, "I was riding through the hills there, toward the rising sun. I saw these horses wandering and did not know they belonged to anyone, so I took them." Although his words seemed conciliatory, his eyes were hard and calculating. "It is our way to take horses without owners and return them only if they are asked for. I did not know this was wrong in the Great White Mother's land." His tone was now almost condescending.

Walsh listened to Levéille translate and waited before answering, allowing White Dog to doubt his intentions. "You may go, but you are not to molest any horse or property as long as you are north of the Medicine Line in the Great White Mother's land."

White Dog nodded stiffly and turned to go, muttering under his breath. *"Ake wancinyankin."*

Levéille quickly translated: *I will see you again.* The threat was clear.

"Halt," Walsh ordered.

White Dog paused and looked over his shoulder as Levéille barked the command.

"Repeat what you just said. I want to understand your intentions."

White Dog refused, but he didn't move to leave either.

Walsh narrowed his eyes. "Withdraw those words you just said," he shouted, and Braden flinched. "If you do not, I shall take you to Fort Walsh."

White Dog cast one last glance to the assembled Sioux, but their faces were mixtures of amazement and amusement. Obviously, they were enjoying the confrontation and attaching no threat to themselves to the incident.

"I did not mean to threaten," White Dog muttered darkly, then turned and plunged through the crowd, followed by his two companions.

Braden released his held breath and only then allowed himself to glance at Steven, who lifted a corner of his mouth in a shaky smile. Finally he looked at the doorway of Sitting Bull's lodge. It was empty.

The Sioux parted to allow the Mounted Police an avenue back to their horses. Although comments swirled around them, Levéille did not translate, and the tone of the voices indicated amazement, but no threat.

When they reached their mounts, Sitting Bull waited for them, one hand on Walsh's horse's withers. "He is young and eager to prove himself," he said, idly patting the horse. "He has not seen what you and I have seen, my friend. He does not yet appreciate a peaceful night's sleep. One day he will."

Levéille translated and Walsh nodded in agreement, then reached out a hand. Sitting Bull took it eagerly, and the two men shook hands.

Braden mounted his horse, realizing only now as his heart slowed that he might never again see Dancing Bird. She and her people could fade back into the folds and valleys of the Cypress Hills or cross back over the border as easily and as silently as they had come. A sense of sharp loss welled up in him, and he scanned the crowd again. Then he saw her standing with her mother, the morning sun glancing off her hair, one hand shielding her eyes.

As the patrol turned to leave, she lifted a hand in hesitant recognition. Braden touched the front of his helmet in response and turned his horse away from the village, focusing his attention on the green hills beyond. Tomorrow, other duties would claim his attention and other responsibilities would occupy his time. But for now, as each stride took him farther away, he would think of crackling fires and mischievous eyes.

Rivulets of sweat rolled down Dancing Bird's face, and she swatted at an annoying fly. Repositioning her knees on a grass mat, she stretched across the staked-out buffalo hide and scraped at another layer of flesh with the scraping tool. Pink tissue rolled up from the underside of the hide, leaving a smooth white path behind. Smiling despite her discomfort, Dancing Bird was proud of her hide preparation skills, even though there were a hundred other things she'd rather be doing.

In the skirt of trees that hugged the river's path, birds squawked at one another, and she wondered at the source of their distress. Was it another bird? Some other creature?

She wouldn't find out today, she reminded herself. This hide had been a gift, and it was a start toward their own home. How wonderful it would be when she and her mother, sister, and brother had their own tipi again, with room and privacy. But that dream was ten buffalo hides away and hours of muscle-torturing scraping.

She sighed and called to mind her father's voice cautioning her to be patient, to finish what she started, and warning against all the others things her impetuous nature urged her to do. A wave of loss swept over her and she sat back on her heels. She missed him deeply. He understood her so well, much better than her mother did.

He understood each day brought endless possibilities for adventure and many things that must be explored and explained. He understood that scraping hides could wait and gathering wood could take hours if the gatherer fully examined every foot of the wood's source.

Not so with her mother. She knew only that each of her daughters must learn good wifely skills so they might marry a man of property and live comfortably. Their stitches must be even, their hides scraped to a perfect uniform thickness, their pemmican delicious and perfectly blended.

Dancing Bird admitted her mother was partly right. A woman's skills were about all she had, save a pretty face, to guarantee herself a home, but all this preparation was endlessly boring. Besides, she was never going to marry, she reassured herself. She would live in her own tipi made from hides she took herself. She would steal her own horses and kill her own food and answer to no one.

She sighed again and returned to scraping the hide. All that was in the future and made a nice daydream, but this stinking, greasy buffalo skin was her present.

"Mother said for me to come and see if you were done yet."

Dancing Bird squinted up at her sister, Walks Lightly. "No, not yet."

"She said to tell you if you were off chasing a bird or an animal that you should be half done with that by evening."

Walks Lightly smiled angelically, a subtle reminder that Dancing Bird, not she, was scraping the hide in the hot summer sun. An accomplished seamstress and hide preparer, Walks Lightly was looking for a husband and finding many suitors, but she was choosy. She was beautiful and could have her choice of any she desired.

"Mother says if you're not at least half done, you can't go riding this evening."

Dancing Bird looked up again. How many of these demands were Mother's and how many were Walks Lightly's? Older by a year, Walks Lightly had been born a pretty baby, grew into an adorable toddler, and then into a beautiful and graceful woman. She had always been the day to Dancing Bird's night, two sisters who were complete opposites. Dancing Bird felt she had come into the world with Walks Lightly's accomplishments ringing in her ears.

Where she spent her days figuring ways to escape her mother's vigilant eye, Walks Lightly followed their mother like a puppy. Where Dancing Bird's quills were stitched a little crooked, Walks Lightly's were perfectly straight and stitched into imaginative patterns. In comparison, Dancing Bird always felt she came up lacking. But as long as her father had lived, she'd had his heart like no other child. Not even her brother, Little Bear, had known the man who sired them the way she knew him. And her sister had never forgiven her for that.

"You've left a string of tissue there." Walks Lightly pointed to the offending glob of fat with a delicate hand. "If you leave it, it will get hard and will tear the hide when you take it off later."

Dancing Bird made a vicious swipe at the bit of flesh and heard her sister draw in a sharp breath.

"If you ruin that hide, Mother will be angry. She should have let me do it."

"I wish she had. Then you'd be out here in the heat and flies," Dancing Bird growled as she flicked the bit off her scraping blade.

"You needed the practice. How will you catch a husband if you can't scrape a hide properly?" Walks Lightly crossed her arms over her perfectly quilled chest and tilted her chin up in superiority.

"I don't want a husband. Why would I want anybody else to order me around when I have you?"

Walks Lightly didn't flinch at the carefully aimed barb. "You might not have me for long. Standing Elk will be outside our uncle's tipi tonight waiting for me to stand in the blanket with him. I heard he has carved a new flute just to play for me." The pride in her voice was undisguised, and Dancing Bird felt a stab of guilt at the envy that rippled through her.

She moved to a new spot on the hide and began to scrape again. "I hope he brings many horses to offer for you. Maybe I can trade some of them for more buffalo hides."

"Does everything have trading value, sister? Can't you see that flute music and warm nights and beautiful sewing can bring pleasure, too?"

Walks Lightly's words stung, for she'd often thought the same things herself, but her brother was interested in establishing himself as a warrior and Walks Lightly was interested in courting. That left her to trade and hunt and try to feed their family. Her mother hadn't been interested in much of anything since her father's death. Dancing Bird didn't see that she had much choice in the matter. In fact, in the months since his death, she imagined he looked down from the stars, happy that she was caring for his family so well.

"Dancing Bird!" Walks Lightly was calling her name. "Are you listening to me? You're going to scrape a hole in that hide."

Dancing Bird looked down and could see that she'd scraped an area much too thin while her mind wandered.

"I'll sew a patch over it," she muttered.

"It'll let in rain. You should save that one for the dew cloth."

Wishing she'd thought of that herself, she murmured, "Yes, the dew cloth."

"You have to help with the chores," Walks Lightly nagged as she turned to walk back to the village.

"I'll be there soon," Dancing Bird called, grateful to

again be alone with the waving grass and the afternoon breeze.

As the heat climbed, the flies grew in number. To keep her mind off their annoying presence, Dancing Bird thought of her nighttime ride, one of her mother's few concessions. During the day, there were chores and sewing and gathering food to be done. But after the evening meal, she figured everyone in the tipi was grateful for one less body heating up the crowded interior.

Her uncle, Sitting Bull, had given her a pony, a little black mare with a white star she had named Wind. As the greens and gold of day gave way to the blue and silver of night and the warbling of birds bowed to insect songs, she and Wind would explore their new home by starlight. Here, among the creatures of the night, she was finally alone with the thoughts that clogged her head by day. Here she could dream and plan without the pressing need of supplying the next meal.

The approach of evening brought boiling black clouds that choked out the setting sun. Swords of lightning stabbed the ground and gouged great holes that the shaman would examine tomorrow. The sides of the tipi were rolled down quickly to shield their meager possessions from the pounding rain, and as she helped with supper preparations, Dancing Bird despaired at missing her ride.

But as quickly as it had appeared, the storm moved across the sky to the east, perhaps to lie in wait for the rising sun tomorrow morning. The storm did not yield the sky easily, trailing skirts of clouds that glowed with lightning. Yet in its reluctant wake, it spread a brilliant field of stars, pinpoints in a sky washed clean. Knowing her mother would hedge on letting her go with such a monster stalking the heavens, Dancing Bird slipped away while her female relatives were moving wet belongings outside to dry and raising the tipi sides.

She galloped away from the village with a sense of guilt and exhilaration and headed into the bosomy rolls of the Cypress Hills, remembering a place she had seen from a distance and wanted to explore further.

She reached a steep bank, a severe change from the surrounding landscape. A wooden structure jutted out of the hillside, as if the hill had swallowed it, leaving part if it hanging out. It was a white man's lodge made of uneven logs. She'd skirted it briefly for the last two nights, watching from a distance, wondering if she dared venture closer. Perhaps the men who built it had left behind something interesting.

But tonight, yellow light spilled from square holes in the lodge, making a warped pattern on the dirt. Windows, the white men called them, she remembered from a trading trip inside one of the white men's forts. They were made of a clear substance that let in the sunlight and opened the inside to full view by any who wanted to look. *Foolish wašíchu,* she thought again and edged closer, curiosity overcoming her caution.

A figure moved past one of the windows. Her heart began to pound. She slipped silently off her horse's back and dropped the reins on the ground. The long fringe on the bottom of her dress swished softly as she crept forward, her moon-cast shadow at her side.

A slick, fat horse cropped grass at the foot of a post where its reins were loosely looped. If she could steal it, she'd be thought of as a brave warrior. Maybe such adulation could buy her even more freedom—or more buffalo hides.

Turning over the possibilities in her mind, she moved closer, cloaked by the moonless night. When she was just outside the door, she whispered softly to the horse, words used by the warriors, a spell thought to make horses willing to follow their captors. The beast made no noise, only eyed her calmly as she took the rope to his halter in her hand.

She quickly untied the knot, then paused. Inside the structure was a table and chairs like the ones she and her people had often seen abandoned alongside the deep trenches gouged in the prairie. A cheery red and white cloth covered the table and a large bear pelt lay on the floor. A fire burned in a fireplace made of river stones and a black pot hung over the flames.

She pressed closer, enchanted by the strange objects inside. A gun lay across the table, a carbine like the warriors carried. With such a weapon she could kill many buffalo and have many hides.

Before she could formulate a plan, a hand clamped down on her shoulder, the fingers digging in like an eagle's talons. She whirled and clawed at her attacker, flinging herself against him, fighting in a flurry of hands and fists.

Hard hands clamped her arms to her body, rendering her helpless against him. But he made no move to harm her, only stood very quietly, his face hidden in the dark. She could not reach the knife tucked into her belt, and every time she lifted a foot to kick him, he tilted her off balance.

"What are ye doin' here?" a familiar voice asked, cutting through her anger.

Braden. A thousand excuses raced through her mind.

"I was . . . looking for you," she tried.

He yanked her along with him the few steps to the doorway. Shoving open the door, he drenched them both in yellow light. Braden's blue eyes stared down at her, and a smile danced across his lips.

"Yer lyin'. Ye were stealin' my horse."

She gazed up at him, hoping her face was covered with a look of innocence. "You are the police. Have you not told us we must not steal?"

"Somehow I'm thinkin' those words were lost on ye, lass. Tell me the truth."

Dancing Bird focused her attention on his hands gripping her arms and how wonderfully warm they were against her skin, how firm and tender they would be if clasped around her waist. His breath ruffled her hair, engulfing her with the smell of him, an unusual scent composed of horse, prairie grass and something else . . . something sweet.

She raised her head and stared straight into his eyes. He stared back, his pupils large and black. "I could arrest ye and take ye to Fort Walsh for this," he said, his voice soft and pliant, not at all the tone he'd used with White Dog only days before.

"You cannot prove I was trying to steal your horse. I have a horse of my own." She nodded toward Wind, now grazing peacefully a few feet away. "Sioux women do not steal horses."

"I'm thinkin' yer not like most Sioux women."

"Will you put the hobbles on me like Walsh threatened, White Dog?" she whispered, then shivered inwardly when his eyes changed from light to dark blue.

Was that anger on his face? Or was he feeling the same strange sensations as she?

"No, lass, no hobbles for ye," he said softly.

He relaxed his grip, then dropped his arms to his sides and stepped backward. Dancing Bird moved toward him, emboldened by the power she sensed she held over him at this moment.

Cheyenne women pressed their lips to their man's lips. A kiss, they called it. A very pleasant sensation, they whispered behind cupped hands, that rendered men helpless in their arms. Since the tribes had been camped together for some time, Dancing Bird had heard much talk of kissing and was eager to try out this magic.

But something more than curiosity drew her to Braden. She was lured to him by some invisible force against which she seemed to have no defense, a niggling urging that whispered in her ear.

"What are ye about, lass?" he asked, alarm edging into his voice as she raised up on tiptoe. She stared into his eyes and saw first fear, then something else flit through his expression. Then, with her eyes closed, she touched her lips to his.

He went rigid with surprise as her hands closed around his muscular upper arms, urging him closer to her. Warmth radiated from the center of her stomach, pouring through her, robbing her of her caution. He gripped her forearms as if to set her away from him, but then he relaxed and his lips grew supple, moving against hers in a sensuous rhythm that made her want him closer, closer. His arms slid around her waist, as warm and comfortable as she'd imagined in her daydreams.

She stepped further into his embrace and his grip, so

soft and gentle, tightened, pulling her hard against him. Her hands slid up his arms, then down his back and across his shoulder blades. As suddenly as he'd yielded to her, he stiffened and firmly set her away.

"Whoa, lass," he murmured softly.

She opened her eyes and saw the distress on his face. Red hot shame burned her cheeks as the realization of what she'd done dawned on her. If she'd done this in her village, she'd have been branded a loose woman, shunned and abused, destined to live out her life without friends or family, for no man would have such a woman. Tears of confusion sprang to her eyes.

"Let me go," she said between clenched teeth.

He released her and stepped backward.

She glanced at her horse, then back to him. She wanted to bolt and run away, ride at a full gallop toward home, hide down by the river and think, try to make some sense out of the last few minutes.

But, she reasoned, she should make some explanation for her behavior, beg him for his silence. If her uncle ever found out . . .

Again, she cursed her impetuous nature and tried to think. Instead she stood before him with clenched fists and tears in her eyes.

Five

"Dancing Bird," Braden began, shock and desire robbing him of his usually glib tongue.

"Please do not tell my uncle." Her large, fear-filled eyes stared up at him as she pleaded with a quivering voice.

Seeing her so humbled turned his stomach, and he cursed his weaker side. He should have pushed her away to begin with, should have gently discouraged her advance. Instead, he'd readily taken her into his arms, drawing pleasure from her touch . . . the touch of a woman he barely knew and of a people he was sent to police.

Braden stepped forward and she moved away, fear making her visibly quiver. "I won't tell anyone a'tall," he reassured her.

"I shouldn't have done that. Father said I do things without thinking first." She twisted her hands and looked away from him. "I . . . I heard some of the women talking and I just wondered . . . what it would be like. If anyone finds out, I won't be able to make a good marriage." Her voice broke on the last word, and the strong, independent woman dissolved into a young girl guided and ruled by strict traditions.

"It'll be a secret between us, I swear," Braden said with what he hoped was a convincing smile as he fought the impulse to yank her into his arms and kiss her again.

"It is the way of my people," she offered, moving even further away from him. "Good women do not show their interest in a man. Men seek them out to bear their children. Only a pure woman will have a good home for her children."

Even as he longed to take away the fear so obviously ruling her at that moment, he conceded the necessity of such a tradition in a people clinging tenuously to life. But not even that rationalization could take away the want that had been resurrected in him. The nights would be longer and lonelier now that he knew the softness of her lips and the feel of her arms around him.

"Have you kissed a woman before?" she asked, her face brightening in anticipation of his answer.

He fought down a grin. Even in the face of impending disaster, apparently her curiosity would emerge intact. "Yes."

"Did you kiss the woman who died?"

Brief, vivid memories flashed by. "Yes, I kissed her."

She looked down at the ground, out into the night and finally back at his face. "Did I do it right?"

Curiosity killed the cat ran through Braden's head like the refrain of a song. "Yes," he said, his stomach tightening, "you did it very right."

"I must go." Abruptly she turned, walked to her horse, and leaped onto its back. "My mother will worry about me."

Braden looked up at her, a hand on her horse's shoulder. "Are you going to come back later and steal my horse?"

She grinned. "No, Long Lance. Your horse will be safe from me."

"Long Lance?"

"That is what all the people are calling you. Because of the lances you carried that day."

The fluttering red and white pennons on long lances.

"Good-bye." She reined her horse around and set out at a gallop. In seconds the night swallowed both her and the sound of her horse's hoofbeats.

Braden walked out beyond the light from his doorway and looked up at the stars. In her innocence she couldn't know how her chaste kiss had aroused him in ways he'd thought never to feel again. He'd had to reach deep down within himself to retrieve the strength to set her away. He wasn't here to seduce Sioux maidens. He was here to keep them from starving.

"The Blackfoot have claimed this territory as theirs." Walsh's quill scraped a black line across the wrinkled piece of brown paper. "And here is where they have agreed to let the Sioux hunt." He drew another square that fit snugly against the first carefully outlined on the rough map, then leaned back in the rickety chair. "Patrols have reported plenty of game and buffalo in that area, but I want you to ride out there and make sure, Constable Flynn. I want to know for sure there are enough buffalo in this area," he stabbed the paper with his finger, "to support this many people."

"Yes, sir. I'll ride out in the morning."

Walsh leaned forward. "I'm returning to Wood Mountain. I've left Sub-Inspector Crozier in charge of Fort Walsh for the time being and have sent Constable

Quinn there ahead of me. I intend to remain at Wood Mountain until we have some indication of Sitting Bull's intentions. I'd like you and Constable Gravel to remain here, where you can closely observe the Sioux. They seem to have accepted the two of you into their midst quite easily. If Sitting Bull intends to use this area to organize attacks across the border, I want to know. We cannot allow that to happen."

He glanced around the small dugout dwelling. "I realize these quarters are small, but hopefully the Sioux will settle in peacefully and constant vigilance will cease to be necessary. At that time, you'll return to Wood Mountain and join the detachment stationed there."

Braden glanced around the dugout. Small was an understatement. There was barely enough room for two men to pass each other without having to open the door.

"Any movement toward the border, any buildup of ammunition and arms, I want to know about. That will require your moving among them. Get to know them, their ways and habits." Walsh stood, picked up his helmet, and shook it in their direction. "Always in uniform. They have come to respect the scarlet jackets. We must use every tool available to us to maintain their respect."

He stepped out into the morning sun and squinted against the glare from the white-blue sky. Looking out across the flat prairie that seemed to extend into forever, he sighed. "This is big country, but we're only fooling ourselves if we believe all these Indians will co-exist without trouble. Be on your guard, Constables."

* * *

Sweet strains of flute music filled the evening air, separate songs played by separate suitors throughout the Hunkpapa circle, and yet the melodies intertwined in a poignant harmony that brought tears to the eyes of old women. Contained in the sweet tunes was hope for the future—new families, new babies, life's continuation.

Evening was gilding the sky with streaks of orange and yellow. The day was winding down. Sleepy children sought their mothers' laps, and preparations for the evening meal were well under way.

Dancing Bird stirred a fragrant soup of buffalo meat and wild turnips bubbling in a buffalo paunch suspended by four stout sticks. She hummed along with the loudest tune as she fished another rock out of the fire, cradled it in the fork of a stick, and brushed off the sand. Then she dropped it into the paunch and watched the steam rise. Outside, her mother tended another fire and another meal. So many people now lived in the tipi that the one firepit could not feed them all.

Dancing Bird sighed and wished she were the one outdoors, but Walks Lightly was standing in the blanket with Standing Elk. A man as good as his word, he had indeed carved a new flute and now played haunting music while they clutched an orange and red striped blanket about them both, even though the night was sweltering.

The couple stood just outside the tipi, and Dancing Bird's mother had forbidden her to come outside while they were together. Last night when Standing Elk had come, she'd amused herself by making faces at him over her sister's shoulder. Although Standing Elk had taken the interference good-naturedly, Walks Lightly had not been so easily amused and had demanded action from their mother.

Dancing Bird stirred the soup again, then stretched out on a buffalo robe alongside the fire pit and folded her hands behind her head. Even with the sides rolled up, a hot breeze twirled the bundles of dried plants that hung from the lodgepoles.

So much effort had gone into the preparation of those precious bundles. In the few weeks since they'd crossed the Medicine Line, she, her mother and Walks Lightly had worked from sunrise to sunset to collect and dry these herbs. Ever mindful of the charity she accepted each day from her brother, her mother had been relentless in her tasks. And even though they were a long way from restoring all the supplies that had been lost, they were better off than before.

Two buffalo hides lay rolled up near her mother's sleeping robe. A second hide had been contributed by her younger brother when, on his first hunt, Little Bear had managed to kill a bull buffalo with a bow and arrow. Heralded as a great hunter, he'd been the guest of honor at a celebration that had lasted long into the night. Sitting across the fire from him, Dancing Bird had remembered with a twinge of sadness his chubby cheeks and fat little hands when he was a baby only twelve summers ago. Now, looking bewildered and a little dazed beneath the huge buffalo headdress, the boy had been thrust into the role of a man.

"Lazy girl." Her mother's voice shattered her daydreams, and Dancing Bird scrambled to her feet.

"Don't let your uncle catch you sleeping when you should be working." Her mother leaned over the paunch and sniffed, then turned toward her, a scowl on her face, but a smile lurking in her eyes.

"I wasn't sleeping. I was looking up at the dried herbs and . . . thinking." The excuse sounded feeble even to her, but it was the truth.

Her mother put her hands on her hips, and Dancing Bird knew she was in for another scolding. "You have your father's ways. He could always charm his way out of trouble." The small smile widened into a grin, but the sorrow that so often lurked in her mother's eyes quickly returned.

Dancing Bird longed to reach out to her mother and offer her the company of a soul equally wounded, but her mother would accept no sympathy—not from her daughters, not from her family. She grudgingly accepted shelter and food from her brother, and only then because of her children.

If she couldn't take away her mother's pain, she could take away the sense of worthlessness, Dancing Bird vowed. Before the snow flew again, her mother would sleep away cold winter nights in a tipi of her own, if Dancing Bird had to skin and tan every hide herself.

On her ride that evening she swung north, following the sparkling, moon-flecked path of the river. Disturbed insects bolted from the grass as she passed, their wings making soft fluttering sounds in the nighttime stillness. She rode until she found the churned, torn sod of a buffalo trail, evidence that a large herd moved slowly north.

Pulling her pony to a stop, she looked over the broad path in front of her and imagined the great bodies dotting the horizon and covering the green hills as far as a person could see. Tomorrow she would return with a gun and ammunition and kill a buffalo. She'd haul the meat home on a travois and tan the hide herself. That would give her three skins. Almost enough to make the bottom row of skins for the lodge.

Secure in her plan, Dancing Bird turned her horse toward home, intending to ride back the way she had come. But as she neared the steep bank where the Long Lances lived, she veered away from her course, drawn there despite a nagging voice cautioning her.

Lights shone from the windows and a thin trail of smoke coiled from the stovepipe that poked out of the dirt roof. Hidden by the night, she watched and waited for a glimpse of Braden. She had returned night after night to watch from the shadows. There were two men there now, Braden and another Long Lance, the one who worked magic with his hands and made things appear and disappear. He might be an evil spirit, her people had worried, sent by Three Stars to torment them. There had been much discussion among the men about the Long Lance with magical hands. But his kind ways and gentle voice had soothed the elders, and they had decided he meant no harm.

The door to the house opened, spilling a path of light out into the darkness. A man moved into the doorway, a slim figure silhouetted against the soft light from the fireplace. He stretched his arms over his head, leaned a hip against the door frame, and crossed his arms over his chest.

She knew it was Braden. None of the young braves who observed her with sly smiles and averted eyes had ever made her heart thump in her ears or made her palms sweat like a brief glance of him did. None had ever enticed her to touch her lips to theirs.

Closing her eyes as a warm breeze arrived to caress her cheeks, she imagined him doing the same. His hands would be rough, but tender, she decided. His palms would cup her cheeks and his fingers would stroke back her hair. And then he would kiss her as she'd kissed him, drawing her tightly into his embrace.

He shifted away from the doorway, abandoned his casual stance and studied the night between them. Somehow he knew she was there, a fact that raised gooseflesh on her arms. Was this how her parents had felt in those moments when a glance took the place of words?

Shaken, she turned toward home, careful to keep her pony to a walk to prevent Braden from hearing hoofbeats. When she was a distance away, she stopped and looked back over her shoulder. His slim silhouette still filled the doorway, still looked in her direction. His presence reached out across the distance between them and touched something deep within her that had never been touched before and never would be again in this way.

She nudged her pony into a gallop and raced through the silky night. Her mind cleared some as the village came into sight and she left him and his spell behind her. What was special about these Long Lances who had come to live among them? They had come to protect them, the talk around camp said. White Forehead and his men were different from other *wašíchu* and were only interested in making sure the Sioux and their neighbors lived together in peace. Her uncle had thought long and hard about this, he often said. The White Mother's police would keep the blue soldiers away and would never do as the blue soldiers had done. The intentions of the Long Lances were much discussed around fires at night. But Sitting Bull held fast to his opinion that the men with the red jackets were their friends.

Dancing Bird released her pony into the herd that grazed near the lodges and crept through the sleeping village to her uncle's tipi. Stepping over sleeping relatives, she slid onto her sleeping robes with hardly a rustle. Her mother sighed and turned over, and she knew her return had been noticed.

A wave of compassion for the woman who had borne so much pain swept over her. Moving-Robe-Woman was a respected woman and yet she risked her reputation to allow her youngest daughter the freedom to heal, a fact that Dancing Bird held dear within her heart even though she and her mother rarely agreed on anything.

Rolling to her back, she stared up at the stars winking at her through the smoke hole and began to plan her buffalo hunt.

He'd often wondered why all things natural were referred to as feminine, as Mother Nature. But on this glorious morning, as a soft wind raked invisible fingers through his hair and the sun lulled him into bliss with warm hands, he knew the answer.

Balancing his helmet on one knee thrown across his saddle horn, he looked out over the voluptuous green hills before him and pushed away a familiar wave of homesickness. Would a decadent display of green always bring this desolate sense of loss? Would he ever again look at a peaceful landscape and not see sunken eyes and gaunt faces instead of grass and trees?

His horse shifted position and he patted Brandy's warm shoulder. A small dot of motion in the distance caught his eye. Instantly alert, he watched as a single horse and rider galloped over the crest of a hill. Cataloging the sight as a hunter, the image nonetheless dogged his thoughts as the horse stopped and the rider dismounted, then fell to the ground.

Braden swung his leg back over his saddle and heeled his mare into a trot. A black Indian pony grazed peacefully while its rider lay prone on the ground. Braden closed the gap between them, concern growing. Had this person fallen from his mount? Was he drunk and was there another source of illegal whiskey to be routed, as the Mounted Police had spent much of their first year doing?

But as he came within yards of the figure he saw it was a woman holding a rifle and staring off toward the east.

Dancing Bird.

Atop a gentle rise, she put the rifle to her shoulder and sighted down the barrel. Braden stopped his horse and swung down.

"What are you doing?" he asked. She snapped her head around, startled. "Shooting buffalo," she said calmly.

A small group of the lumbering beasts grazed down in a coulee, cropping the new grass.

"By yourself?" he asked, wondering what she'd do with the beast once she'd dispatched it.

She threw him a disgusted look. "Of course by myself."

He stretched out on the ground at her side, enjoying the moment of discomfort that flitted through her expression. He knew she'd been riding by their outpost at night, sitting out beyond the light, watching them from the dark. He'd seen her, a silent shadow, more than once, and always sensed she was there, a fact that disturbed him more than he wanted to admit.

"How will you get the meat back to your village?"

Doubt ruined the confidence in her expression. "I will put it on my travois." She nodded toward her pony, and he noticed the long poles tied securely along its side.

A bull buffalo weighed several hundred pounds. Butchering it was a daunting task for several people, much less one. He glanced up at the sun, now climbing in a clear sky, promising a hot day. Her jaw was set firmly, working the muscles beneath her skin as she again sighted down the barrel of the gun.

Three riders emerged from the coulee, directly between them and the buffalo. Braden opened his mouth to warn her, but the roar of the gun drowned out his words and engulfed them in a cloud of smoke. She dropped the weapon and grabbed her shoulder, rolling over onto her side with a groan.

Braden scrambled to his feet. One of the distant riders pitched backward off his horse, and his two companions dismounted and fell to the ground, sighting down the long barrels of their rifles. His own weapon several feet away, Braden threw himself down on Dancing Bird and rolled them both over and over until he lay atop her in a small depression of ground. Bullets zinged overhead. Both horses threw up their heads and trotted further away, taking Braden's Springfield rifle out of reach.

She struggled for a few seconds, moaned deeply, then lay still. Her shoulder was probably dislocated from the recoil of the heavy rifle, and his weight on her was surely causing her agony. He called back from memory his brief glance at the riders. They weren't white men.

They were probably Blackfoot, and he imagined the map Walsh had drawn on a piece of brown paper.

She'd been hunting in Blackfoot territory, a simple mistake that could well cause a major incident. Somehow, without getting shot, he had to defuse this situation immediately.

His white helmet lay on its side a few feet away. Rolling off Dancing Bird, he crawled on his belly toward it, bullets gouging the dirt behind him. He jammed the helmet on his head and glanced back at Dancing Bird. She watched him with huge, dark eyes. Then he stood, praying the scarlet of his jacket would speak for itself, as Walsh believed.

A bullet buried itself at his feet and threw a spray of dirt onto his boots. His heart hammering, he stood his ground. "I'm Constable Flynn of the Mounted Police. Put down your weapons," he shouted in what he hoped was passable Blackfoot.

The men lifted their heads and looked at each other. He thanked God he'd learned to speak Blackfoot at Fort McLeod. Then the men slowly stood, still clutching their rifles. Their unseated companion stumbled to his feet, holding his arm. They remounted their horses and rode forward.

Braden positioned himself between them and Dancing Bird as their horses scrambled up to the rise of the hill. Scowling, the men pulled their horses to a stop.

One was Dog, a Canadian Blackfoot who wandered the Cypress Hills and frequented Fort Walsh to trade buffalo robes for supplies and rock candy. With him was Young Eagle, a young Blackfoot from the Fort McLeod area. The third man, blood dribbling from between his fingers as he held his upper arm, was named Red Elk.

He lived with his family in a settlement just outside Fort Walsh, one of many Indian settlements that had sprung up like mushrooms since the fort's establishment. What the three men with seemingly little in common were doing riding so far from the fort crossed Braden's mind briefly, and he filed it away for later consideration.

Dog looked over at Dancing Bird, then back at Braden. "Why did your woman shoot us?" he asked, pointing at the gun lying on the ground.

"She was huntin' buffalo." Braden nodded toward the small group of animals just disappearing over the crest of a hill. He said a small prayer of thanks that the lumbering beasts rarely moved quickly.

Dog looked over his shoulder toward the receding buffalo, suspicion still in his eyes. "Why does a woman hunt? You not hunt for her?" he asked, this time in English.

"I don't have a man," Dancing Bird shot back from where she lay on the ground, disgust in her voice. Braden wished he was close enough to clamp a hand over her mouth. Did she realize just how much trouble she was in? Or didn't she care?

"She is the niece of Sitting Bull, of the Sioux who have come to the White Mother's Land. They have no lodges, no food. Her father was killed by Three Stars, and she hunts to feed her family."

The three men grunted and murmured among themselves, and Braden tried without success to understand their quick words. Even the Indians north of the border, those who lived in peace, had heard of Crook's relentless pursuit of the Sioux.

"You are from Fort Walsh," Dog stated, swinging his gaze back to Braden to look him over from head to foot, then glancing beyond to where his rifle rested in its scabbard.

Braden nodded. "Yes."

Dog smiled and nodded toward him. "Red shirt protected you," he said, a glint of mischief in his eye.

"Sure and I hoped it would." Braden smiled.

Dog laughed, then pointed at Dancing Bird. "She is hurt?"

"Her shoulder is dislocated."

Dog nodded slowly, then looked to his companions. He pointed to his shoulder, then back to Dancing Bird. "You pull like this," he said, grabbing his own wrist with one hand and yanking his arm straight out. "Hurt bad, then better. You tie like this." He crossed his chest with the imaginary injured arm, palm down. "She better soon. Go back to woman's work." He frowned in her direction, and Dancing Bird scowled at him.

"Is he hurt?" she said between clenched teeth and nodded toward his companion, who had a thin trail of blood dripping off the ends of his fingers.

Dog smiled. "I will wrap his wound, but we will not tell he was shot by a woman."

The wounded man threw Dog a dark glance and slung the blood off his fingers.

The trio turned to ride away, but Dog suddenly reined in his horse and looked back at Dancing Bird. "Many buffalo over hill there." He pointed in the direction from which they'd ridden before the shooting. Then he smiled. "You need husband, you come see me." His laughter pealed across the open expanse, and their chuckles floated back as they rode down the incline and out of sight.

Six

Braden knelt at her side, where she'd pushed herself into a sitting position with one arm. He reached out a hand to touch the bulge that marred the smooth line of her shoulder and she flinched away, her eyes large with fear and pain.

" 'Tis only a dislocation." He touched her, running his fingers across her shoulder, testing the degree of damage with a gentle squeeze. He swallowed and looked into her face. The damage was severe. He'd have to reset it, and soon, before it started to swell.

"I have to reset your shoulder," he said, hoping his voice sounded steadier to her than it did to him. "Pull it back into joint. I won't lie to ye. It'll hurt like the very devil."

She blinked slowly, her long dark lashes briefly sweeping away her façade of bravery. "I know. I've seen the warriors do this to each other after a hunt."

He helped her to her feet and gripped her arm tightly, a mild wave of nausea rippling through him. Placing the palm of his hand on her collarbone, he hesitated and looked into her eyes again. He'd seen grown men faint into limp, boneless heaps.

She locked gazes with him and lightly rested her fingers on his forearm. "I'm ready," she whispered.

Braden issued a silent, brief prayer that he wouldn't have to do this twice, and yanked her arm. The shoulder slipped back into joint with an audible pop. Her eyes slid shut and her knees buckled. Braden caught her in his arms and lowered her to the warm, soft grass. She moaned against his chest, then moved her head and blinked several times as if trying to focus her eyes.

Braden pulled off his belt and joined her on the ground, sliding her between his legs, propping her back against his chest. He wrapped the belt around her to secure her arm against her chest, then leaned her head back against him and waited for her to regain full consciousness.

A warm, morning wind blew her hair across his cheek, strands of silk sent to torture his sensibilities. She was barely an armful, and yet she evoked a sense of protectiveness in him that told him he'd do foolish things to protect her if he wasn't careful. Images of her flight to freedom that before were mere visions conjured from her words became painful realities within him as he held her fragile body in his arms.

Finally, her head slid to the side and she opened her eyes. She stared up into his face—not quite seeing him, he realized, as she fought for control.

"I'll take you home." The warmth of his breath against her hair released her scent, which swirled up and held him prisoner.

He stood, then scooped her into his arms. Carefully positioning her shoulder, he lifted her into Brandy's saddle and swung up behind her.

She gripped the saddle horn with her uninjured hand

and hunched forward as the horse turned and started toward her village. Braden eased her back against him and lightly wrapped an arm around her. Despite his efforts, her back slid against his chest in a sensuous waltz, but the pleasure quickly became torture.

Little demons of fire danced through her shoulder, burning here and there, threatening to rob her of consciousness again and again as the mare's rolling gait ground bone against bone. But through the haze of pain that made her vision dance and ripple, his arm around her remained a touchstone in her misery. The one thought that circled through her mind was she would require this touch again and again. The memory of his warmth would disturb her sleep and dominate her daydreams.

Their arrival at the outskirts of her village sent out a ripple of curiosity that quickly reached Moving-Robe-Woman. Dancing Bird leaned out of his embrace and tried to sit upright when she saw her mother's stricken face emerge from their lodge. Forcing a smile, Dancing Bird watched her mother's gaze flicker over her, checking for injuries and harm as she'd done since childhood.

Braden swung down, his departure leaving a cold void behind her. Before she could gather her wits, he reached up, pulled her into his arms and set her feet on the ground. She swayed for a moment and felt his hands touch her waist to steady her. Gathering her strength, she stepped away from him before she couldn't.

"I will heal," Dancing Bird said softly when her mother's eyes misted as they focused on her shoulder.

"How did you do this?" her mother asked.

Despite her mother's controlled voice, Dancing Bird knew a tight ball of fear lay curled inside Moving-Robe-Woman. She'd not survive the loss of another of her family, and she'd allow nothing that courted that possibility. If her mother knew Dancing Bird was hunting buffalo alone, she'd never allow her daughter out of the village again—at least until she proved she was a capable hunter.

"Her horse stumbled and she fell." Braden's voice was innocent and convincing. " 'Twas a stroke of luck I found her," he finished, smiling.

Her mother narrowed her eyes slightly and looked between them, judging, weighing their words, already sensing a conspiracy. He thought with amusement that the poor woman had probably spent a good deal of Dancing Bird's life doing just this.

Without waiting for the verdict, Braden's hand cupped Dancing Bird's elbow and urged her forward.

"I'm going to rest," Dancing Bird said and ducked under the rolled-up edges of the lodge. To her surprise, Braden followed her, and the curious crowd dispersed.

"I'm thinkin' we didn't convince yer mother," Braden whispered as he moved to the back of the lodge and unrolled her sleeping mat.

Dancing Bird turned to face him, aware of her mother's vigilance just outside. She wanted to kiss him again, to have him kiss her as she'd imagined in her daydreams. She wanted to feel his arms around her in passion as they'd been around her in comfort. But as he stood staring down at her, there was no spark of desire in his eyes, only gentle concern and the kindness that often lurked there. Her heart began to ache more than her arm. He didn't want her at all.

"Thank you," she muttered, staring down at her feet so he wouldn't see the tears gathering in the corners of her eyes.

A finger touched her chin and raised her head to look into his face. "Stay out of trouble?"

She nodded, unable to speak the retort in her mind past the lump in her throat.

When she dared look up, he was a flash of red swinging into his saddle. Dancing Bird stood alone in the tipi and listened to his muted voice as he offered her mother a few more details, then bid the rest of her family goodbye. She sat down on her uncle's sleeping robe, fighting tears, straining to hear his horse's hoofbeats as he rode away. For a few seconds, she could pick out the horse's gait above the village noises. Then he was gone . . . and so was her happiness.

The battered gates of Fort Walsh had never looked so good, Braden surmised as he rode beneath the Union Jack fluttering in a July breeze. Two weeks in the muddy, cramped quarters he and Steven occupied were enough to drive any man to drink, he thought, with a wistful memory of smooth Irish whiskey.

He dismounted in front of the low log building that contained Walsh's office and looped his reins over the railing, noting several new buildings now squatted among those of weathered lumber. Traders had set up shop in wagons and shacks, advertising their wares with gaudy signs. Beyond the gates, a sprawling community of Indian encampments had sprung up like mushrooms around the fort. Saulteaux, Assiniboins, Sioux, and Blackfoot lived side by side, each bringing with them problems to be laid at James Walsh's feet.

Braden rapped on the door, then shoved it open and ducked to step inside. Walsh stood, his hands braced on the desk top, staring down at a disorderly heap of papers. Clumps of mud crusted his usually shiny boots.

"Constable Flynn," Walsh said, and straightened slowly.

"I came for a bath and supplies," Braden said bluntly, hoping to belay the dread rapidly growing in Walsh's eyes.

A relieved smile spread slowly across the assistant commissioner's face. "There's a report I wish I heard more often. Water and supplies I can provide. Universal happiness I cannot."

"Have there been problems?" Braden eyed the pile of papers.

Walsh snorted and ran a hand through his hair. "Problems. That's using a mild term. Missouri traders started arriving two weeks ago, bringing with them an assortment of illegal whiskey, weapons and women. The Assiniboins are complaining about the Blackfoot and the Blackfoot are complaining about the Sioux. All in all, we're straddling a powder keg. What about Sitting Bull's Sioux?" Walsh asked the question with obvious trepidation in his voice.

"They're recoverin', makin' new lodges, huntin'. Sure and the buffalo seem plentiful enough."

"Any signs the old man wants to venture south?"

Braden shook his head. "No signs of trouble. They seem content where they are."

Walsh stamped his foot to dislodge a clump of mud from his boot, then grimaced at the floor. "But for how long?"

"Do ye think they'll go back across the border?" Even as he asked the question, his heart sank queasily at the thought of the vast American plains swallowing up Dancing Bird and her people as if they'd never existed.

Walsh skirted the desk and sat heavily in his chair. "Sitting Bull's defection is an itch Crook can't reach. The whole American Indian campaign was wagered on the white man being more human than the Indians. The Indians were less experienced in games of betrayal, but more experienced in defending their homes, a point Crook overlooked in his arrogance." Harsh words from a genteel man.

Braden propped a hip on the edge of his commander's desk. "Have ye had any dealin's with a Blackfoot named Dog?"

Walsh looked up, fatigue dimming the blue of his eyes, then frowned and shook his head. "Why?"

"I ran across him and two friends a few days ago, ridin' in the Blackfoot huntin' territory. Strange friendship, I'd say. He was with Young Eagle and Red Elk."

"I agree, a strange combination. What were they doing?" Walsh asked, pushing himself forward to prop his arms on his desk.

Braden shrugged. "Nothin' except ridin' together that I could see."

"But you thought they were up to something?"

Braden nodded. "Couldn't put my finger on it, but yes."

Walsh smiled. "We'll make a policeman out of you yet, Flynn. What did your gut tell you?"

"That they were out of place, brewin' up trouble."

Walsh slid a stack of papers toward him, thumbed through the first few, then pushed them away again. "I've been expecting some of the native tribes to try and stir up trouble with the Sioux. Maybe you stumbled onto their plan. Keep an eye out, Constable."

Braden slid off the desk and walked to the door.

"Constable Flynn."

Braden turned. Walsh waved a small white envelope at him, a smile on his face. "Constable Fraser and his wife have a daughter."

"And are the mother and babe well?"

Walsh laughed. "Mother and daughter are fine. The father may never be the same. Constable Fraser had to deliver his daughter on the banks of the Old Man's River after Maggie decided to go fishing."

Braden laughed, and felt a wave of nostalgia for Fort McLeod and Colin's company. " 'Twill be a strange day that Maggie Fraser does anythin' the easy way."

After leaving Walsh's office, Braden walked across the parade ground, leaving behind the whitewashed, stockaded walls of Fort Walsh. Ahead, the trader's village beckoned.

Abraham Dillon's tent was a colorful mixture of the useful and the absurd. Bright copper pots dangled on pieces of rope from the center pole and clanked together merrily in a summer breeze that sailed underneath the rolled-up sides. Colorful lengths of fabric lay folded on a table and jars of beads squatted nearby, all intended to catch the passing Indian's eye.

"Constable Flynn." Abraham winked at him with his one good eye and came forward, a gnarled hand extended. "I have missed your Irish."

Braden grinned and shook hands with the old man, trying to remember just which one of Abraham's eyes worked—the one that wandered or the one that stared straight ahead.

"You come to buy pretties for a lady?" He waggled bushy white brows that wrestled for dominance in the center of his forehead.

"Maybe," Braden said. "Do ye have any rock candy?"

"Do I have rock candy? What kind of trader would old Abraham be without candy?" He shuffled to the side and picked up a jar filled with irregular chunks of color. "Catering to the sins of the palette and the eye, that's what I do," he said, his smile wide.

"Give me four or five pieces of that," Braden said. Then a length of cloth caught his eye. Demure in its beauty, the calico fabric reminded him of the prairie flowers now blooming, their thousands of tiny blooms combining to make carpets of color in the sun. The red, yellow, and blue print played across a background of white.

"How much fabric does it take to make a dress?" Braden asked Abraham.

Abraham laughed. "You're sorely ignorant in the ways of women, Braden, lad. Depends on the woman, her size, her height. Here." Abraham bent and pulled out a worn and tattered volume from behind his shelf. The front cover exhibited a woman in a dress with an exaggerated rear end that threatened to tip her forward.

"They're wearin' this?" Braden asked incredulous. "How do they sit?"

"Sittin' ain't the purpose, lad. Saunterin' is." Abraham cavorted in imitation of a lady in a bustle.

Braden thumbed through the book, reminded of just how long he'd been in the wilderness. Smoothly groomed drawings of women posed in ladylike and demure positions smiled coldly from the pages. One section exhibited women in hunting dress, leaning benignly on the stocks of rifles. None of them would attempt to heave the weapons to their shoulders and shoot a buffalo, he'd wager.

"Well, just give me"—he paused, calculating how easily Dancing Bird had fit within the circle of his arms—"four yards."

Abraham whipped out the bolt of cloth and neatly cut the length with a sharp, evil-looking knife. He folded it carefully and handed it to Braden, wrapped in brown paper along with the separately wrapped candy. Braden paid him and turned to go.

"Constable."

Braden turned around. Abraham's face had grown sober. "Sometimes I hear things," he began, casting a cautious glance at the tent opening.

"What is it, Abraham?"

"I'm a friend to all, you understand."

Braden nodded, the hair on the back of his neck standing to attention. Abraham was about to tell him something he didn't want to hear.

"There's talk."

"What kind of talk?"

"Talk 'bout makin' it so them Sioux's gotta go back across the border."

"What do you mean makin' it so?"

Abraham looked at the scuffed dirt floor. "If'n there was to be a killin' and if'n it was to be blamed on the Sioux. . . ."

"Who said this?"

"Weren't nobody in particular," Abraham said, casting another glance at the door. "Just heered gossip."

"Can ye give me a hint, old man?"

Abraham stepped to the tent opening and stood looking toward the settlement on the rise of land to the west and nodded in that direction. "The Blackfeet been huntin' this land fer years, a-thinkin' all these buffalo was put here for them and their young'uns. Now here comes the Sioux, hungry and wantin' to hunt. You know as good as me, Constable, that there ain't enuff buffalo to go around. Now whatta you think's gonna happen if'n two or three men put their heads together and figure out how to get all this back fer their families? Can't blame 'em much, can you?"

Braden stared out at the white lodges, peaceful and pristine in the sun. And yet behind the lodge flaps, families worried about starvation, worried about losing the one thing that supplied their homes, fed their children, sustained their lives. The gut-twisting fear he'd thought never to feel again, the fear he thought he'd left an ocean behind, gripped his insides again as memories of hunger and misery returned. No, he couldn't blame 'em much.

"Does Dog have anything to do with this?" Braden asked without looking at Abraham.

Silence at his side answered the question. "Red Elk?"

"Man's got a family to feed, a young'un on the way. Fear like that'll make a man do strange things."

"Indeed," Braden said, sickly guilt sliding into his already churning stomach. He thought he'd left that behind, too.

"I just don't want nobody killed," Abraham said, a plea in his voice. "Nobody on neither side. Them Sioux's lost their home, lost their food and supplies. The Blackfoot's afeared of losing their food. I feel sorry for the lot of 'em. Reckon them boys in blue down there think about that?"

Braden doubted they did. No one could understand

the complexity or the heart-wrenching reality of the situation until they walked among the people affected, as he had. Again he imagined Dancing Bird's people fading back into the Cypress Hills, clutching what little they'd managed to accumulate, possibly never to be seen again once they crossed the border.

"I'll keep an eye on things," Braden promised.

"I hope yer girl likes them bolt goods."

Braden glanced down at the package in his hand. His girl. "I think she will."

"They come! They come!" shouted Red Moon. She dashed wildly through the village, her long dark hair streaming out behind her, her light eyes wide with fear.

Dancing Bird struggled to her feet, grimacing at the pain that shot through her arm and at the foul-smelling poultice her mother had placed on her injured shoulder. Confined to the sweltering tipi, she was irritable and out of sorts. There was nothing to do inside but count the lodgepoles and sort herbs with one hand. Outside, the sun and wind beckoned. Birds sang their summer songs and perched on swaying stalks of grass. Her pony grazed peacefully, waiting. And beyond it all was Braden in his dirt house.

She hadn't seen him since her accident five suns ago. She'd been tempted more than once to sneak away when the family was asleep, but Little Bear would tell on her if he found out. Somehow he'd discovered she'd gone hunting buffalo. Embarrassed and afraid his sister would injure his newly acquired reputation, he'd threatened to tell if she ever attempted to do it again. In return, she'd threatened that if he told, she'd make him sorry as only a sister could do. And so they spent their days, held hostage by each other.

"They come!" Red Moon's voice carried over the camp, and as Dancing Bird poked her head outside, she noticed the people did not scurry as she'd expected. Instead, they viewed Red Moon's panic with sympathy and mild interest.

"More blue soldiers! They come with the black shirts!"

Dancing Bird strained up onto her tiptoes to try and see the source of the crowd now building toward the center of the village. She listened and heard no shots, no shouts, no galloping hooves. Catching her mother looking the other way, she edged into the crowd. Protecting her arm with her other hand, she plowed a path until she stood at the center of the excitement.

A tall man wearing the long dress of a black shirt stood calmly talking to her uncle. He spoke Sioux easily and fluidly, the words rolling off his tongue as if he'd spoken it all his life. Her uncle was listening carefully, casting furtive glances at the two men with the Father.

Father Andrew Michaux.

"Father!" she called, but her voice was lost in the noise. Her heart joyous, she strained for a closer look at the man who'd taught her English as a child. His once dark hair was now a beautiful silver, offset by the dark simplicity of his dress. His face was no longer youthful, but lined with experience and days beneath the prairie sun. But his eyes were the same soft, gentle blue.

As he spoke, she glanced at the men with him. One indeed wore the blue uniform of the Long Knives. The other man wore a brown suit, like the ones she'd seen the white men wear at the forts where they'd once traded. His face was red with heat and the neck of his shirt seemed to be choking him.

She squeezed further into the crowd, wincing as someone jostled against her arm.

"I come in peace, Uncle, and bring these men to talk to you. They have come from the White Father and bring his words to you."

"I do not hear the White Father's words anymore. I am a child of the White Mother, and so are my people. We are safe here. We sleep peacefully. Our women and children do not disturb the moon with their sobs. We are happy here. Why would we want to come back to live out our lives on land that is not ours?"

Father Michaux listened, his face calm and serene, and when Sitting Bull was through, he spoke again. "Uncle, this land is not yours, either." His voice was soft, almost like a caress, a soothing tone he'd once explained was born of a peaceful soul. "You and your people are not British citizens. The Canadian government will only allow you to stay here. They will not feed you when the buffalo are gone."

"The Long Lances are our friends. They have promised they will protect us, and I believe them. Why would we return to a country determined to kill us all so that we will be no more trouble?"

"The Long Lances are obeying the orders of the White Mother. She has told them to keep you safe while you are on her soil, but she and the Long Lances wish you gone."

He paused and she caught his eye. He smiled gently, then quickly turned his attention back to the task at hand. "Will you counsel with these men?"

Sitting Bull glared at the two men, and they recoiled

a step. With a twinkle in his eye, Sitting Bull whirled and stalked toward his lodge. "I will sit in council with the white men tomorrow morning."

The crowd swelled after Sitting Bull, leaving only Dancing Bird standing in front of the three men.

"Dancing Bird," Father Michaux said with a smile and a sweep of her from head to foot. "You have turned into a beautiful woman."

She felt her cheeks heat. "Thank you."

"Ah, you have remembered your English."

"I have been talking for the Long Lances."

"It was fortunate you knew how to talk the white man's talk."

"Yes, it was fortunate."

"Do you have a family of your own? Children?"

Dancing Bird shook her head. "I have no man."

"I cannot imagine young men have not asked to stand in the blanket with you."

She shrugged. "They think I am odd."

Father Michaux laughed. "You are not odd, Dancing Bird, but you are a very different woman. Someday a young man will recognize that as a gift. How are your father and mother?"

"Father was killed in the winter." Even saying the words still hurt.

Father Michaux stepped forward, concern in his eyes. "I am sorry. He was a good man, and I counted him a friend. What happened?"

Dancing Bird glanced at the men behind him. "The blue soldiers chased us after Long Hair died. They chased us through snow and cold. Father was killed by one of them." She jerked her chin in their direction and wished she had a knife so she could show it to them and see them tremble.

"Your people have suffered much, Dancing Bird. I'm here to help bring an end to that. There are reservations waiting for you, large tracts of land where you would have a house of your own, cows to raise, land to plant in crops. The White Father will feed you until you can feed yourselves, and you will never have to run away again. The White Father whose name is Grant has promised these things to you, and he is a man of his word."

Dancing Bird scanned his face. Dear Father Michaux, her childhood playmate, teacher, confidant. He believed he spoke the truth. But she had listened at the bottom of too many council lodges to believe as he did. White Father Grant had waged a war on his own people, she'd overheard. He'd sent armies to burn and destroy homes and land, to force all of his people to believe as he did. And the generals who'd fought and defeated their own brothers were the men sent to lead the Sioux onto the reservations, cruel men who craved blood and power.

Many times she'd lain in the grass and watched a hill of ants with her father at her side while he tried to explain the white man's desire to conquer. His soul was not at peace, her father had explained. In their land there were no buffalo to hunt, and they did not know of Buffalo Woman and her prophecies. They were a tormented people, he'd said, and asked her to keep this in mind so that one day she might understand the white man.

She looked back at Father Michaux, a kind and gentle man, yet willing to argue for the white men eager to destroy the Sioux, and she knew for once her father was wrong. She would never understand the white man.

Seven

"We must send word to the Long Lances that these men are here," Sitting Bull said as he arranged robes on the floor of his lodge.

Dancing Bird looked up from her place by the fire and glanced at Spotted Eagle, chief of the Sans Arc and her uncle's confidant. A tall, handsome man, he met the world head-on with a sharp wit and finely honed sense of humor. He winked at her and she smiled. Her uncle would never have made such a comment in front of a woman if he were not upset.

"Send a rider to the Long Lances' house. Ask men to come here and hear what these men have to say."

Spotted Eagle nodded, bobbing a crown full of coup feathers. His large hands straightened the breechcloth at his waist and then tugged at the quilled vest that hung around his neck. "I will go myself so they will know this is important."

Dancing Bird cradled her aching arm and wished she could ask to be the messenger. How she longed to feel the wind against her face and smell the grass-scented air of the prairie.

As if reading her thoughts, Spotted Eagle threw her

a glance. "Should I ask them to send to Fort Walsh for more men?"

"No." Sitting Bull shook his head and straightened. "We do not want the whites to think they are too important."

With a nod, Spotted Eagle ducked out of the lodge, leaving Dancing Bird alone with her uncle. His gaze settled on her and he looked uncomfortable for a moment, as if he'd forgotten she was there. "You were glad to see Father Michaux?"

She nodded. "Yes, I was glad. He looks well."

"He traveled far to bring the white men here." His comment was more of a musing than a statement.

"Do you think he believes what they say?"

Sitting Bull frowned, and Dancing Bird wished she could bite her tongue. She wasn't supposed to know these things or be interested in them.

"You have made good use of your ears, niece," he said with a sly smile.

"Father said I should learn to understand the white man."

"Your father was right, but do not talk of this outside this lodge." He glanced at her again as he moved another robe. "Otherwise all the women will want to disobey their husbands and fathers, and then who will cook buffalo and turnips?" He slanted her a laughing glance and she grinned in return.

The sun made a grand exit, leaving the sky in a splash of lavender, brief in its glory, that was quickly chased from the stage by the elegant black of night.

Stars glimmered brightly, reminding Braden of starshine reflected off a gray Irish sea.

He leaned a shoulder against the open doorway and watched the sun and moon struggle for dominance of the sky. Was she out there? Watching him from just beyond the light's reach? She'd visited him several more times since the night he'd caught her trying to steal his horse. He never saw her, but he could sense her presence, feel her there a few yards away, satisfying her curiosity about him while he was deprived of the same privilege.

"She's not out there." Steven marched past him, dragging his saddle.

At Braden's surprised look, Steven stopped and laughed. "You're wearing the same look Maggie Fraser pasted on Colin's face about five minutes after she met him. You'd just as well surrender now, old man, and save yourself the misery of resistance."

"I'd never thought . . ."

"Don't add lying to your sins." Steven laughed. "I know a goner when I see one."

"You think I'm in love with Dancin' Bird?"

"Don't you?"

"Yes, saints help me."

Steven laughed and dropped his saddle into the dust at his feet. "Who'd have thought you and Colin would have a taste for rebellious women?" He pulled a briarwood pipe from his jacket pocket and filled it.

"When did ye start smokin' a pipe?" Braden asked, wondering how he could have missed such a trait about a man he'd lived so closely with for the past two years.

Steven shrugged and turned the carved pipe over in his hands. "Always had a taste for it. Got it from my father, I guess. I never smoked it much back home. It just didn't seem to fit with Bubbles's personality."

"Bubbles?"

"My clown name." Steven had been a professional clown before joining the Mounted Police, a fact that had caused quite a stir at the time in the ranks of the newly recruited. Steven rarely talked about his past, leaving an explanation to the imagination of the listener. "My mother shed many a tear over the fact that her eldest son made a living entertaining children at birthday parties. You're changing the subject."

Braden looked back out into the night and imagined her there in the darkness, her hair wild. " 'Tis a fact I never thought I'd love anybody again. Not after Anise. And then suddenly there she was, her little claws firmly around me heart."

"It's called healing, old man." Steven lit the bowl of his pipe and a milky column of smoke coiled into the night. "It happens when you're not looking. What are you going to do about it?"

"Nothin'." Braden turned toward Steven, a dim silhouette, the bottom half of his face lit by the warm glow of the pipe. "Try to ignore it."

Steven sputtered and chuckled. "Like you can ignore a toothache?"

" 'Tis worlds apart we are, she and I. She and her people could vanish back across the border tonight and I'd never see her again."

"So marry her."

Braden jerked his head around. "Marry her? Walsh would have me head, and after the flap over Colin and Maggie's marriage, so would Ottawa. And McLeod would have the heart attack he's so richly earned."

"Dunno," Steven mumbled around his pipe stem. "McLeod's a family man and a long way from a fool. He realizes he can't keep all his men single forever.

"Besides, she doesn't know I'm in love with her."

Steven sniffed and chuckled. "I'd wager she knew before you did. Women are quick on that sort of thing. They can read us like a book. Nothing escapes 'em."

"Things are too unsettled now with her people. Something like this might cause trouble. No, it's best I don't tell her."

"You might have a point there," Steven said solemnly.

They both stood silent, staring out into the deepening night, when suddenly an image appeared, a feathered apparition on a charging horse. Steven dropped his pipe and leaped backward to dive for his gun. Braden struggled to draw his revolver, backing way from the horse's flailing hooves, which threatened to rip him to shreds. But before either of them could arm themselves, a rich, deep chuckle wrapped around them and Spotted Eagle's grinning face emerged into the dim light.

"Long Lances should be more careful. This is Indian country," he said, comically waggling his eyebrows.

Braden laughed and sagged against the door frame, half relieved and half embarrassed. They had indeed been caught badly off guard.

Spotted Eagle sat his mount as most men wished they could—long legs dangling below his pony's belly, his body fluidly absorbing every fidgety step the pony made. He was an intimidating figure, the half-light shadowing his gaunt face. Despite the laughter sparkling in his eyes, Braden could well imagine him coldly sighting down Custer's men.

"Sitting Bull says you come. Three men have come

to our village from the Long Knives. We want no trouble."

"Long Knives?" Braden said, his senses instantly alert.

Spotted Eagle shook his head. "They make no trouble yet. We know the Black Shirt Father that brought them to us. One is a blue soldier."

"You speak English." The incongruity suddenly hit Braden.

Spotted Eagle grinned. "Smart man not give away all secrets at first."

Quickly, Braden's mind spun back over past meetings, assessing what might have been inadvertently said. To his relief, he could remember nothing untoward. Apparently enjoying his joke, Spotted Eagle grinned again. "You will come now?"

Steven's hand shook slightly as he reached to pick his pipe up out of the dirt. "Yes, we'll come as soon as we saddle our horses."

"I wait." Spotted Eagle crossed a leg over his horse's neck and lay down on the length of his pony's wide back.

Show-off, Braden thought with wry amusement as he went around the corner to saddle Brandy.

"Nearly scared the wits out of me," Steven mumbled as he saddled his mare.

"A carefully planned display," Braden answered.

"Meant to intimidate us?" Steven whispered.

"Meant to remind us who and what they are. Their pride is all they've got left."

Braden checked the ammunition in his belt and in his revolver and swung into the saddle. As they rode around the corner of their dugout, Spotted Eagle sat up and picked up the single rein that controlled his horse. Steven went inside the dugout and put out the lamp, casting them all onto the mercy of starlight.

Silvery shadows emerged as the safety of the warm, yellow light disappeared. They started in the direction of the Sioux village, every hair standing up on the back of Braden's neck.

For a time, Spotted Eagle rode alongside them in silence. Then he turned to Braden. "You have family? Woman?"

Braden shook his head. "No, not anymore."

"Woman die?"

"Yes, she died before she was my wife."

Spotted Eagle considered the answer for a few minutes. "She die in battle?"

Braden glanced at Spotted Eagle. They seemed to define a person by who their family was instead of viewing them as an individual. Perhaps that was a way to see not only who a person was, but who they might become, a clever advantage. Braden launched into his explanation of Anise's death and his journey to Canada, gauging Spotted Eagle's reaction from the corner of his eye.

"You come here to get another wife?" he asked.

"No," Braden responded, not daring to glance at Steven's face.

"Man needs woman," Spotted Eagle said as they came into sight of the village's flickering fires, dotting the river bank like fireflies in the grass. "In Sioux village, without woman, man has no home, no warm fire. Woman owns tipi, robes. Man living alone makes own food, sleeps alone." Spotted Eagle made a face. "*Wakantanka* make two." He held up two fingers.

"Woman keep man warm, give him children." He put down one finger. "Man bring food, protect children." He put down the other finger to form a fist. "Make Sioux strong."

Braden looked up at Spotted Eagle's angular face, and Spotted Eagle winked at him. "We will find Long Lance a woman."

A few people milled around in the sleeping village. A brown dog trotted across a dusty expanse, stopped in front of a tipi, and flopped down with a grunt. Campfires burned low, some merely glowing embers, lending an eerie and yet peaceful aura to the village.

Braden glanced at Steven, who raised his eyebrows, as close as he'd get to a comment. And as they passed home after home, flaps began to open and heads poked out. By the time they reached Sitting Bull's lodge, a small crowd was trailing them.

Braden swung down, threading his reins through his fingers, and wondered if Spotted Eagle had told him the truth. Were the men truly visiting, or were they prisoners? Had they been summoned to carry a message of defiance to Walsh, or merely to confirm there had been no trouble?

As the possibilities swam through his mind, Braden saw Sitting Bull hurrying toward him. Wearing only his breechcloth and leggings, he could have been mistaken for any other Sioux man and not the legendary killer he'd now been dubbed.

When he reached Braden, he extended his hand and Braden grasped it.

"I am glad you have come," he said as he pumped Braden's arm, obvious relief in his voice. "These men have come to us from the Long Knives to ask us to come and live on reservations. We want no trouble. We only want to sleep peacefully," he said, echoing the statement he'd already made many times.

Braden glanced over Sitting Bull's shoulder and met Dancing Bird's eyes. She wore a strip of leather across her shoulder to hold her arm in place. Despite the late hour, her eyes sparkled with curiosity and delight. Braden wondered if her uncle knew she was there, listening where she wasn't supposed to be. She met his glance and his heartbeat doubled. Her eyes narrowed and she smiled slyly. If he wasn't careful, she'd find some way to be in his arms before he left the camp tonight.

And if she didn't, he would.

"I know one of these men," Sitting Bull was saying. "He is Father Michaux. He lived with us many years ago and taught my niece to speak the white man's words. The other two men come from the Long Knives."

Before he could explain further, three men emerged from a tipi near Sitting Bull's and walked toward them. An armed guard walked closely by their side.

"They are *akicita*, our police," Sitting Bull hastened to explain. "I asked them to guard the men while they were here so there would be no harm to them."

Braden glanced at the angry expressions of the people now crowded around and at the scalps hanging from the ends of lances and the tips of lodgepoles. These men were either incredibly brave or incredibly stupid.

"Constable," the man in the blue uniform said with a nod as he stepped up beside Sitting Bull. "I'm Colonel Niles Ashton, sent here on orders from President Ulysses S. Grant. And this is Tom Worth, reporter for the *Chicago Tribune.* Father Michaux was kind enough to volunteer to bring us here and act as our interpreter."

The Father's expression didn't hold the enthusiasm of a man acting totally on the basis of his own will, but neither did he seem to have been forced. He stood calmly to one side, wearing a slight smile. He'd been Dancing Bird's teacher when she was small, a fact that should have at least given the good Father a permanent crease between his eyes. But his face was lineless and unreadable, and he stood with his hands concealed inside his black robe.

The reporter, on the other hand, was a brown little man. Brown hair, brown suit, brown hat, shoved back at a jaunty angle. He scribbled away at a pad of paper as the conversation swirled around him.

Braden swung his attention back to Colonel Ashton. "And why did ye not see fit to inform Assistant Commissioner James Walsh that ye were comin' to visit?"

Ashton looked taken aback for a moment, but he rallied quickly with a slow smile. "I hardly felt this was a matter for the Mounted Police. These are our Indians—refugees from justice, really. I'm only doing them the courtesy of asking them to come back instead of riding in with an armed force and herding them back across the border. We've learned in dealing with the American savage, Constable, that leaving them some dignity makes them more manageable."

Did the man think him such a fool that he wouldn't see through his goading? He was testing his mettle, trying to see if Walsh would back up his much publicized promises with action.

"Sure and the last time I looked, Colonel, this was Canadian soil yer standin' on. Are ye contemplatin' an invasion? Did we not whip yer American asses once before when ye came chargin' across the border, beatin' yer chests and yellin'?

Braden delivered the speech with a smile pasted on his face. The smile became real when the colonel's face blanched.

"I meant no threat, Constable. I merely meant that the Sioux are our problem and perhaps you shouldn't involve yourself in this."

Braden dropped his reins and, with a glance at Steven's amused face, began to circle the group of three. He'd had enough arrogance to last him a lifetime. Arrogance had kicked at him and shunned him when he'd stumbled off the ship from Ireland. Arrogance had denied him jobs and lodging as soon as his Irish brogue escaped his lips. And arrogance had wished all Irishmen dead or sent packing back to their starving island.

"I'd say the problem came to us, Colonel. And as long as they abide by the rules Assistant Commissioner Walsh laid down, they're welcome to stay."

"And if they don't obey those rules?"

"Then they will have to go back across the border."

Ashton glanced at Sitting Bull.

"It is as he says," the chief said with a nod.

"Perhaps we can sit down and discuss this," Ashton tried, changing the tone of his voice.

Sitting Bull whirled around and pinned Dancing Bird with a glare. "Go and tell your mother to prepare for guests."

With a surprised look on her face, Dancing Bird scurried away without a backward look.

A young warrior tentatively approached them. Steven handed him the reins and smiled. The young man smiled back and led their mounts away with soothing words and a pat to Brandy's shoulder.

By the time they reached Sitting Bull's tipi, it was empty and prepared for a council. Sweetgrass burned on the altar, its pungent smoke curling upward. Buffalo robes had been spread on the lodge floor, and Dancing Bird was nowhere to be seen. He'd bet his sidearm her ear was firmly pressed to the back of the tipi, Braden thought as he ducked inside.

They all sat down, and Sitting Bull passed around a clay pipe that had been left for them. Each man in turn drew on the pipe. Steven raised his eyebrows at Braden when the fragrant tobacco smoke coiled up to his nose. Ceremony completed, Ashton launched into his pitch, saying nothing Braden hadn't heard discussed before.

The Americans offered the Sioux sanctuary on reservations where their weapons and horses would be collected and sold to buy cattle and farming implements. Each family would be given land to own, and they would be expected to feed themselves from this portion of land for the rest of their lives. They would not be permitted to hunt buffalo or leave the reservation. They would never again make war on the white man.

Sitting Bull's face was impassive as Ashton spelled out the end to all the Sioux valued, prompting Braden to mentally add a few mandates of his own.

They would never again ride through thigh-high buffalo grass with the warm summer sun on their naked backs.

They would gladly give the *wašichu* all that they held dear, all that was sacred, and do so with obedience and reverence for their conquerors.

"No." Sitting Bull shook his head. "We will not return. We are happy here. Our women do not cry and bury their babies."

Ashton was nonplussed. "You won't have to work so hard, risk your lives hunting the buffalo. You won't have to roam and move from place to place. You can live out the rest of your life in one place."

Sitting Bull's lips twitched in a half smile at the man's ignorance. "The life you have just described seems like a difficult life to you, but it is what makes us Sioux. *Wakantanka* gave us this land and all that is on it to feed and clothe our children. What you have just said, would you like this life?"

Ashton looked puzzled. "What do you mean?"

"These things you have told us, would you like to live this way?"

Ashton was shaken, his mask of confidence sadly slipping. "Why . . . sure."

"Then have blue soldiers live on these lands, farm, and raise cattle. We will stay here in the White Mother's Land."

Having driven home the slight, Sitting Bull rose and stalked from the lodge.

"That arrogant—"

"If I were ye, Colonel, I'd choose me words carefully," Braden said with a knowing glance at Spotted Eagle, who glared at Ashton from his robe beside Sitting Bull's now empty spot. With a final sneer, Spotted Eagle and the rest of Sitting Bull's sub-chiefs rose one by one and filed out, leaving Braden and the visitors alone.

"I thought you said you could convince him." Ashton lashed out at Father Michaux.

"I said I could get him to listen to you. Convincing

was your job," the Father replied. "But I can see diplomacy is not your strong suit."

Ashton reddened and Worth scribbled frantically on his pad. "There's not enough food to feed them all indefinitely. I'm sure your commander knows this," Ashton sputtered at Braden, his face growing redder.

"He's aware of that fact, as are we all. But forcin' 'em back into the hell ye created for 'em isn't the answer, either."

"The free bands of Sioux roaming the Dakotas were ordered to give themselves up last spring, before Custer's massacre. Their refusal to comply is what caused Grant to send troops to enforce the order."

"And just how did ye think the word was goin' to get to all of 'em, and why did ye think they'd believe ye? Ye've never given 'em any reason to believe ye before." Braden felt his temper slipping. Ignorance was right behind arrogance on his list of intolerances, and Colonel Ashton was a shining example. If the rest of the United States cavalry were like him, no wonder they'd made such a mess of things.

"I demand to see your commander. I insist you take me to Fort Walsh immediately."

"I'd be glad to accompany you there." Steven slid smoothly into the conversation. "Constable Flynn has other duties that demand his attention. We'll return to our post and leave in the morning." Steven's voice was as smooth as milk, his tone even and calm, the perfect salve for the situation. Braden threw him what he hoped was a glance of gratitude.

Ashton and Worth rose and stalked out of the tipi, followed by an embarrassed Father Michaux. A small knot of curious people waited for them, which Ashton and Worth waded through without comment. Father Michaux paused and turned to Braden.

"Despite his woeful lack of tact, Ashton's right about the food supply."

Braden glanced at the faces surrounding him and felt an edge of dread slice through him. Would starvation always be his shadow, like some wraith sent from hell to haunt all his days?

"I know that. So do McLeod and Walsh. But sendin' 'em back to the likes of Ashton isn't a solution."

The Father smiled at the upturned faces and spoke softly in their language, assuring them all was well and they could go back to their sleeping robes.

Father Michaux watched them shuffle away, dragging sleepy children behind them, and his eyes grew misty. "They were a grand and glorious people in the old days," he said, his voice slipping curiously. "They commanded their world from the back of a horse and answered only to their God."

"Sure and wasn't it your job to convert 'em, Father?"

The priest smiled. "And so it is. But to see a love of God so strong, so confident." Father Michaux slanted a sidelong glance at Braden. "The Holy Church sometimes seems from another world."

Braden nodded as Father Michaux moved away with a soft swish of robes. He was left alone in the center of the still village. An occasional soft snore issued from a lodge and somewhere soft moans suggested lovemaking.

Shoving his hands into his pockets, Braden walked toward the outskirts of the village, where Brandy grazed on knee-high grass. Overhead, quivering stars popped out of an ebony sky, bathing the sleeping earth in silvery starshine. Alone in the dark, Braden gazed up at the vastness of the heavens above and wondered about Father Michaux's last words.

How fitting and natural the Sioux beliefs seemed, he thought, hearing his old village priest's horrified voice hissing *blasphemy.* How right that a people would worship the things that nourished them in body and spirit—the sun, the earth, the buffalo. Raised in the grandeur of the Catholic church, the simplicity of the Sioux beliefs was almost overwhelming.

Brandy whickered softly and nudged his jacket with her nose as he ran his hand across her shoulder. Steven had left with Ashton and Worth, and Braden was reluctant to follow. He'd had all the politics he wanted for one day.

Brandy raised her head, pricked her ears forward, and stared at something over his shoulder. Braden turned and found Dancing Bird standing close behind him.

She was temptation personified in the silvery light. A dark mantel of hair hung over one bare shoulder where her dress had slipped to the side to reveal smooth, brown skin. The leather strap that bound her arm stretched across her chest and defined the swell of her breasts beneath the soft leather of her dress. She moved toward him with no hesitation in her steps.

Assailed by a wave of want that nearly buckled his knees, Braden threw an arm over his mare's neck and pulled her closer for distraction. Dancing Bird stopped inches away from him, the toes of her soft moccasins nudged against the toes of his dusty black boots.

She raised her face to look up at him and he knew, for the second time in his life, that he was lost.

Eight

He lowered his head, hesitating only a second while the voices of reason screamed in his ear. This was insane. Irresponsible. Impossible. He barely knew her, barely understood her or the life she led. And yet he was drawn to her as surely as the sun sailed across the sky.

Was there truth in the romantic Irish legends he'd heard all his life? Was there a destiny for everyone, an undeniable and inescapable calling that propelled lovers over obstacles and pitfalls into each other's arms?

And then he shut his mind to the voices and kissed her. She tasted smoky and sweet and forbidden, and his heart hammered frantically as she responded with an eagerness he hadn't expected. Drawing her closer, he ran a hand down her back, over the swell of her hips, and fought the urge to cup her flesh in his hand and pull her hard against him.

Unfortunately, she felt none of the same reserves. Her hands smoothed down the length of his jacket and out across his hips. Then her hands moved forward, sliding across the fabric of his pants toward the small space between them. Her lips curved into a smile beneath his kiss. Shocked, he pulled away first.

"Yer a naughty lass," he wheezed as she looked up, her eyes twinkling.

"You are firm and strong. You would be a good warrior . . . if you were Sioux."

Shaken, he struggled to regain his sense and listen to her words, fearful of what he might find himself committed to if he missed a single word. "If I were Sioux, your mother would have me skinned and hanging in little pieces on her drying rack."

A warm night breeze swept across them, rustling the grass at their feet and inspiring the insects into a new symphony. One chirping voice was joined by two and then more until their voices swelled and filled the night, then fell silent as suddenly as they'd begun.

Braden thought his heart would burst from his chest as he closed his eyes and fought back the fantasies cavorting through his thoughts. There was no hiding his response to her caresses, nothing to prevent her from seeing how far she'd pushed him except the dim mantle of night. Her eyes swept down his body and back up and she smiled. He felt as if he stood before her naked . . . physically and emotionally.

Her eyes lost their twinkle and filled with concern as his cheeks burned with embarrassment. What must she think of him? Worse, what message was he sending her? She caressed his cheek with soft, cool fingers. "This is an honor you pay me," she whispered, toying with the edges of his ear.

He turned away from her, fighting to regain control of both his body and his dignity, neither of which was listening at the moment. " 'Tis not a proper thing where I come from."

"Why? Do men not want women in Ire-land?" she pursued without mercy.

Saints above, he was in it now. "Of course they do, but . . . not quite so obviously."

"There is nothing to be ashamed of. This is how it is between women and men. How else will a woman know her man wants her?"

"Well"—Braden half turned, wondering if anyone had ever really died of mortification—"we usually tell 'em."

Dancing Bird smiled, stepped around him, and trailed her fingers across his lips. "White men use too many words. Words can lie. Bodies cannot." She moved close again, pressing against the length of him, and he winced. Looking up at him with wide eyes, her fingers traced a crooked path down his jacket, weaving in and out between the brass buttons, across his broad leather belt. He caught her wrists.

"Please don't," he begged.

"I have done something wrong?" she asked, concern darkening her eyes.

"No, ye've done nothin' wrong." He relaxed his grip and rubbed the insides of her wrists with his thumbs. "We come from people with different ways. My people marry before we are . . . close with each other." Even as he said the words, memories of a passionate, storm-racked afternoon rose to haunt him.

"We marry, too, before we sleep with our men, but not always. If the man and woman are promised to each other . . ." She shrugged her shoulders.

Braden gathered her hands in his and brought her fingers to his lips. "I was sent here to watch over your people, to make sure there is no trouble that would make the White Mother send you home."

A sheen of tears brightened her eyes. "You do not love me?"

The words stuck in his throat. Was she asking for a declaration? Did she mean *love* in the sense of commitment or did she simply mean fondness? Even though her English was excellent, there was the chance she would misinterpret anything he said from this point forward, and the consequences of that could be disastrous both personally and diplomatically.

"I am very fond of you," he said, choosing his words very carefully. "You are my friend."

He couldn't tell her how much he wanted her, how much he loved her, not now. Perhaps never.

She recoiled as if he'd slapped her. "I have seen that you want me with your body," she said. "And in here"—she laid a hand over her heart—"I know you want me, too. Why do you lie?"

Braden gathered her hands in his and absently rubbed her fingers. " 'Tis a dangerous time for you and your people. There are people who do not want the Sioux here in the White Mother's Land, people that would do anythin' to see ye sent to the blue soldiers' reservations. It is these people I am here to stop. If I were to . . . love you . . . then these people would use that against me. Do ye understand what I'm sayin', lass?"

She held his gaze for so long he thought she was about to agree. Suddenly, she snatched her hands away and stalked off. "You are like the other *wašíchu*," she threw back over her shoulder. "You lie. And you are man, so you lie twice."

Her gait was so jaunty, he would have sworn she was

stomping her feet. "You see woman, you want her, then you say stupid things." Her voice grew fainter as she widened the distance between them. "This is why I do not want a husband. Then my days would be filled with stupid things." She waved her one good hand over her head in exasperation and marched down a dip in the landscape until she was out of sight.

Braden turned to Brandy. The mare stared back at him quizzically, a tuft of grass sticking out either side of her mouth.

" 'Tis a blessin' ye can't comment on the fool I just made of meself."

Brandy returned to her chewing, quivering the sprigs of grass caught in her bit.

Moving-Robe-Woman stood in the shadows cast by a lone willow and watched her daughter stalk past. She followed the line of a hill to where the Long Lance with red hair stood with his horse, staring off into the night. The time had come to find her headstrong daughter a husband . . . and quickly.

"Big Dog has asked to stand in the blanket with you."

Dancing Bird looked up from her quilling and stared at her mother, hoping she had not heard correctly. "What?"

Moving-Robe-Woman sawed at a buffalo hide suspended on a slanted tree branch, raking a hair remover back and forth across it. Bits of hair floated at will on the breeze and found their way into everybody's mouths, food, and beds. "I said Big Dog wishes to court you."

"He is an old man!"

"He is not so old."

"His hair is turning white."

"White hair makes him look wise."

"It makes him look old. You told him no, didn't you?"

Her mother didn't answer. She raked harder, sending fur flying.

"Mother?"

"I told him you would see him," Moving-Robe-Woman said shortly, keeping her eyes on her task.

"He's ugly," Dancing Bird protested.

Moving-Robe-Woman glanced up with narrowed eyes. "Handsome doesn't fill the paunch or warm the sleeping robes."

"But it helps. Besides, he's already killed one wife."

Moving-Robe-Woman shook her head and tightened her lips. "She died in the flood."

"Only because he stumbled and knocked her into the water."

Her mother was undaunted. "It is time you took a husband. He is a good man."

Big Dog was indeed a decent enough man with a good reputation, but he was a shining example at nothing. He lumbered through the camp, snapping tree limbs with his large feet and scaring children with his looming presence. Nothing about him made her want to crawl into his sleeping robes.

"I will find a husband for myself," Dancing Bird countered, wondering what had brought her mother to this moment of panic that she would marry her daughter off to the village clown.

"No. You are like your father. Your mind is on the trees and the birds when it should be on gathering food." The hair removing stick whizzed through the air and a thick layer of hair floated around them.

Dancing Bird picked a hair off her tongue. She'd never heard her mother say a single word against her father. Ever. To hear her do so now meant that something deeper was wrong than a simple search for a husband.

Her mother sighed and stopped scraping the hide. "Your father thought I was too serious, and he loved to laugh and play. I was taught to prepare for bad things. He lived from sunrise to sunrise. I never understood that way he had."

"Didn't you love him?"

Moving-Robe-Woman looked across the prairie, where shadow and sun danced in merry abandon. "With everything in me." She swung her face back toward Dancing Bird. "But if he had been cautious that day, and not foolish, he would be here with us now."

Dancing Bird touched her mother's arm. "You cannot blame him for dying."

Moving-Robe-Woman pulled her arm away and again scrubbed frantically at the hide. "Big Dog will be here tonight. Go and prepare yourself."

"I won't be courted by him. I don't like him, Mother."

Moving-Robe-Woman stopped her rubbing again and looked at her daughter. "We have lived with my brother long enough. Your sister will be married in three suns. Your brother will soon have his own lodge and take a wife. When you are married, I will become a second wife, and your uncle will have no more responsibility for us."

Her mother's eyes were desperate, driven. Dancing

Bird dropped the quilling she held and crawled through the pile of hair at her mother's feet until she knelt at her mother's side. "You said you would never be a second wife," she reminded softly. "We agreed we would have our own lodge and live as we chose."

Moving-Robe-Woman raised troubled eyes. "I said many things after your father died to ease your pain."

"But you still love Father."

"Love is a luxury. Better to have a man who is a good hunter."

Could the kind of love her parents shared, the love she craved, disappear so easily, like flower petals on a spring breeze?

"You don't really believe that," Dancing Bird whispered.

Her mother dropped the hair removing stick and pulled Dancing Bird close. "I only want you safe, little one, safe and happy. A woman alone is not safe. She needs a man to protect her, to provide for her."

In her mother's world, those words were true. A man was a necessity. But not in the world she hoped to create for herself. Times were changing for her people, and she sensed that soon, the world as her mother knew it would cease to exist and they would be left to forge a new one. Perhaps this destiny was what her father had been trying to prepare her for all these years.

"Now go and prepare. Big Dog will be here soon." Her mother held her at arm's length and smiled a rare smile.

Her knees buried in buffalo fur, Dancing Bird stared into her mother's face, into dim brown eyes that had once danced with merriment. Maybe she could stand an hour or so in a blanket with Big Dog if it would bring back that light.

"I made a bloody fool of meself. Even Brandy there thought so." Braden sawed at a strip of sinew, then sat back and wiped the blood off his hands onto the soft, green grass. He and Steven had traded their uniforms for buckskins, now streaked with blood, in order to butcher a buffalo Steven had shot.

Steven glanced over at the mare, who raised her head at the mention of her name. He stood, straightened his back with a groan, and spread a blanket across the buffalo carcass before them. Then he sat down on the beast's hindquarters and filled his pipe, his arms braced on his knees.

When smoke curled up from the carved bowl, he took it out of his mouth and studied it. "Ah, well then, I trust Brandy's opinion."

Braden scowled at him, and Steven laughed softly.

"I acted like a ruttin' buck and she knew it."

"You aren't the first man to get carried away in the arms of a beautiful woman, and you aren't likely to be the last."

"She touched me in ways . . . in places . . ." Braden lifted a chunk of meat and placed it on the waiting travois.

"She's from another culture, a people not terrified by their own humanity. They've learned how to incorporate lust into their lives without the devastation the church would have us believe will ensue."

"Still, I gave her the wrong idea."

"I'd say you didn't give her anything, old chap. She

had her own ideas before you ever touched her. The proud men of Troop B are falling one by one." Steven grinned at him, and Braden glared back as he straightened the kinks out of his legs.

The bull buffalo they'd killed would provide them with enough meat to last the winter, once it was salted and dried. The rest they'd take to Sitting Bull's village. The shaggy hide lay rolled neatly to the side, a gift for Dancing Bird, an addition to her lodge collection.

Braden walked away from the carcass and drew a breath of fresh air untinged with the scent of blood. He toed the fresh hide with his boot and wondered if she'd accept his gift. A soft breeze blew through his hair, and he imagined her fingers doing the same. "I never wanted Anise as badly as I wanted Dancing Bird at that moment."

"When my wife died, I vowed I'd never take another woman."

Braden whirled around. "You were married?"

Steven nodded, his pipe firmly clamped in his teeth. "For four years. We'd known each other since we were children."

"What happened?" He never would have guessed that sorrow lay behind Steven's calm gray eyes.

"Complications of childbirth. I lost her and my son."

In the years he'd known him, Braden had never seen melancholy in Steven, never seen the anguish that had seemed to eat at himself and Colin in those early days.

"At first I considered it punishment for so sorely disappointing both my parents and hers, and I shook my fist at the heavens, as they say." He took the pipe out of his mouth and studied its lines and angles, all the while still perched on the bleeding buffalo carcass.

"They didn't see the art in clowning and thought I'd lost my mind, reverted to childhood, couldn't take responsibility—all the objections you might imagine. After Catherine died, I left my job and worked exclusively as a clown in a small circus. I found catharsis in hiding behind dear old Bubbles. And then I realized that that was exactly what I was doing—hiding—and Catherine would have been furious with me."

"Is that when you joined the force?"

Steven nodded. "The point of these ramblings is that in those dark days I discovered two things." He slid off the carcass and stood. "The first was that Catherine was dead. She had lived, and quite enjoyably, I might add, a full and wonderful life. But she was gone and would never return. I awoke one morning dreaming she was pulling my ear, something she did quite frequently when I made a fool of myself. And I realized then and there that she was raving at me from the other side about the precious time I was wasting."

Steven picked up the fresh hide, tossed it up behind Braden's saddle, and tied it down while Brandy danced nervously, rolling her eyes at the scent of fresh blood.

"The second," he continued as he wiped his hands on the grass, "was that regret is a curse we place on ourselves. Only we can remove it. Left alone it will consume us."

He picked up the reins and handed them to Braden. "Act, don't think, old chap. Thinking, as my Catherine used to say, will only get you in trouble."

Sunset stained the sky by the time all the meat was loaded onto the two travois. Steven took one to their outpost to begin the arduous task of smoking and drying the meat. The other now skidded behind Brandy's heels. Flute music wafted on the last wisps of day as Braden rode into the outskirts of the village.

He was grateful that crowds had stopped gathering at his appearance. Now only smiling faces and nods greeted him.

Courting couples stood in front of their parents' lodges wrapped in colorful blankets, only their heads and shoulders visible. Blushing maidens looked up as he passed, covering their giggles with cupped hands. Steven's words circulated through his head. The blanket was symbolic of union vows, he supposed. Two people both bound and protected by their promises, and yet their degree of intimacy was hidden by the folds of cloth—a unique blend of lust and social mores.

As he approached Sitting Bull's lodge, he saw Walks Lightly and her husband-to-be wrapped together in a gray and red blanket in front of the home. They were to be married in a few days, and he and Steven had been invited to the celebration.

A familiar laugh reached his ears and he glanced around for Dancing Bird, hoping for a candid glimpse of her, but she was nowhere to be seen. Standing Elk let the blanket slide off his shoulder just as Braden drew to a stop in front of the tipi. Curious, Braden thought. He didn't remember Standing Elk being so tall or so broad shouldered. He swung down from the saddle just as Dancing Bird peeped around the towering man, a brilliant smile on her face . . . until she saw Braden.

Words fled, and Braden stood slack-jawed. Dancing Bird's smile melted into shock and her cheeks flamed. Moving-Robe-Woman hurried out of the tipi, concern etched across her face. With a nervous glance at Dancing Bird and her partner, she turned and smiled at Braden.

"We killed a buffalo, and there is too much meat for us to use. Will you take the rest?" he managed to say with as much aplomb as he could muster. Dancing Bird translated softly and her mother nodded and answered.

"She says she will take the meat so it will not spoil."

Only then did Braden turn toward the couple, his heartbeat pounding out the word *stupid, stupid, stupid* in his ears. The man of her choice was gray-haired, easily old enough to be her father, Braden guessed with a nauseous roll of his stomach, and he stared at Braden with a vacant expression that gave neither welcome nor suspicion.

Dancing Bird's cheeks still glowed pink with the heat of embarrassment as she stepped out of the blanket and sidled away from her suitor.

"I brought you two gifts," Braden said, struggling to keep his face and words impassive. He pivoted, untied the pelt, and laid it on the ground at her feet. Then he opened his saddlebag and withdrew the brown-paper-wrapped length of calico and placed it in her hands.

Dancing Bird looked down at the skin and the package, then raised her eyes to meet his. Everything that had passed between them was still there in her eyes, and yet his sense of reason rushed to provide him comfort. *This is as it should be,* the voice argued. She was seeking a husband, planning a family, a stable life. Wasn't that his job? To see that this came to pass?

The man at her side frowned and spoke sharply. Dancing Bird barked a reply at him, and he looked both chagrined and surprised. She gathered the blanket and shoved it into his arms. He strode away with a dark, backward glance.

She squatted down and examined the pelt. "I cannot accept this."

"Why not?"

"Because when a man brings a woman gifts, he is asking to court her." She looked up into his face, and his confident voice of reason fled as his heart turned a somersault.

"Sure and that's not my intention."

The remark hurt him more than the pain that passed through her eyes before she looked down. He wanted to fall to his knees and beg her forgiveness for his heartless remark, but the memory of her tinkling laughter, expended on someone else, foolishly hardened his heart. He was angry, but at himself. He could not give her what she could find in the arms of this warrior. His home was the dirt dugout, for the moment, and his wife was the Northwest Mounted Police.

"I meant that I intended for you to use it for your lodge cover."

She looked up again, her eyes bright with a suggestion of tears. "My family and I thank you." She unwrapped the paper and shook out the colorful calico. Clasping the fabric against her chest, she returned her gaze to his face and his heart pooled in the bottom of his stomach. "Thank you."

He put a foot in his stirrup and gripped the saddle pommel.

"Are you coming to the marriage celebration?" she asked, stopping him with a hand on his knee.

Warmth spread from her touch, crawling into intimate places in his body, chasing away the voice of reason, stripping him of his carefully controlled nonchalance. He looked down at her small hand, rough and scarred from work, and wondered at the power it held over him.

"Yes, Steven and I are coming."

She released him and stepped back as he swung into the saddle.

"Mother arranged for Big Dog to come here tonight."

The confidence she wore like a suit of armor was gone as she looked up at him. He longed to sweep her up in front of him and carry her away to some place where they bore no responsibility for others and played no roles, someplace where they'd be free to explore their love and each other.

"She says it is time I found a husband."

But no such place existed. They were both trapped in their separate roles, walking predetermined paths that would never intersect—like deep wagon ruts.

"Perhaps she is right," he said softly.

Nine

Dancing Bird pillowed her cheek on her arm and drifted through the cobwebs of her dreams. She was in Braden's arms. The night was warm and sultry with insect songs and a caressing breeze that fingered through their hair. And he looked down at her with eyes that were open to his soul.

He belonged to her and she to him.

A marriage ceremony went on around them—their marriage ceremony.

She smiled and snuggled deeper into the soft sleeping robe until someone pushed at her leg. She fought leaving the dream.

"Dancing Bird," a voice chastised. "Get up and tend the meat."

The voice of authority worked its way into her mind and she cracked open an eye. The dream vanished and the smell of roasting meat consumed her.

"Get up and tend the meat," her mother said again.

She rolled to her back and looked up at her mother's scowling face.

"You would let the food for the marriage feast burn if I let you."

Dancing Bird pushed herself to a sitting position and

rubbed her eyes. A chunk of meat hung over a struggling fire, dripping fat, providing a path for flames to sizzle and blacken the outside of the roast.

Quickly, she extinguished the flames with a stick and spread the orange coals further apart.

"What were you dreaming?" her mother asked, squatting by her side to tend a paunch of bubbling greens.

Dancing Bird spun back the last few minutes of her dream and decided to lie. "I dreamed I was riding on the prairie with Father."

Her mother slanted a suspicious glance at her. "You were smiling."

"Was I?"

Her mother picked up a stick and stirred the contents of the paunch. "I haven't seen you smile like that in a long time."

"It was summer and the wind was in my face. We were riding very fast." The lie needed a little improvement.

"Hmmm." Her mother grunted and put down the stick. "Do you have your sister's dress ready?"

Dancing Bird glanced toward the back of the tipi where Walks Lightly's new dress hung, beaded and bright. She'd put the last touches of beading on it last night while struggling to stay awake and see to the meat that was their offering for the marriage feast. "It's ready."

Her mother rose and stepped over sleeping relatives. The number of people in the tipi had finally thinned as new lodges were finished and erected. Now only Dancing Bird and her family remained with her uncle, his wife, and their young son, White Elk. Moving-Robe-Woman fingered the beadwork and smiled.

"You did well," she said, beaming.

Dancing Bird didn't comment that she'd hated every stitch she'd put in. Sitting for hours chasing tiny little beads with a bone needle was not her idea of fun.

"One day soon your sister will do this for you," Moving-Robe-Woman said, smoothing the already smooth garment.

Dancing Bird stiffened. So far, she'd been able to avoid the subject of Big Dog and herself. He'd returned for three nights with his blanket in his arms. Each time she'd managed to keep the conversation short and his hands where they belonged. In the three nights they'd spent with their heads covered by the blanket, she felt no closer to him than before. Their communication consisted of either silent breathing or a listing of his battle accomplishments. He knew no endearments or romantic words, and she sensed a directness in him that would probably translate into painful and frequent coupling in the marriage bed.

In those nights they spent beneath the blanket, she endured the time in his company by remembering the feel of Braden's lips against hers, by remembering the light in his eyes, by keeping alive the small flame of hope that he would return and declare his love. But he hadn't. Part of her understood, but none of her accepted it. And as the days crawled past, her family's interest in Big Dog grew.

"It is time to prepare," her mother declared and went to shake awake Little Bear.

The morning passed in a flurry of activity and Dancing Bird found herself mindlessly moving from one task to the next, a welcome respite for her weary mind. By the time the sun was straight overhead, the preparations were complete.

"Are you nervous?" Dancing Bird asked Walks Lightly as she smoothed a braid into place.

Her sister's hand shook slightly as she reached up to check Dancing Bird's work. "A little."

Dancing Bird moved around in front of her sister. After today, nothing would be the same between them, she realized, her stomach churning. Funny that in all the scurrying over the last few days, that thought hadn't entered her mind. As different in nature as the sun was from the moon, they were still sisters, each a silent shadow to the other in times of joy and pain.

Now that circle would be broken. Walks Lightly would be an integral part of another family circle, tend her own fire, raise her own tipi. There would be no more nights of giggling and whispering and no more shared secrets with sly glances hidden from their mother. Soon after the ceremony, her love with Standing Elk would be consummated, and as she slept in her husband's arms, she would pass from the ranks of girl to woman.

Dancing Bird pushed aside a strand of her sister's hair and Walks Lightly raised tearful eyes. "I will miss you," she whispered.

"I will miss you, too." Dancing Bird touched her sister's cheek. "But you will not be far away."

Walks Lightly shook her head. "Not in distance. I had not realized until now how different we will be."

Dancing Bird forced a laugh. "You are a nervous bride. Tomorrow morning you will see nothing has changed," she lied, overwhelmed with the same protective urge to make things right for her family she'd felt since her father's death.

Walks Lightly was not fooled. "You know this is not true. If Standing Elk decides to join another band after this summer, I must go with him."

"Has he talked of this?" Panic gripped Dancing Bird's throat.

Walks Lightly shrugged. "Some people are talking of returning home. They say soon there will be no buffalo here and we will be hungry again. They say it is better to farm than starve."

Dancing Bird gripped her sister's shoulders, fighting down the panic now rolling through her. "You must not let him go. We have sacrificed much to come here to the White Mother's Land. Father died so that we could come here."

Walks Lightly hung her head as a tear dripped off her nose. "He will be my husband, and I must follow him."

"Then don't marry him. Stay here with us. It is not too late."

Walks Lightly's head came up and she smiled. "Of course I must marry him. I love him, and I must go where he goes. That is the way it is. One day it will be this way for you."

"No." Dancing Bird shook her head. "I will never give up my family and my will for a husband."

"Big Dog has spoken with Uncle and our brother about you. They are talking about how many horses he will bring."

The panic she felt shifted into full tilt. "When?"

"I heard them talking about it last night as they planned a buffalo hunt."

"What exactly did they say?"

Walks Lightly frowned. "Uncle said that Big Dog has many coups in battle, that he is a brave warrior. He has stolen many horses. His wife would be well provided for. Uncle thinks he will make an offer for you after my marriage."

Suddenly, the world was a narrow, dark place. The role in life she'd shunned and stepped around now yawned before her. If Sitting Bull gave his consent, she would be Big Dog's wife. She would cook his food, clean his clothes, endure his lovemaking, and bear his children. His will would become hers.

"What did Uncle say?" she asked, dreading the answer.

"He said he must talk to you first."

Given a reprieve, at least for the moment, Dancing Bird pasted a smile back on her face and pushed the problem away for later consideration. She would see Big Dog today, but she would try to ignore him. Perhaps he would lose interest.

A stir outside caught their attention, and they hurried to look outside the open tipi flap. Three Long Lances rode into the village abreast, the two scouts following behind. Dancing Bird stepped outside, leaving her sister inside in her wedding finery.

Braden rode on the outside of the three, carrying a bright red and white flag on a tall lance. Beside him rode Steven, and on the end was Long Lance Walsh. Their uniforms were brilliant red, cleaned and smoothed. Long, white gloves came half way up their arms and their boots gleamed in the hot, midday sun.

None looked right or left as they passed through the village and stopped where Sitting Bull and his chiefs sat in the shade of bending willows, awaiting the ceremony. Dancing Bird slipped into the crowd following them, ignoring her sister's warning.

Walsh dismounted first and stepped up to Sitting Bull. *"Hí ha ni wašté."*

Sitting Bull smiled. "Yes, fine morning."

Braden swung down, his uniform pants stretching smooth over his hips and legs. His gleaming white helmet all but hid his face, the strap secured beneath his chin. He pulled the end of the long lance from a leather strap on his saddle and planted it in the soil at her uncle's side.

Sitting Bull gazed up at the fluttering red and white material, then smiled and nodded. Braden said something to him and smiled himself, flashing white teeth. Too far away to make out the words they exchanged, Dancing Bird was content to simply watch him and memorize the way his every muscle moved. His jacket hugged his wide chest and flared out across narrow hips. Long, black boots covered his pants nearly to his knees and defined his legs. He was beautiful.

And even if he had been as ugly as Big Dog, she'd have loved him anyway, she admitted, leaning back against a sapling willow, the hopelessness of her situation taking the strength out of her knees. One day, these memories of him would be all she'd have.

Bitter tears started at the corners of her eyes, and she swiped at them angrily. She wouldn't cry now. Her family was depending on her. Her sister needed her strength as she began to walk a new and strange path. She would cry tonight when she was alone, sob out her sorrow to the wind and the moon with only the prairie grass as witness.

"We are ready," her mother whispered at her elbow.

She hastily dried her tears on the guise of pushing back her hair.

"I am coming." She turned toward her mother. Moving-Robe-Woman frowned, slanted a glance toward the Long Lances, then smiled softly. "Walks Lightly is waiting to see you."

Dancing Bird pushed through the crowd unnoticed and entered her uncle's tipi. Walks Lightly stood in the center with her hands folded in front of her. Whatever doubts she'd had moments ago were now safely locked inside her. She lifted serene eyes to Dancing Bird's face and smiled. "Good-bye, sister."

The tears started again and Dancing Bird let them run down her face. "Do not say that."

Walks Lightly stepped forward and caught a tear on her finger. "This is a strange day when you are the one crying."

"Everything has ch-changed too quickly," Dancing Bird stuttered.

Walks Lightly pulled Dancing Bird into her arms. "You are our strength. Father gave his strength to you before he died. It has comforted us to know that you carry him within you. Do not fail me now," she said with a trembling voice.

"If you don't love Standing Elk, then don't marry him. We can escape out the back of the tipi and run away until I can think of an explanation." Dancing Bird pulled away and looked into her sister's face.

Walks Lightly smiled. "Only you would think of that, sister. I love him with all my heart. I can think of nothing I would rather do than be his wife. It is you I worry about."

"Me?"

Walks Lightly pulled her close again. "You love the Long Lance named Braden, don't you?"

"Yes."

"Has he offered horses for you?"

"No."

Walks Lightly hugged Dancing Bird tightly. "You are like Father, like the butterflies that live for the summer and think nothing of the winter. Mother and Brother and I are like the ugly grasshoppers that ignore the beauty of summer and prepare for the winter. You have given your heart to a man you cannot have. Your pain is deeper than ours and your joy brighter. This is why I worry about you."

"Do not worry about me," Dancing Bird said with as much courage as she could muster. "I will find a way. Don't I always?"

Walks Lightly smiled. "Yes, you do."

"Then come. Standing Elk is growing weary of waiting for his wife." Feigning happiness she didn't feel, Dancing Bird led her sister outside, where a black and white pony waited. A blanket covered the pony's ample back and prairie flowers bobbed in its mane.

Walks Lightly paused long enough to hug her mother, then leaped onto the pony's back. Eager villagers opened a path for her as she rode toward the river where Standing Elk and her uncle waited beneath the bending willows. When she stopped before them, Standing Elk reached up and plucked her from the horse's back to stand at his side. He wore the quilled vest his mother had worked on for months. Smooth tan buckskin leggings reached up to a beaded breechcloth.

Sitting Bull rose to his feet, his long eagle-feather headdress sweeping the ground, one of the few possessions that had survived the desperate flight from their home. For the first time in more than a year, he looked the part of leader of his people.

Dancing Bird faded into the crowd, fighting a lump in her throat. Braden and his party stood to her uncle's immediate right, apparently given this position of honor. Holding their helmets in front of them, the three red-clad men kept their gazes on the couple before them.

"Today you take my niece as your wife," Sitting Bull began, a kind smile on his face. "From now on she will be your responsibility."

Standing Elk nodded and looked down at Walks Lightly with open adoration.

"You ask her to cook your food and bear your children, to bind your wounds and tend your home. Do you agree to these responsibilities?"

"Yes," Standing Elk said.

"Do you, Walks Lightly, agree to do these things as your duties as his wife?"

"Yes, I do," her sister answered.

"Then take her. She is yours," Sitting Bull said.

Standing Elk lifted Walks Lightly and placed her on the painted pony's back. He vaulted up behind her and, taking the reins, issued a whoop. The crowd burst into laughter and talking as the couple rode through their numbers to stop in front of the new tipi that had been erected in front of Sitting Bull's. Standing Elk and his brothers had contributed the hides that now stretched new and painted across the freshly cut lodgepoles. Dancing Bird and Walks Lightly had sewn the cover.

Festoons of fresh flowers hung from the flap pole and bobbed in a warm breeze. Standing Elk slid off first, then pulled his wife into his arms. His friends shouted ribald comments and encouragement as he carried her inside, closed the flap, and pulled the fastening strap in behind them.

The crowd turned toward the feast laid out in the center of the village. No one would see the couple again until morning. Later tonight, after the marriage had been consummated, they would enjoy the meal Dancing Bird had left inside their tipi beside a banked fire.

Above the crowd, Dancing Bird could see her mother and brother greeting the wedding guests. Tall and looking older than his years, Little Bear nodded and spoke with the aplomb of a man, not a boy. Occasionally she saw her mother's gaze sweep the crowd, looking for her. But Dancing Bird didn't feel like celebrating. She'd done her duty to her sister and now all she wanted to do was go someplace private and cry out her sorrows.

Shadows were beginning to lengthen, and soon the welcoming curtain of night would make it easier for her to hide. She only had to avoid everyone for a few more hours.

Milling with the crowd, she caught occasional glimpses of Braden. He was standing at her uncle's side, engaged in a serious conversation, judging from the look on his face. He had made no attempt to find her—and why should he? He was aware she was being courted.

So what had their kisses meant? She'd satisfied her curiosity with him, felt the curves and hard planes of a man's body, known the physical evidence of being wanted. And he'd enjoyed her touch, quenched the desire to hold a woman's soft body, and neither carried any scars for their experiments.

Even as she spun the lie, she accepted it as fact, for

only that way could she put to rest the memory of his hands on her skin.

"I spoke to your uncle." Big Dog's deep voice boomed in her ear and she flinched.

"You did?" she asked as she turned to face him.

He stared down at her, not a hint of joy in his face. "I offered him five horses for you."

"Why would you do that?"

He frowned in confusion. "What do you mean?"

"Why do you want me? You care nothing for me. You only want someone to tend your fire and sew your clothes."

"Those are the duties of a wife."

"I don't want to be a wife."

His face softened, relaxed into an almost sympathetic expression. "Your mother is worried about you. She fears you will have no home, no family."

Dancing Bird looked up at Big Dog in the dim light, noticing for the first time that keen intelligence shone from his eyes. Perhaps he was not the monster she had imagined, but neither could she ever love him.

"You think I am worth only five horses?"

"They are all I have. With them, your mother's horses would be ten, enough to attract a husband."

His face changed when he spoke of Moving-Robe-Woman and a flicker of realization was born within Dancing Bird.

Big Dog wanted her mother, not her. But if he was willing to offer for her, who was the most desperate—Big Dog or her mother?

"And what do the others say is the price to win me?"

He averted his eyes, looking beyond her, and didn't

answer immediately. "Five horses is considered a generous offer."

His words cut deeply. So that was the story circulating about her, that she was unmarriageable, odd, undesired. She glanced over the heads of the crowd to where her uncle was still talking to Braden. "Yes, I guess you would be a fool to offer more horses for an unwanted bride."

"Dancing Bird—" he began, then stopped, as if at a loss for words.

"What did my uncle say?" she ventured, bracing herself for the answer.

"He said he would think about it and let me know in five suns."

Dancing Bird turned abruptly away from him and hurried toward the pony herd. Sunset was quickly gilding the sky with rose and gold. The huge campfire would soon be lit and the celebration would go on into the night.

She dragged the long fringe of her dress through calf-high grass, scattering grasshoppers into startled flight ahead of her. The air was warm, and the evening promised to be soft and studded with brilliant stars. But all she could think of as the herd came into view was Braden.

She'd hoped to find some opportunity to tell him her courtship was not her idea. But there'd been no chance, and people would talk if she sought him out. His visits to the village had grown infrequent of late. By the time he returned after today, she might be promised to Big Dog—or worse, married to him.

The trailing branches of willows hid her retreat along the river. Stars began to pop out of a deepening purple sky, and soon the noise of the celebration was a distant hum. The pony herd had wandered down to the river to drink and now grazed among the trees. She walked through the herd, pushing aside the dangling branches as she searched for Wind.

She heard a soft nicker and Wind trotted toward her, her ears pricked forward. She slid her hands across the pony's shoulder, then put her arms around her neck and breathed in the pungent, comforting scent of horse. Wind's lips fumbled with her dress, searching for a treat.

"I don't have a present for you this time," she said into the horse's mane. "I'm sorry. I forgot."

She slipped the soft grass rope around Wind's nose and led her toward the edge of the willow grove and the wide, star-speckled plains beyond.

Braden stepped into her path just as she reached the last wind-gnarled willow.

"I thought I'd find you here," he said, his voice soft and rough. "I didn't see ye at the weddin'."

"I was there." She wound the end of the rope around her hand. "I have to go."

"Where? Where are ye goin'?" He moved a step closer.

The tears that had threatened all day were now closer, thanks to his appearance. She wasn't up to sparring with him, to cleverly keeping her sorrow and her love for him out of her eyes. He'd come to ask questions she wasn't sure she could answer.

"I'm going for a ride." She pointed to the prairies behind him.

"Ye've done enough runnin' for one day, haven't ye?" He narrowed the distance between them with two steps.

"What do you want from me?" she asked when he was an arm's reach away.

He spread his hands. "I just want to know that you're happy."

"Yes, I'm happy," she lied, gripping the soft weave of the rope.

"Yer uncle tells me Big Dog has offered horses for ye."

"Yes, he has. But my uncle has not yet accepted."

"Do you think he will?"

"I don't know," she answered honestly.

He moved closer yet again until now he stood a breath away. She couldn't look at him, couldn't risk touching him, so she stared at her feet.

"Is this what you want, Dancin' Bird?" He cupped her elbows in his hands and urged her toward him. "Do ye love this man?"

She resisted, knowing once she was in his arms, she'd abandon every tradition she'd been taught.

"I am a burden on my uncle's household and I am old enough to wed. It is time I looked for a husband."

"But do you love him?"

She raised her chin and commanded the tears not to flow. "There is no one I love and no one who loves me. We do not marry for love like the *wašíchu*. We marry a man who is a good provider and a strong warrior."

A slight flicker of reaction darted through his eyes, but his face remained impassive. "And Big Dog is all of that?"

"He is a brave warrior with many coups."

In the dim light, his eyes were the color of the sky before a summer rain, a deep, dangerous blue that darkened as the storm approached.

"But do you love him?"

She should lie, she knew, end this between them once and for all, grow up and accept her place among her people. But she chose honesty instead. "He is a man. He needs a wife. There have been no other offers for me."

The chirping of crickets swelled to a crescendo, then faded into silence. Still he held her gaze, studying her, testing the truth of her words.

"I don't understand your ways, but I respect 'em. If this is yer choice, I won't interfere." He released her arms and stepped backward, retreating behind his wall of self-control, returning to his role of guardian and diplomat.

He turned on his heel and started back toward the distant clamor of joyous voices, jamming his helmet on his head as he walked. She watched him go with a sinking feeling that ended with a dry, hard burning in her chest. One night's ride might not be enough to spend all the tears waiting to be shed.

Tears had started down her cheeks when she heard the crunch of Braden's boots stop. Turning around, she saw him standing still, hands on his hips, staring at the ground. He remained that way so long she began to think he was ill. She had dropped the rope and started in his direction when he suddenly pivoted and walked back toward her with deliberate steps.

They met where the river tumbled over a half-rotten log and complained with a throaty gurgle. Braden wasted no words on his intentions. He swept her into his arms and kissed her without preamble.

"Ye'll not be Big Dog's wife. If yer anybody's wife, ye'll be mine," he said against the soft cleft of her collarbone.

Then, without further explanation, he released her and walked back toward the village, his scarlet jacket fading into the deepening twilight.

Ten

Braden smacked Brandy's ample rump and sent her trotting into the corral with Steven's horse. He took off his jacket, tossed it over a fence post, and placed his helmet on top. Then he climbed onto the top rail and hooked the toes of his boots behind the second rail for balance. Brandy crumpled to her knees and rolled, legs flailing, cheerfully coating herself with the fine, dry prairie soil. Sufficiently dirty, she stood and shook, sending a cloud of dust to engulf Braden.

Propping his elbows on his knees, Braden gazed out across the wide, dark prairie and wondered at the sudden turn his path and his heart had taken. Proposing marriage to a woman he'd known only a short time, a woman from a world so foreign to his, had to signify some sort of mental unbalance, he thought wryly. But he'd learned long ago that the heart and the head often don't think the same.

The simple fragility of what he'd witnessed at the wedding ceremony had touched him deeper than he realized. A warm spring breeze and smiling faces were only fronts for the difficult and uncertain life Walks Lightly and Standing Elk were embarking upon. Life was lived in minutes, not hours or days. As he'd stood and watched the couple take their vows, his eyes had roamed the crowd for Dancing Bird. Was she thinking the same as he? Was she counting those seconds empty when she wasn't with him?

The fence shifted slightly and the scent of tobacco smoke swirled around him.

"Is Walsh gone?" Braden asked as Steven threw a leg over the top rail and joined him on his perch.

"Yep. He left right after the ceremony. He said he had to get back to Wood Mountain. There's talk about a commission coming up from the states."

"A commission?" Braden turned to face Steven. "What kind of commission?"

"All the appropriate brass to take another run at convincing the Sioux to return home."

Braden shivered inwardly and recalled his previous thoughts.

"Talk is they're sending Terry himself."

"Terry? Sitting Bull hates him, and rightfully so. He's the one who forced them across the border."

"Ah, the ingenuity of the military mind. Still and all, that's who they're sending."

"When?"

Steven shrugged. "Don't know. Sometime in the fall, Walsh thinks. No date's been set. All I know is McLeod himself is coming down to meet them, if and when they come."

Suddenly, the short summer seemed even shorter.

"Walsh said to give you his good-byes," Steven ventured.

Braden glanced at Steven, then smiled. "I guess I just disappeared, didn't I? What did he say?"

"I told him you were working out some territorial disputes."

Braden looked up at the sky. "Think he bought it?"

"Not for a minute."

Braden laughed. "I guess I owe him an explanation. He's not going to like what I have to say."

Steven elbowed him and held out a brown crockery jug. "Take a little of this before you tell me the story that's going to give James McLeod the heart attack he's so richly earned."

Casting a sidelong glance at Steven, Braden uncorked the jug, took a whiff, and then jerked his head away. "Whiskey? Bootleg whiskey?"

"As bootleg as it gets. Brewed under some of the finest cots in Fort Walsh."

Braden tipped the jug and winced as the bitter liquid burned its way down his throat. He wiped his mouth on the back of his hand and handed the jug back to Steven. "Does Walsh know this is goin' on?"

"Sure he does." Steven took a sip and replaced the cork. "It's only brewed in small amounts and used for medicinal purposes, loneliness being one of those ills needing a cure. As long as its existence isn't known outside the ranks of the troops and none makes its way into the hands of the Indians, he turns an informed blind eye."

Brandy shuffled over and shoved her soft nose into Braden's hands. He absently scratched her forehead. "I asked Dancing Bird to marry me. At least I think that's what I asked her."

Steven clapped him on the back. "Good show, old chap. What do you mean you think you asked her? I wouldn't think that's something a man would be in doubt about."

"I heard Big Dog's offered her uncle five horses for her. 'Tis an insult, that, but the lass thinks she's a burden to her uncle's hospitality. I followed her away from the celebration and she looked so . . . vulnerable."

"Are you saying you regret your proposal?"

"No, not a'tall," Braden fired back. "It's just . . . I don't have anythin' to offer a wife. No home, a job that might disappear if I marry." He shook his head. "I'm not even sure she understood what I meant."

"Women don't usually miss that sort of thing. Believe me, lad, she knew. But what inspired words did you use to turn the maiden's head? If you don't mind my asking," Steven hurried to add.

"I told her if she was goin' to be anyone's wife, she'd be mine."

Steven didn't comment for several seconds. "I'm surprised at you, old man. I had you pegged for a down-on-one-knee lad."

"Impetuousness is one thing I've never been accused of—at least not until now. I'm goin' to Wood Mountain tomorrow to talk to Walsh. 'Tis true he holds me future in his hands."

Steven struck a match and relit the bowl of his pipe. Soon, a fragrant cloud filled the space between them. "I wouldn't be so quick to do that just yet."

"Why?"

"I did a little hunting with her new brother-in-law the other day."

"Standing Elk?"

Steven nodded. "Her family's worried about her. She seems determined to make a life for herself and her mother outside the bonds of marriage for either of them. Makes 'em appear a little strange to their neighbors, you know. Her mother says her father planted this seed of independence in her and when he died, she was determined not to be dependent on anybody. You might have your work cut out for you."

"What are ye sayin'?"

Steven clamped the pipe between his teeth and braced both hands on the corral rail. "Remember that horse we broke at Fort McLeod that first winter?"

"The roan? My backside remembers well."

"She couldn't stand the sight of a bridle. You could walk up to her all day, lean against her, put the saddle on her back. But as soon as you brought out a bridle, she'd gallop to the back of the corral and glare at you."

"Yer sayin' Dancing Bird's like that mare?"

"I'm saying that despite that mare's good nature, she couldn't take that last step into captivity, couldn't accept the one thing that would control her will—the bridle and bit."

"I should court the lass first?"

"Yep, that's what I'm saying. Give her a little time to get used to the idea before you give Walsh a headache. It'll ease her mother's mind, too. Moving-Robe-Woman's had enough surprises in her life to last a while. You've got the summer. Things might change in the fall."

Suddenly, the canopy of stars above him that defined infinity seemed to lower, and time became very precious.

With mixed envy and pride, Dancing Bird watched Walks Lightly and Standing Elk emerge from their tipi.

Yellow ribbons of sunrise colored the sky as he paused and lowered his head to speak with his wife in hushed tones. Neighbors watched the couple with quick glances and sly smiles, perhaps remembering their own tentative emergence from their tipis after their wedding nights.

Walks Lightly smiled up at her husband and handed him his bow and arrows. Their fingers touched briefly and he leaned in closer, almost touching her lips. He said something softly and she smiled and colored. Then he turned and hopped onto the back of his horse tied nearby.

He was going hunting, Dancing Bird knew. A large herd of buffalo had been sighted nearby and a hunting party had quickly formed. Dancing Bird could barely wait until Standing Elk was gone so she could tell her sister her own news.

Walks Lightly smiled and blushed again as Dancing Bird approached her. Awkwardly, they faced each other, and neither knew what to say. Walks Lightly's face wore a continuous blush, and her lips were slightly swollen.

"Good morning," Dancing Bird said after she'd mentally sifted through several other opening lines.

"Good morning," Walks Lightly answered, then said nothing further. Nervously, she twisted her hands in her dress.

Dancing Bird waited, but her sister said nothing, only glanced around at the people watching them both.

"It will be a beautiful day," Dancing Bird tried again.

"Yes, a good day for a hunt," she replied and blushed some more at the distant reference to her husband.

"This is foolish," Dancing Bird said on a rush of breath. She grabbed Walks Lightly's hand and dragged her inside the tipi. "Tell me all about it. How was he?" she said once they were inside.

Walks Lightly laughed and her eyes sparkled. "Oh, it was wonderful. He was wonderful." She reddened to her ears.

"If you don't stop blushing, people will think you have the fever," Dancing Bird scolded playfully. Walks Lightly's wedding dress lay in a heap on the floor. Next to the firepit lay two strips of birch bark still bearing partially eaten meals. The sleeping robes were tousled and intertwined in a heap. Walks Lightly followed her sister's gaze and looked away.

"Don't blush again. I know what you did last night," Dancing Bird said and flopped down onto the bare floor next to the tangled robes. "So does everybody else in the village. It is expected. The old ones did the same themselves."

Walks Lightly picked up the plates and dumped the uneaten food into the fire. "You don't have to make it sound so ordinary. It was not." She slanted her sister a sly glance, and Dancing Bird grinned.

"Now that's more like it. Come over here and sit down and tell me everything. Then I will tell you a secret." She patted the nearest silky buffalo robe.

Walks Lightly sat down gingerly and related the loss of her innocence, describing in detail Standing Elks' elaborate seduction.

"Ohhh," Dancing Bird breathed when Walks Lightly finished. "Can two people do that?"

Walks Lightly grinned. "Yes, because we did. Now tell me, what is your secret? Has Big Dog offered Uncle horses? Have they reached an agreement?"

"Yes and no."

"How many horses?"

"Five."

Walks Lightly frowned. "Only five? What did Uncle say?"

"I haven't talked to him yet."

"Then what is your secret?"

Dancing Bird leaned closer. "Braden has asked me to be his wife," she said in a whisper.

"Marry a white man?" Walks Lightly exclaimed.

"Shhh. Someone will hear." Dancing Bird clamped a hand across her sister's mouth.

"Has *he* offered Uncle horses?"

"No, not yet."

"How do you know he meant it if he does not bring horses? Maybe he was making a joke."

"That's not what his lips said," Dancing Bird countered with a smile.

"You kissed a man you are not promised to?" Walks Lightly's voice rose in alarm. "People will talk," she added in a whisper.

"No one saw. We were out with the horse herd."

"So far away from the village? If someone were to find out you had seen him there, you might never find a man who would have you."

"I've already found a man who will have me."

"What if he did not mean what he said? What if he lies like the other *wašíchu?"*

"He meant what he said," she said defensively. "He does not lie."

Walks Lightly paused, then leaned in close. "How does a white man kiss?"

Dancing Bird laughed. "The same as a Sioux man, I'm sure. They both have lips . . . and hands."

"Do not tell me any more." Walks Lightly shook her head. "I do not want to know."

"Oh, Walks Lightly, I have done nothing wrong. You worry too much about what people will say."

"What people think of us is who we are," Walks Lightly replied with wisdom beyond her years. "That is how it is."

"I only want to be as happy as you, sister. I want to share my bed and my body with a man I love, not some rutting bull with many coups. I want Braden to do to me what Standing Elk did to you last night. That is what I want."

Walks Lightly studied Dancing Bird's face, then smiled softly. "That's what I want for you, too. I believe you will do what is best. You are smart like Father in ways Mother and I do not understand. You've always walked outside the world we understand. I will trust your judgment."

The sound of a horse outside the tipi brought Walks Lightly to her feet. She hurried to the flap, expecting her husband, then stopped half in and half outside.

"What is it?" Dancing Bird pushed her sister out of the way.

Braden sat astride his mare, holding another buffalo hide in his arms. Walks Lightly threw Dancing Bird a sly smile and ducked back inside her house. Dancing Bird stepped outside and stood uneasily before him. She hadn't expected to see him again so soon after his confession.

"Finding out all the details?" he said, nodding toward the tipi, a twinkle in his eye.

Dancing Bird rose to his challenge as the warm honey of desire slid through her. "Yes, I am."

He grinned slowly. "And did you learn anything?"

She stepped to his side and looked up, certain their words would not be overheard. "I learned many ways to make a man beg for a woman's attention," she whispered.

His eyes darkened to a stormy blue. "Is that so? And what ways are those?"

She smiled. "I think you do not want to know now. I think you would rather learn on our wedding night."

His neck reddened, and she stifled an outright laugh. How she loved to best him at his own game. And as his eyes seemed to look through her clothes, she imagined ways in which she might also best him once he was her husband.

"I brought ye another hide for yer collection."

She lifted the hide from his arms. "This will help make a good lodge for my mother."

"Yes, she'll need her own lodge," he said, his point understood. So far he'd backed away from none of her hints of their marriage, renewing her hope his words last night had not been hastily spoken in passion.

"I'd like to speak with your uncle," he asked, and her heart began to thump.

"He has gone on a buffalo hunt. The herd is close, near where the horses graze. I will take you there."

"No," he said, gathering his reins. " 'Tis something should be discussed between him and me alone."

"You will need an interpreter."

"I will have Standing Elk to speak for me if needed, but your uncle speaks English well."

She waited, but he offered no further explanation. With a last look, he reined around and trotted out of the village.

* * *

The churning cloud of dust gave away the location of the hunt. Topping a rise, Braden reined Brandy to a stop and watched the warriors single out an animal, then flatten themselves against their horses' backs and pursue the beast to within arrow range. Then, legs clamped firmly around their horses' sides, they would drop their reins, take aim, and send an arrow swiftly into the buffalo's neck. After a stumbling step or two, the beast would crash to its knees in a quick, ground-gouging death.

He picked up his reins and rode down to where Sitting Bull sat astride his pony, safely away from the melee, watching the younger men hunt and kill their prey.

The old chief kept his eyes on the hunt as Braden stopped at his side. "Young man's game." He pointed toward the hunt.

"I would like to speak with you," Braden signed, touching his lips with the ends of his fingers.

Sitting Bull nodded, then waved at Standing Elk as he paused in pursuit. He waved back and galloped toward them. When he drew to a halt, he looked between the two men. Sitting Bull spoke to him and pointed at Braden.

"What do you wish to say?" Standing Elk asked.

"I would like to ask permission to court his niece, Dancing Bird."

A sly smile slid across Standing Elk's face as he turned to the chief and spoke. Sitting Bull raised his eyebrows, spoke, and Standing Elk repeated his words. Braden felt panic slide into his veins. If the chief said no, he'd stand no chance at all.

They exchanged comments and finally Standing Elk turned back to Braden. "Sitting Bull wants to know why."

"Why what?"

"Why do you want to court Dancing Bird? He says she is his niece, but she would make a poor wife."

"Ask him why he thinks she would make a poor wife."

Standing Elk repeated the question. Sitting Bull answered, shrugging his shoulders.

"He says," Standing Elk said, "that she is disobedient and never does as she is told."

"Tell him that I want a wife like her, that I am in love with her and think she will make me a very good wife."

Standing Elk stared at him as if he'd suddenly grown another head. "Why would you want a disobedient wife?"

"Ah, we Irish treasure the lass who can think for herself and knows her own mind."

Standing Elk shrugged, delivered the message, then threw back his head and laughed.

"What did he say?" Braden finally asked.

"Are you sure you want to know?" Standing Elk asked with a crooked grin.

"Yes."

"He says he wished more *wašíchu* wanted women like this. That way there'd be less *wašíchu*."

Braden laughed and nodded at Sitting Bull's smile.

"He also says you have his permission to court Dancing Bird, but he warns he is not responsible for anything that happens to you at her hands." He paused, then continued. "Her sister will be very happy. Walks Lightly worries about her."

"Tell him I'll be takin' that chance and tell your wife that her sister's heart is safe with me."

Walsh drummed his fingers on his desk and studied the swirled pattern in the dust that covered his desk top.

"Every night I have the same dream," he said after an interminable silence.

Braden fidgeted in his chair and wished his commander would just shout at him or scold him or cut him to ribbons with his cool logic. Instead, Walsh had decided to prolong the torture with anecdotes.

"I am walking across the prairie. It is a lovely, warm spring day and the grass is green and waving gently in the breeze. Suddenly rabbits begin to appear out of the ground. At first there are only one or two, then more. Then there are tens of them all hopping around me. I blink and the rabbits have turned to women, lovely, young women."

He leaned forward. "I thought at first it was Jackson's cooking, but now I know the meaning goes deeper than that. It is a representation of the tenacity of man. Each and every time mankind has been denied something, humanity has found a way to provide that forbidden thing. And so it is with women and my men."

He rose from his desk and walked to the window. "I forbade the men to make, possess, or drink liquor, and it is brewing as we speak underneath bunks in the men's quarters. Not in large quantities, mind you, just enough to provide the thirsty a taste on special occasions. The men of the Mounted Police have been forbidden to marry and bring their families out west. Ottawa judged the life and sacrifices too great to ask of the women and children. Yet you and Constable Fraser have found a way around that by choosing native daughters."

Walsh turned from the window. "So, Constable, you have unwittingly done me a favor. You have solved the mystery of my nightmares, even if you will give them to James McLeod when he hears of this."

"Sir, 'twas never my intention to cause problems for you or the force."

Walsh waved his hand and returned to his desk. "I'm aware of that, Constable. You have a fine service record. But I'm sure you realize that this situation is potentially explosive."

"Sir, I have developed a congenial relationship with Sittin' Bull and his family. 'Tis a fine view they have taken of this, and I don't think this will be a problem a'tall."

"What do you intend to do if Sitting Bull's band eventually chooses to return across the border and live on the reservations?"

"I have thought of that. Since she will be me wife, I see no reason why she can't remain with me."

"That would be the reasonable assumption, Constable, but no one can know or guess the contents of the politician's heart. As you know, the Americans have requested a commission be formed to meet with Sitting Bull and try again to convince him to lead his people home. We anticipate their arrival sometime this fall. Commissioner McLeod has been asked to meet them at the border."

"Yes, sir. I have heard of these plans."

"Do you also know it is the generally held opinion

that the Sioux will not last the winter here, that the buffalo will be so depleted by the time the snow flies that widespread starvation may further reduce their numbers?"

The pit of Braden's stomach grew heavy as unlimited possibilities for difficulties unrolled before him.

"No, sir. I did not know that the situation was so critical."

"And General Terry is relentless. That's one of his better qualities," Walsh quipped sarcastically. "If this commission is not successful, he will try again . . . and again. And so you see, Constable, while I would gladly open my arms to these poor, hunted people, the government of Canada will not. We must live alongside the Americans as long as this continent remains in one piece, and politics will continue to make the world spin. Think carefully of this decision, Constable Flynn. For if you marry Sitting Bull's niece, the eyes of two countries will be upon you."

Eleven

A fierce storm crossed Braden's path between Wood Mountain and home, delaying his return. When he finally arrived at the edge of the Sioux grazing grounds, the sun was casting long shadows, and the rasp of the grasshoppers had grown lazy and slow. The thicket of willows where he'd found Dancing Bird the night of the wedding now beckoned cool and green, a respite from the blazing June sun.

Intending to follow the path of the river and take advantage of the shade, Braden guided Brandy into the thicket. A flash of motion to his left startled him, and he hauled back on the reins.

Behind the curtain of drooping willow branches, a figure moved. He leaned down to peep beneath the branches. Dancing Bird sat in the current of the stream, the graceful curve of her back naked and smooth. Her black hair was pulled up on top of her head and secured with a stick. An unfinished buffalo hide was staked out in the sun, now host to a cluster of flies. An abandoned awl lay in the grass nearby.

She stood and stretched her arms over her head, and her graceful back curved into slim hips and long legs. She pulled the stick out and her hair tumbled down her back, nearly to her waist. Unashamed and unaware, she splashed the water onto herself and laughed softly at the joy of it.

Every curve he had held and imagined now was open to his view. As he watched, desire and embarrassment warring within him, she turned to the side, giving him a profile of her soft curves.

Escape was impossible. She'd hear any movement he made now. And so he sat, praying Brandy wouldn't sneeze or paw or rattle her bridle. And for a span of miraculous minutes, all was perfectly quiet—until Dancing Bird slid her buckskin dress over her lithe body. As if reading his mind, Brandy jingled her bit.

Dancing Bird whirled, her eyes large with fear.

"It's Braden," he said as she bent and looked under the tree branches.

"How long have you been there?" she asked, caution in her voice.

"I saw your hide staked out and thought you might be here . . . out of the sun."

She stepped lightly through the leaf litter, her bare feet making tiny squishing noises on the damp soil, and stopped when she reached his side. A latigo strap dangled by the front of the stirrup and she picked it up and slid its narrow length through her fingers.

"You have come to speak with my uncle?" She looked up at him.

"No, lass. I came to talk with you." He swung down from the saddle and threaded his reins between his fingers. Had she truly understood the meaning of what he had asked her under these very trees? Or had their earlier bantering been just that? What did she expect of him now? Where would he begin to explain?

"The other night . . . I spoke too quickly."

Her color fled and her eyes hardened. "You regret your words?"

"No, no." He reached for her, but she took a step backward.

"I should have spoken to you before I said that."

"What do you mean?" She tilted her head, her expression filled with suspicion. He was making a terrible mess of this.

He stepped closer. " 'Tis a custom among my people that a man court a woman before he asks her to become his wife, just as it is among your people. I've spoken to your uncle and now I'm askin' you. I'd like to come and stand in the blanket with you."

There. It was out. He wondered if any of it had made any sense to her. She stared at him so blankly that he began to wonder if she'd understood him at all. Then she laughed.

"You do not have to court me. I want you, and you have said you want me." She stepped closer. "Young maidens look forward to flute music and blankets, but I only want you."

"Perhaps one day ye'll regret I didn't court ye proper."

"Or perhaps you will."

Braden stopped her advance by cupping her shoulders in his hands. "Grant me this, lass. Let me court ye like should be done. Let me give ye this one piece of . . . the old ways."

Something within her chest tightened. In all her misbehavior and mischief, what had she done to deserve this man? "When should we begin this courtship?"

"Tonight?"

She stepped away. "We must not arrive together. Mother will be angry." She ran to the hide and snatched it from its restraining stakes, then quickly gathered her other things. "I'll be waiting," she threw back over her shoulder as she ran along the river's path, around a bend, and out of his sight.

Braden sat down on a half-rotten log and scratched Brandy's face when she lowered her nose to sniff at his hair. "I feel like I've been run over by a herd of leprechauns, lass," he said, raking his fingers between her eyes, "all bent on mischief."

As with any small settlement, word had traveled quickly. Sly smiles and covert glances greeted him at every lodge until he arrived at Sitting Bull's tipi. He dismounted, pulled his gray wool blanket from behind his saddle, stepped up and rapped on the lodge flap. Moving-Robe-Woman swung the flap of hide back, smiled slightly, then turned and spoke in Sioux. Dancing Bird emerged immediately.

Braden lifted the blanket and raised his eyebrows. She took it from his hands and flipped it over his shoulders until it was wrapped around them and covering their heads.

"Has anyone ever died of the heat in one of these things?" he asked as the wool quickly accumulated their body heat despite the sun's final plunge toward the horizon.

"Most people don't care how hot it gets," she whispered and ran her palm down his chest.

"What are we supposed to talk about?"

"Our future together, plans for our lodge, how many

children we will have together. But you must speak softly, because everyone will be listening."

"Am I allowed to look outside and see just how many people *are* listening?"

"Un-uh." His brass buttons surrendered to her nimble fingers and she slipped her hands inside his jacket.

"Are ye supposed to be doin' that?" he whispered.

"No, but I know the rules of this game and you do not, so I have the advantage." She slid the pads of her fingers up and down the ridges of his ribs.

"Spoken like the daughter of a warrior."

"I know many things about standing in the blanket that you do not. Would you like me to whisper them in your ear?" Her warm breath was already brushing the hair at his temple.

"No, please."

"Then I'll save them for next time."

"When I leave tonight, I have to be away for several days." Her fingers stilled their exploration, and he felt her stiffen.

"Where will you go?"

"I have to go to another Long Lance fort to speak with our chief. I have to get his permission to marry you."

She relaxed with a soft sigh.

"Did ye think I was goin' to say I wasn't comin' back?"

"No . . . I didn't think that. I thought . . . you might change your mind while you were away."

The independence and assurance he so valued in her dissipated like morning mists, leaving behind, if only for a brief moment, a woman scarred by uncertainty.

He caught her against him and heard her mother clear

her throat nearby. He didn't care who knew he was holding her in his arms. What he was about to say was the most important thing he would ever say to her.

In the semidarkness, he could barely see her eyes as she looked up at him. "I would never change my mind, Dancing Bird. You are the woman I love, the woman I want. But there will be times I will be gone for many suns and you will have to wait for me alone."

"I will not be alone. You will give me a son. I will have the medicine man make a potion so that I may bear a son soon. Then he and I will wait for his father to come riding home."

If he could have made love to her at that moment, standing upright inside a sweltering blanket, he would have done so without regret. Instead, he kissed her, bending her back against his encircling arms, ignoring the intakes of breath that said their every movement was visible to the onlookers.

When he released her, she tossed the blanket back over their heads and welcome cool night air rushed in. A small group had gathered around them, including Moving-Robe-Woman, Walks Lightly, and half a dozen other women. Braden half expected to be clubbed for his actions, but he saw amusement on the surrounding faces instead of anger. Except for Moving-Robe-Woman. He'd have to describe her expression as shock.

Dancing Bird stepped demurely away from him and folded her roving hands in front of her. Never mind that his jacket gaped open in front with no plausible explanation. He held the blanket strategically and walked to his waiting horse. Facing Brandy, he took his time folding the blanket and tying it securely behind his saddle. Then he rebuttoned his jacket and turned around.

"I will be back in one moon," he said, and Dancing Bird nodded, understanding the deeper meaning of his reassurance.

As he trotted out of the village, he passed Big Dog standing by his tattered lodge, arms crossed over his chest, his gray eyebrows knitted together. Braden tried to push it from his mind.

Dancing Bird loved him. Her uncle was in favor of their union. Nothing could go wrong. But still, as he left the grazing grounds and broke into a canter toward their outpost, the nagging premonition that had risen this morning returned to perch on his shoulder.

Braden pulled Brandy to a stop on the same rise of land he'd topped more than a year ago. Then the broad sweeping arc of the Old Man's River had shielded only a brushy island in its midst. Now a neat stockaded fort sat on the island, its soft browns and tans a sweet contrast to the brilliant greens of the surrounding trees.

James McLeod's empire sprawled out in the valley below. Fort McLeod, built and named for the beloved commander, was the only established law and order in the Northwest Territories, the touchstone upon which potential settlers hung their hopes and wishes. James McLeod and the 150 tired men who'd ridden over this hill on that bright October day in 1873 had eliminated the illegal whiskey trade in western Canada in record time, restored normalcy to the lives of the Blackfeet, and established a place for themselves in history. And as Braden viewed the scene before him, he wondered if he would be part of that history.

McLeod had made improvements, he saw. The buildings, which last winter had sported leaky mud roofs, were now covered with fresh wooden shingles. New buildings of milled lumber instead of odd-sized cottonwood logs had been added, and a collection of houses and stores clustered outside the massive gates. The town of Fort McLeod had been born.

A wave of nostalgia swirled up around him, a sense of home and belonging. As he basked in the sensation, he realized the old pain had faded to a dull, unpleasant memory in the back of his mind. No more did he feel rootless, drifting, without purpose.

But would he have a future with the men who milled below? Would McLeod and Ottawa permit another of their number to marry, to take on the responsibility of a wife and family as well as the responsibility for thousands of acres of wilderness? He heeled Brandy and she lifted her head from grazing and trotted down the incline.

Colin's offices had been improved and, with Surgeon Kittson's reassignment to Fort Walsh, Colin now cured the ills of Fort McLeod. The door swung open and Maggie Fraser's beautiful blue eyes widened with wonder.

"Braden!" she exclaimed and threw her one free arm around his neck, pressing a squirming baby against his jacket.

Braden returned the hug and glanced over her shoulder, where Colin looked up from his white ceramic mortar and pestle. He smiled broadly, wiped his hands on a cloth at his side, and crossed the floor in two long steps.

"Old man, what brings you here?" he said, extending a hand, which Braden grasped and shook heartily.

"I came to see McLeod," he replied without explanation, and Colin threw him a curious glance.

"Supper's almost ready. You'll stay, of course."

"Depends on what Maggie's cookin'," he teased. "I've lost my taste for beaver and muskrat since I've been gone."

Maggie arched her eyebrows. "That paunch around Dr. Fraser's middle ain't from beaver and muskrat," she replied smoothly.

"Leave me out of this," Colin said, taking his daughter from his wife's arms. "Come on, Mary, let's get out of their line of fire." The baby cooed softly, and Colin's face softened as he gazed down at her.

A perfect picture of family life, a home filled with love and good humor, if not material wealth. Suddenly, Braden wanted this very much. In fact, he craved it, the way dry ground craves a summer storm. He'd ridden across a continent with Colin, seen him angry, sad, joyful, and filled with want so strong he'd risked his life to fulfill it. But until now, he'd never seen him content. And contentment had, in Braden's mind, become the nectar of the gods.

"Do you want to hold her?" Colin asked, his face full of pride and expectation.

Braden nodded, and Colin placed the baby in his arms. Tiny blue eyes gazed up at him with intense scrutiny. She cooed softly, wiggled, and spit up a handful of milk on Braden's jacket.

"Oh, Lord, I'll be so glad when she gets over this stage," Maggie said, rushing to retrieve her daughter.

"I've had worse on me clothes and put there by folks far less attractive." He held the baby up, and she grinned and shoved her fist into her mouth. "Looks like she's hungry."

"And I'm glad she is. I'm a-fixin' to start lowin' like an old milkcow." Maggie took the baby into her arms, handed Braden a rag, and shuffled off toward the bedroom that opened off Colin's examining room.

Braden glanced over at Colin, who grinned sheepishly. "Still delicate with her language, is she?"

Colin smiled after the wife he obviously adored. "She has her own way of getting her point across."

Braden wiped away the sour milk, then took off his jacket and spread it over a chair. "Yer a lucky man, Colin Fraser. The saints have smiled on ye."

"Yes, they have. But this time last year, I would have sworn I was cursed." He stared at the closed door another moment before swinging his full attention to Braden. "What brings you back to Fort McLeod?"

Braden shoved his hands into his pockets. "I've come to ask McLeod's permission to marry."

"You still have a taste for living dangerously, don't you? Marry? Congratulations!" Colin rose, gripped Braden's hand and clapped him on the shoulder. "Who's the lucky girl?"

"Sitting Bull's niece, Dancing Bird."

Colin whistled low. "I was right. You do like to live dangerously. You may yet surpass my and Maggie's reputation for trouble. Sitting Bull's niece. What does Walsh say about this?"

Braden grinned. "I think, in his own way, he passed the responsibility to McLeod. Walsh gave me his permission—a wee bit too easily, I thought at the time."

"And so he sent you to talk to McLeod?"

"An interview I'm not lookin' forward to, thanks to ye and lovely Maggie in there."

"Do you plan to stay on with the force once you're married?"

"Of course. 'Tis my home. Besides, what else would I do?"

"Married? Who's gettin' married?" Maggie emerged from the other room, the sleeping baby tucked in her arms.

"Braden here's taking the plunge."

Maggie grinned broadly. "Where on earth did you find a woman in the Cypress Hills?" She frowned and glanced down at the sleeping child. "You ain't marryin' one of the them trader whores, are you?" she whispered.

Braden laughed. "No. She's Sitting Bull's niece."

"Yore marryin' an Injun?" Her eyes widened. Until that moment, the thought that his marrying a Sioux woman would be viewed as anything but normal had never entered his mind.

"Yes, I am." The feeling of camaraderie in the room cooled a bit as he waited for Maggie's next comment.

"Well good for you," she said with a decisive nod of her head. "At least you're marryin' somebody who knows how to look after themselves out here. You won't believe the sort of women who've come here just because they're in love with a red coat." She slanted a glance at her husband and Colin smiled.

At that moment, Braden could have kissed Maggie Fraser, but for a totally different reason than a year ago.

"What's her name and when do we get to meet her?" she asked, eyes shining with excitement.

"Her name is Dancin' Bird and I was hopin' both of ye would come for the weddin'."

"Dancing Bird. That's a purty name." She shifted the baby to the other arm. "I'll be right back. Let me put her down. She's as heavy as a sack of grain." Maggie disappeared back into the bedroom.

"We've heard that things are uncertain with the Sioux, that the Canadian government considers them refugees, as do the Americans," Colin said.

"That's true enough."

"And that the buffalo herds won't last."

"Also probably true."

"Do you think they'll ever return home?"

Braden stared over Colin's shoulder and into the fire. "I think the time will come when they will have no other choice."

"And Dancing Bird will remain with you?"

Braden stared down at his hands. "Yes. I hope so."

"Supper's ready," Maggie announced as she tiptoed out the bedroom door and eased it shut behind her.

Over the meal, they turned the conversation to fort small talk and old friends. As soon as the dishes were done and the table cleared, Maggie said her good nights and was off to bed, citing the baby's nocturnal feedings as her reason. Braden suspected she was giving him and Colin time to talk.

"How is it, livin' with the same woman day in and day out?" Braden nodded toward the bedroom door now gently closing.

"I'm not sure how I lived without her," Colin replied without hesitation. "There were some difficult times at first. Maggie couldn't stand the confines of the fort. She was used to having all the territory to roam in. I couldn't stand for her to be out of my sight. So we reached a compromise. Before Mary was born, she'd disappear for a day or two to go hunting or just ride the wilderness. She promised to always come back, and I promised not to try and find her. She kept her bargain and I . . . well, I sort of cheated."

"Cheated?"

Colin laughed and leaned closer. "I had the daily patrols on the watch for her. They kept me posted on her every move. But since the baby's come, she seems content here at home."

"Think that'll last?"

Colin shook his head. "Probably not. She'll always be a child of open spaces. But I know she'll always come back to me. Now, tell me how you met Dancing Bird."

Braden related the meeting between Walsh and Sitting Bull, his and Dancing Bird's ensuing relationship, and the beginning of their courtship.

"When is the wedding?"

Braden shrugged. "I don't know yet. I felt I owed it to her mother to court her accordin' to their customs, to put her mind at ease. There's already been so much uncertainty in their lives, I was reluctant to bring 'em one more upset. And I have to arrange for some sort of housing near Fort Walsh for after we're married. I'm buyin' horses from Tom Forbes while I'm here to take back to Sitting Bull as her bride price. Sure and it better be soon." He slanted Colin a glance, and Colin laughed.

"Tempted to jump over the nuptials, are you?"

Braden shook his head. "She lives a life of such simple beliefs, and yet her curiosity knows no bounds."

"Seems you and I had a similar conversation one evening not so long ago," Colin said with a grin, referring to Maggie's ardent pursuit of him in the early days of their courtship.

"She can set me on fire with just a touch or a look. 'Tis all I can do to behave meself."

"It's a pitfall of being in love." He nodded toward the bedroom door. "She can look at me across a room, and it's off to home early. Trouble is, she knows it and tortures me mercilessly."

"Have ye ever thought how strange it is that two people would find each other in a place so far from their homes, so far from everything familiar?"

"That's why God invented Fate," Colin said, smiling, "and I've learned that once Fate has you on her list, there's no use resisting."

Braden paused with his hand on James McLeod's door. McLeod was an honest and fair commander, a compassionate man deeply devoted to his family waiting back east. And yet to him fell the responsibility and supervision of the 150 men who'd followed him across a continent plus the needs and wants of an entire territory rapidly filling up with settlers.

Braden rapped on the door and received a pleasant 'Come in' from the other side. James McLeod dominated the room with his benevolent presence, his pipe clamped in his teeth, his shirt sleeves rolled to his elbows. Black suspenders stretched tightly across his flawlessly smooth white shirt.

"Constable Flynn," he said, a smile wrinkling the corners of his eyes. "What brings you back to us?"

Braden closed the door behind him, his courage fleeing for a moment. A small sliver of concern passed through McLeod's expression.

"I have a matter I'd like to discuss with ye," Braden began, praying for the proper words. He sat down across the neatly organized desk and watched as McLeod carefully laid down his pen, folded his hands, and gave Braden his complete attention.

Best to meet things head on, Braden decided, a thousand ways to lead into the conversation darting through his mind. "I'd like to get married, sir."

McLeod smiled slowly. "Has Constable Fraser started an epidemic here?"

"No, sir."

McLeod looked down at his desk. "Assistant Commissioner Walsh sent you to me for permission?"

"Not exactly, sir. He gave me his approval first and sent this for you." Braden handed McLeod the sealed letter. McLeod took the letter, broke the seal, and read the contents.

"Humph," he grunted around his pipe stem and carefully refolded the letter. Then he removed the pipe from his mouth and propped it carefully in a waiting bowl. "Well, Constable, I'd say you have successfully usurped Constable Fraser's penchant for trouble making."

At McLeod's request, Braden related the events leading up to his proposal to Dancing Bird. McLeod listened attentively, then folded his hands and stared at the wood grain of his desk.

"I have to be honest with you, Constable. I don't feel Ottawa will greet this request favorably. Their heart's desire at the moment is to get rid of the Sioux, not give them reason to stay. I fear they would look at this request as another reason for Sitting Bull not to lead his people home."

"Then I'll leave the Mounted Police." Even as he said the words, he felt the loss of something important, something vital to him. What would he do? How would they live? He wanted something more than a life of subsistence, even though such life had its charms. But he owed Dancing Bird more than that.

"Now, don't jump off and do something rash, Constable," McLeod said, raising his palm. "Let me write some letters and ask some questions. I just wanted you to be aware of the answer I anticipate. Perhaps I will be found pleasantly wrong."

An urgent rapping on the door caught McLeod's attention.

"Come in," he called.

Constable Jackson stepped into the room, a young man recently enlisted and assigned to Fort Walsh. He smiled as he saw Braden. "Good, I have a message for both of you." His smiled quickly faded and the premonition Braden had felt earlier returned in full force, enough to prompt him to stand.

"There's been a murder, one of Sitting Bull's Sioux. Constable Gravel found him three days ago. Looks like he was hunting close to Blackfoot territory. The Sioux are stirred up. Same with the Blackfeet. Assistant Commissioner Walsh sent me to bring you home," he said, nodding toward Braden. "He said to ride straight through."

"Did you ride straight through to get here, Constable?" McLeod asked in his deep and controlled voice.

The young man nodded, his face pale and tired.

"Then you are to stay here. I'll send someone else with Constable Flynn."

A flash of gratitude went through the young man's eyes. "Thank you, sir."

"Do you know who was killed?" Braden asked, fear rising in his throat like bile.

"A young man—a boy, really. Little Bear, I believe was his name."

Dancing Bird's brother.

Another loss.

Braden felt McLeod's eyes on him and wondered if his face had paled as had his heart. "It's her brother."

Twelve

Leaden skies oozed a sad, gray rain that slid down the bare backs of the assembled lodges. Where before the tipis had seemed to dot the river's edge happily, they now huddled together in misery. Streaks of ash smeared the tipi sides, a sign of mourning, and Braden mustered every ounce of self-control to keep himself from charging straight into the village and sweeping Dancing Bird into his protecting arms.

But before he saw Dancing Bird or any of her people, he had to have the facts in hand from both sides. Cool, logical thinking and careful words might be all that would keep this from developing into a full-blown Indian war. Reluctantly, he turned Brandy toward the dugout and wiped a trickle of water from between his eyes.

Evening fell with no prelude or fanfare, just a gradual darkening from miserable gray to starless black. He let the reins lay slack and trusted Brandy's unerring sense of home and supper. And when the yellow pinpoint of light from the dugout windows appeared, Brandy pricked her ears forward and shifted her swaying walk into a trot.

He rode past the front of the dugout and into the lean-to where he unsaddled a sodden Brandy, rubbed her down with handfuls of dry, fragrant hay, and dumped a generous portion of grain into her feed box. She shoved her nose into the grain and began to chew with a soft, grateful whicker that did little more than jiggle her sides. With an affectionate pat to her backside, Braden stepped around her and walked to the front door. Steven swung open the door.

"Been this wet all the way?" he asked as Braden slogged past, dumping his white helmet in a handy chair.

"Aye, all the way for the past five days." He unbuttoned his coat and shrugged it off, sighing with relief. Despite its weight, he supposed he should be grateful, for once the serge was soaked and warmed by his body, it was as warm as a coat.

"You rode from Fort McLeod in five days?"

Braden sat down, pulled off a boot, and dumped water onto the thirsty board floor. "I don't think I can eat pemmican again . . . not for a year or two, anyway." He yanked off the other boot and dropped both to the floor with a thump. "What happened?"

Steven sat down in a chair across the table and laced his fingers together. "I was riding patrol up by Blackfoot territory. Off in the distance I heard a shot. Thinking it was a hunting party, I rode in that direction. I found him lying on his stomach in the grass, a hole dead center above his eyes."

Braden winced at the starkness of the words, picturing the young man who'd been struggling to grow up before his time. "He wasn't shot with a long gun, then?"

"Nope," Steven said, relighting his pipe. "Appeared

to be done with a sidearm. At close range, too. I loaded him up on my horse and took him to his family."

Braden yanked off each wet sock and sat with his elbows propped on his knees, wet socks dangling from his hand, and let the fatigue pour over him. "What do you think happened?"

"Hunting territory dispute, I'd say. The Blackfeet are growing mighty nervous about the buffalo herds now that the summer hunting season is in full swing."

Braden passed a hand over his eyes, struggling to keep his thoughts straight. "How did Dancing Bird take the news?" Sioux mourning customs were self-destructive and harsh, he'd learned, and his anxiousness for her grew.

Steven removed the pipe from his mouth and looked Braden directly in the eye. "I won't lie to you. She took it hard."

A sharp knife wouldn't have pierced him any deeper, but there were still details to collect and his thoughts were growing fuzzier with each passing minute. "Sitting Bull?"

"Sad. He looked sad and years older. He just sat in his tipi and shook his head. Moving-Robe-Woman hasn't said a word to anyone since."

Braden stared at the floor, studying the lines and cracks of the board floor. Vaguely, he heard Steven scrape back his chair and soon dry clothes were shoved underneath his nose.

"Here. Won't help anything to have you dead of pneumonia."

Braden stood and stripped down to his damp, shriveled skin. The sensation of warm, dry cloth sliding over his body was the last assault on his consciousness. He stepped over the wet heaps and tumbled into his bunk. "Wake me up in an hour or so," he heard himself say with a distant, muted sound.

Visions of passing landscape mixed with jumbled remnants of thoughts that gradually floated away into a deep void. The next sound he heard was the early warble of a meadowlark heralding the first hint of sunrise.

The dawn was new, a subtle mix of night and day on the eastern horizon, when Braden rode away from the outpost. By the time he reached the Sioux village, the grass was a bejeweled carpet of quivering drops of rain left behind by the previous night's storm. Lazy columns of smoke drifted up into the sun-streaked sky from the rain-darkened lodges, but Braden knew he wouldn't find Dancing Bird there. He swung north.

He found her where the buffalo grass grew tall and unruly, dried by the sun that now commanded the sky, and combed by the west wind. She sat on Wind atop a slight rise of ground that rose toward the tree-lined Cypress Hills. Her hair, which had once skimmed the small of her back, now hung in uneven lengths just below her shoulder blades, severed as a symbol of her grief.

Braden pulled up short of hearing distance and committed the image to memory. Soon, very soon, this luxurious freedom would cease to exist for her people, and they would no more feel the wind in their hair nor be free to sit and watch the birth of the morning. And although she looked at peace, he knew she was anything but peaceful.

Time grew heavy and an urgency gripped him. She was Hunkpapa Sioux, a child of warrior stock, a ruler of the wind and the seasons. And in the span of a moment, her destiny might change and she could spend the rest of her life relegated to obscurity and confinement on a reservation, gouging at the unyielding ground.

He was sure she heard him approaching as Brandy waded through the tall grass, but she didn't turn her head until he stopped at her side. Streaks of ash marred the smooth planes of her cheeks. Fresh slashes ripped across her wrists and smears of dried blood dribbled down the skirt of her dress, disappearing into the long fringe. His throat tight, Braden could think of nothing to say to such raw grief, and yet the pain in her eyes found a companion buried deep within his own chest.

She slid off Wind's broad back and stood facing him, one hand on her horse's withers. "You are well?" she asked in a voice husky from mourning wails.

He dismounted, took off his helmet, and hooked it over his saddle horn. "I'm fine. I'm so sorry. I came as quickly as I could."

She lifted one corner of her mouth in an effort to smile. "Mourning is something the Sioux have learned to do well."

"Do you know what happened to Little Bear?"

Dancing Bird shook her head. "We only know that Long Lance Gravel found him and brought him home."

"Do you know what he was doing so far from home?"

She swallowed, and new grief brimmed in her eyes. "He had gone hunting. He wanted to bring me more hides for my lodge."

Braden wanted to pull her into his arms, but he sensed in her a reluctance to give over her self-control just yet.

"You spoke to your chief?" she asked, blinking away the new tears.

Braden nodded.

"What did he say?"

Braden swallowed. "He said I would have to ask the council of the Long Lances in Ottawa."

"This council. What will they say when you tell them you want to marry the niece of Sitting Bull?"

She looked so alone standing there in her blood-streaked dress, her world teetering on the brink of an abyss. Everything within him urged him to take her in his arms and never let her go. But somehow he sensed she would not give herself, either heart or body, until she had sorted things out in her mind.

"They will probably say no." He, at least, owed her honesty.

Her expression didn't change; she wore the studied calm of a warrior. "And what do you say, Braden Flynn?"

He stepped forward, and she stood her ground. She wanted a commitment from him, wanted some touch-stone around which her tattered world could turn. He was more than glad to give it. He picked up her hand and kissed the ends of her fingers, cold despite the July heat. "Yer already me wife where it matters most, in me heart. We're only satisfyin' the minds of others now."

Her solid countenance began to slip and her eyes grew misty. "What if the chief of the Long Lances says you can no longer be a Long Lance if you marry a Sioux woman?"

"Then I'll leave the Long Lances and be your hus-band."

Tears carved a path through the smudges on her face, but still she didn't come to him. Instead, she stood stoic and alone. Braden gathered her against him. She sobbed on his shoulder and entwined her arms around his neck, gently at first, then with a tightening grip as her body tensed and the sobs grew in intensity.

He pulled her down into the soft, deep grass and cradled her in his lap as she clung to his neck. Through her tears, her lips found his and she scratched at the brass buttons on his jacket. Her kisses were wild and passionate, the product of a tortured and wounded soul seeking solace, and yet he knew she loved him and wanted him as a wife wants her husband. Walsh's words rang faint in his ears. She might never be his wife in the eyes of his church, but she would be his wife in the eyes of his God and hers.

She unbuttoned both his jacket and shirt and plunged her hands inside to encircle his ribs. He sucked in a deep breath, closed his eyes, and called into battle every shred of self-control he possessed. Gently, he took her damaged wrists and held them in his hands. They might never know another time when she would so desperately need the comfort of his body, but he couldn't let her sacrifice the last shreds of her self-respect and pride. One day soon he would give her that comfort, but not today. Not while grief fueled her desire.

"Not now. Not like this," he said gently. She raised questioning eyes to his. "I can't give ye much, but I can give ye the honor of a courtship." Braden scrambled to his feet and pulled Dancing Bird up beside him. "We'll wait for the Long Lance council. And if they say no, then I'll marry ye anyway."

She raised up on her toes and kissed him again, not the wild desperate kisses of before, but a gentle kiss that nearly made him take back all his noble words.

Then she carefully buttoned his shirt and jacket and adjusted his belt. "Someday I will do this for you every morning," she whispered against his cheek and stepped backward out of his reach.

Together they rode back to the village. The tremolo of mourning wails reached them before they could see the cluster of tipis. When they reached the village, a slow procession of women circled inside the rows of Hunkpapa tipis, their faces darkened with ash, making the haunting tremolo that heralded death.

They dismounted, and Dancing Bird took his hand and led him inside her uncle's tipi. The sweet-sickly smell of death floated heavy on the hot summer air. Little Bear lay flat on a buffalo robe, his hands crossed over his chest, his bow and arrows tightly gripped in his dead fingers. Moving-Robe-Woman fiddled with his headdress, adjusted the feathers, tenderly straightened his hair. Then she pulled a smooth, tanned skin over his face. Dark dried blood streaked her legs and pooled on the tops of her feet.

"We have already observed the *wacekiyapi,* and we will take his body to the scaffolding today," Dancing Bird explained in a whisper, then stepped to her mother's side. But Moving-Robe-Woman was oblivious to all except her dead son stretched out before her.

Dancing Bird ducked outside the tipi, then quickly returned, followed closely by Sitting Bull, Standing Elk, and her cousin Elk's husband. The three men lifted the body that lay on a travois of poles and woven branches. Standing Elk glanced at Braden, then at Dancing Bird. He raised his hand and crooked two fingers in Braden's direction, then indicated the corner lacking a carrier.

"You come," he said, "for her." He nodded in Dancing Bird's direction.

Braden moved to Standing Elk's side and took the weight of that lone corner on his shoulder. The scent of human decay enveloped him, and he swallowed quickly.

They stepped outside into the heat of the morning and waded through the crowd that parted, then closed in behind to follow. A short distance from the village, a new scaffolding had been built, its freshly stripped poles gleaming yellow in the sun. They placed the body on the scaffolding and tied it there with soft, woven ropes. Then Sitting Bull turned and held out his hand. A man stepped forward leading the delicate pony Little Bear had ridden.

He smiled, wrinkling his leathery skin, and patted the horse's cheek. "She has been a good pony. She carried Little Bear bravely on his hunts," he said, and Dancing Bird murmured the translation. A creeping sense of dread spread through Braden as he looked into the horse's dark eyes.

"She will miss him, but she is young and should live to carry another warrior." Sitting Bull twitched his fingers at a young man standing on the front edge of the crowd. He was about the same age as Little Bear, and tear tracks unashamedly webbed his cheeks. "Little Calf, take this pony and treat her well. She once carried a brave warrior."

Little Calf nodded and took the leather reins in his hand, pools of tears brightening his dark eyes. Braden remembered seeing the two boys together often, one moment solemnly discussing details of manhood, the other cavorting through the village like children. They'd balanced together on a delicate precipice, walked a fine line between childhood and manhood, a time in life when deep friendships were forged.

The crowd slowly peeled away from the burial site and shuffled back to the village. Moving-Robe-Woman was accompanied by two of her friends, each supporting an arm, but Dancing Bird remained behind in the shade of the scaffolding and stared up at the shrouded body.

"Father was so proud the day he was born," she said softly, trailing her fingers down the smooth pole nearest her. "He'd almost given up hope of ever having a son. Walks Lightly and I knew he loved us, but . . . a man wants a son." She allowed her fingers to fall away from the wood. "Now they walk the Spirit Path together." She raised her eyes. "And we must go on living."

Braden tried to swallow the lump that sprang into his throat. Her last words sounded like a sentence of punishment instead of the gift of life. Every chivalrous thought he'd had only hours ago dissipated like the morning mists. Customs and traditions and social mores suddenly seemed trivial, erratic wanderings born of human minds struggling to suppress their natural instincts. Life was very short and, here among these tortured people, so very precious.

He took her hand in his and cleared his throat.

She looked up at him, questions in her eyes.

" 'Tis a fact I can wait no longer to have you as my wife."

Her brows drew together in concern and alarm grew in her eyes.

"I cannot guarantee my council will allow us to marry."

She said nothing, waiting.

"So I'm askin' ye to become my wife now. We'll make our vows to each other and wait on no one."

A slow smile spread across her face.

"Tonight when the moon rises, I will be beneath the willows where the horses graze. Will you come to me there?"

"I will come," she said softly.

The sun was sagging on the western horizon when Braden finished his lonely patrol and the dugout appeared over the rise of a hill of land. He'd ridden for hours without a single glimpse of another human being. The green, rolling hills lay serene and calm beneath his gaze, but someplace in their gentle folds they hid a murderer.

As he'd ridden, he'd mulled over the events of Little Bear's murder. Was it a chance encounter? A foolish accident? Or was Little Bear's death planned before he left home? And why had he gone alone?

Braden swung into the corral, unsaddled Brandy, and sent her trotting toward Steven's horse with a swat to her rump. He'd stopped and bathed in the creek in mid afternoon. As the time approached to meet Dancing Bird, a thousand doubts hammered within him.

Steven raised his head from where he pored over a stack of papers on the plank table. "Any trouble?"

"No," Braden replied. "I didn't see another livin' soul."

"See any buffalo?"

"None. They must have moved further north."

Steven ran the feather of his quill through his fingers. "I had a visitor today."

Braden shrugged off his jacket and draped it over a chair. "Who?"

"White Dog. He said he wanted to know if we'd seen buffalo, but in the course of the conversation, he managed to get around to his real purpose. He asked if we'd found out what happened to Little Bear."

"And I don't suppose he could shed any light on the mystery?"

Steven shook his head. "I asked. He denied any knowledge of what happened."

Braden stepped to his bunk, took his saddle bags down from the wall peg, and laid back the leather flap. A wave of memories stared up at him.

The loose white shirt he'd worn when he enlisted.

Dark gray pants, patched and stained.

A neatly coiled belt.

A thumb-worn Bible.

The journal he'd kept on the miserable voyage from Ireland.

He plunged his hand past the other items and felt around in the bottom of the saddlebag until his fingers brushed against lace, and he withdrew the delicate handkerchief.

His mother's scent still clung to the yellowed fabric, despite the miles of ocean air and months in the leather pouch. Ignoring Steven's curious stare, he brought the bit of linen to his nose and inhaled, closing his eyes and allowing himself to go back in time just once more.

Then he untied the knot in the corner and cradled the silver ring in his hand. He hadn't touched it since the day he'd slipped it off his mother's still hand. A dirty string was still wound around it, and tarnish had turned it a dark gray. It was the only thing he could ever remember his mother owning that didn't have a practical purpose. She'd worn it on her right hand. When the hunger set in and her soft, smooth hands began to thin and narrow, she'd encircled the silver with string to make the band fit. As the months rolled by, she'd added more and more string. Still it nearly hung from her bony hand.

Somewhere in his boyhood memories, he remembered her telling him his father had given it to her, a trinket purchased with precious coin on a marketing trip to Dublin, a huge extravagance on the part of a frugal man. But he'd brought it home with a wide smile, slipped it onto her hand and told her she was wearing the family wealth. Then he'd lifted her into his arms and spun her around while Braden hung onto their legs.

Now he couldn't separate what he'd been told from what he actually remembered. He gazed down at the ring and smiled. The truth of the story didn't matter now, only the warm memory. Tonight he'd pass the ring to his wife, the sum and total of their fortune, a tangible promise she could touch when time and distance yawned between them. He ran a finger over the filigree work and let the childhood memory of touching his mother's soft hands and this ring fill him for a moment before he turned to face Steven.

He slipped the ring into his pants pocket and closed the leather flap of the saddlebag.

"You know, a man galloping toward the edge of a precipice wears a certain expression," Steven said, his eyebrows raised.

Braden looked up into his friend's slate-gray eyes and saw Steven had guessed his secret. "At moonrise, I'm meetin' Dancin' Bird. We're going to say our vows to each other. After that I will consider her me wife. Maybe not in the eyes of the church or the law, but in our own hearts."

"I think you should follow your heart."

" 'Tis a sin I'm about to commit, ye know."

Steven shrugged. "I don't recall God defining the marriage ceremony. Man did that." Steven grinned. "As an excuse to eat and drink to excess, mostly."

Then his face fell suddenly serious. "A constable from Fort Walsh was by here this afternoon. The US has appointed a commission to come here and negotiate with Sitting Bull for their voluntary return home. Lord Dufferin is insisting the Americans take some action on this matter with the Sioux."

"Is the commission still due to arrive in the fall?"

Steven nodded. "With Terry in the lead."

Braden shook his head.

"My thoughts exactly."

"What kind of fool do the Americans think Sittin' Bull is? He's not going to listen to Terry."

"Sounds to me like it doesn't matter who's the best negotiator, but more like who can swing the biggest stick."

The world, already plunging headfirst into the unknown, lurched into high speed. Braden looked back at Steven and found his friend watching him closely.

"I can't wait for Ottawa to sort this out. I can't wait another day. I'll leave the force before I lose her."

* * *

Walks Lightly's wedding dress rolled up neatly and fit perfectly in the parfleche Dancing Bird now laced shut. Preparations for supper were taking longer than usual, and she'd had to make her clandestine plans in bits and pieces as family members came and went. When she dropped a bowl for the second time, her mother had sent her inside with a stern frown to tend the firepit, giving her exactly what she wanted—privacy.

She'd managed to steal her sister's dress by wiggling underneath the tipi from behind and snatching the dress while Walks Lightly and her husband were outside. She'd felt a little guilty at first, taking it without permission, but if her plans went perfectly, it would be back in its carefully tied parfleche tomorrow morning and no one would be the wiser.

She peeped underneath the rolled up tipi sides. The sun had set, and a subtle lavender softened the hard lines of the distant bluff. The moon would soon rise and take her sister's place in the sky. And before the sun returned, she would be Braden's wife. She smiled at all the implications of that title.

"Dancing Bird." Her mother's sharp voice cut into her thoughts.

"Yes?"

Moving-Robe-Woman stood in the doorway of the tipi, her hands on her hips. "I thought you were sick. I called your name many times."

Dancing Bird felt her face flush. "I'm sorry. I . . . was thinking about a bird I saw today."

Her mother scowled. "Big Dog is here. He will make you think of things other than birds."

Panic rolled through her. She'd forgotten she was supposed to stand with him tonight. How was she going to get out of this?

"I do not feel well," she blurted and bemoaned her own lack of imagination.

Moving-Robe-Woman frowned at her, then raised a finger. "You will not hide from this. You need a husband. Big Dog is as good as any."

"Mother, I do not love him."

Moving-Robe-Woman shook her head. "What do you know of love? You live with a man, cook his meals, give his body comfort, and he provides for you. That is all that is necessary."

"And as long as you don't love him, you will not hurt when he is killed? Is that what you mean, Mother?"

Moving-Robe-Woman's face blanched. "When you take a husband, give him your body, your hands, and your time, but never give him your heart." On those words, her mother turned and ducked out of the tipi.

Dancing Bird remained in the lodge and heard her mother gently send Big Dog away. Their exchange was soft and pleasant, and Dancing Bird heard a lilt in her mother's voice she hadn't heard in a long time. Or did she imagine it?

After some time she peeped outside. No one waited for her and her mother was nowhere in sight. She gathered her parfleche and mounted Wind, whom she'd tied out behind the tipi earlier, explaining she wanted to ride later and did not want to hunt for her in the dark. As she gathered the reins to ride away, a hand grabbed her calf and her heart leaped into her throat.

"You forgot these." Walks Lightly looked up at her, her own wedding moccasins dangling from her fingers.

Dancing Bird reached down slowly and took the shoes from her sister's hand. "Thank you," was all she could think to say.

"Where will you meet him?"

"He is waiting for me in the grove of willows by the creek."

"I will move the horses so no one will come there for their mount. It is time they were moved anyway." Walks Lightly stood at Wind's side and scuffed her moccasins in the grass. "You have chosen a difficult path."

Dancing Bird nodded. "I know. But it is the only path for us."

Walks Lightly stepped backward into the shadows when someone passed close by. "Love him tonight as if there will be no other time."

"I will."

Walks Lightly stepped back into the light and touched Dancing Bird's thigh. "I love you, sister."

"I love you, too," Dancing Bird replied, her voice deserting her on the last word. She gathered her reins and turned Wind toward the north.

Thirteen

The moon hung white and serene, rivaled only by the twinkling stars vying for her attention. Braden swung down off Brandy's back and breathed in the damp, musty scent of rotting leaves. He glanced around the grove, but Dancing Bird was not there. He briefly wondered if she'd changed her mind.

As if conjured by his thoughts, Dancing Bird rode out of the darkness. The white dress she wore caught the feeble moonglow and spun a soft cocoon of light about her. She slid off Wind's back in a flurry of long fringe and dark hair.

"I have a gift for you." She untied a bundle from behind her blanket and withdrew a soft buckskin shirt, crooked rows of beads marching across the shoulders and chest. Braden took the velvety material in his hands and wondered at the hours she'd spent on the beading.

"I have something for you, too." Braden reached into his pocket and withdrew the ring. Taking her hand in his, he slid the cool metal onto her finger, then folded her fingers inside his. "It was my mother's, a gift from my father."

Dancing Bird stared down at the shiny band, turned her hand and watched the moonlight play with the silvery surface. Then she lifted a distressed face. "I cannot wear it. Mother will see."

"Here." He took his knife and cut two of the ankle-length fringes from her sister's dress, tied the ends together, threaded the ring onto the length and tied it around her neck. The sparkling silver band slipped beneath the neck of her dress, settling between her breasts. She looked up at him, her eyes dark, deep pools.

The wind whispered through the willow branches, seduced into a silent and graceful waltz. Evening insects chirped, their voices following some silent conductor's signals. Over it all, Braden could hear the rush of blood in his ears.

Moonlight dappled the leaf-strewn ground, having found its way through the canopy of leaves above. Braden took her hand in his. Her skin was rough from work; her hands strong and capable. Moonlight sprinkled lacy patterns across her cheeks. A tiny wisp of hair fell forward from her ear, begging to be punished for its disobedience. A tiny freckle graced her left chin—or was it another trick of the moon?

How could he find mere words to express the depth of his devotion to the woman at his side? How could twenty-six letters make up enough words to say what was in his heart? He closed his eyes and she squeezed his fingers, a quiet courage he was quickly learning to rely on.

"I promise—" he began, then cleared his throat. "I promise that I will love ye and only ye all me days. I will protect ye and make a home for ye at me side. I will care for ye through sickness and when misfortune comes."

She smiled at him from her halo of moon-dappled light.

"From this moment on, I am yer husband."

Dancing Bird squeezed his hand again and smiled up at him. "And I promise to love only you all my life," she said in a strong, steady voice, full of confidence. "I will care for you and give you many healthy children. I will gladly leave my home and my people to walk by your side. I will never again fear misfortune, because you will be with me. From this moment on, I am your wife."

Braden removed his helmet and lowered his head. "We Irish kiss our wives at the end of our weddin's," he whispered, his lips barely grazing hers. She reached up on tiptoe to meet him.

The night was suddenly quiet and soft and dark. The woman who had tempted him to the brink now stood before him demure and bashful. An intoxicating sense of protectiveness washed over him and a slow heat began in the pit of his stomach and spiraled outward.

He took her in his arms, and she melted and reformed beneath his touch. Her trembling fingers worked loose the brass buttons on his jacket, then pushed the heavy material off his shoulders. He dropped the jacket to the ground. Next, she attacked the buttons on his white shirt, but stopped when his suspenders prevented it following the jacket to the earth. Chuckling, Braden lowered the straps and took off his shirt.

" 'Tis unfair, ye know. Ye have on yer dress and I only have me trousers."

Tilting her head, she smiled slowly. "But when you untie my dress, I will be wearing nothing."

The slow spiral of heat widened. His muscles tensed

and his heartbeat increased. Braden sat on a stump and removed his boots and socks. The cool earth squished against the heated bottoms of his feet as he stood and stepped toward her. He slid his fingers into her hair, around to the back of her neck and found the tiny leather thong that held her dress. Slowly, the leather slid apart and the garment drooped to the edges of her shoulders, where she stopped it against her chest.

"I will see you first, husband," she said, her grin wicked.

God help him, she fired his blood. And as his desire grew, so did his embarrassment at undressing so casually in front of her. As if reading his discomfort, her smile widened and she motioned with her hand for him to finish.

He popped loose the button on his trousers, dropped them to the ground, and stepped away. The chill of the damp air wrapped around his skin and gooseflesh sprang up, wonderfully arousing.

She gave him a slow perusal—satisfying, he knew, a long piqued curiosity. Then she released the dress. It slid down her body and pooled at her feet. Delicately, she stepped to the side and stood before him as naked as he.

"Do you like your wife, husband?" she asked with complete abandon, her hands planted on her hips.

Braden moved forward, his hands shaking badly. Surely when he touched her, she'd think he was having some sort of fit. But her warm skin stilled his quivering fingers and his heart began to thump in his ears. She glowed honey rich in the moonlight, her skin dark and flawless against his own ghostly glow. Her cool, soft fingers laced through his hair, combing against his scalp, lulling and exciting.

Taking her wrists in his hands, he raised her arms and kissed the gaping wounds that marred her wrists. "Say you will always be my wife, even if others say no." Trailing kisses, he followed the line of her arm up to the softness of her shoulder.

"I will be your wife." She tilted back her head to allow him access to her neck. "I will bear you many sons."

"And no one will become between us. Not your people or mine."

"No one."

He cupped the weight of her breasts in his hands and marveled at the gifts of a woman's body, gifts that so perfectly answered needs in a man.

She traced her fingers through the fine scattering of hair on his chest. A soft evening breeze caught her hair and lifted it in a dark cloud around her head. Had a man ever so wanted and loved a woman as he did at that moment?

Her wandering fingers left his hair to smooth out across the sensitive spot on his collarbone that made him shiver. She laughed softly and continued her journey down his arms, leaping to his ribs and across his hips, around to his back, where she abruptly clasped him against her, her hands locked at the small of his back. "Make love to me," she whispered against his cheek.

Could men melt into pools at the feet of the women they loved? The irrational thought bounced through his head as he acknowledged the fact the seduction had just changed hands.

She urged him down to the leafy ground along with her, and he wished he'd had the forethought to bring a blanket. But somehow the feel of the damp ground beneath them and the swirling scent of water and earth seemed fitting and right.

Face to face they lay, their cheeks propped on bent arms, their breath stirring errant strands of hair. With a lazy smile, she examined the length of him, no virginal fear in her eyes.

Moonlight made an intriguing shadow in the dip of her waist, deepened by the angle of her body. Braden leaned forward to kiss the beckoning shadow, but she captured his lips first. One slim hand feathered down his arm, across his hips and down across the flatness of his stomach to cup him protectively.

He grunted in surprise and felt her kiss widen into a smile beneath his lips.

She chuckled softly, her breath making little swirls against his cheeks. "You are a willing husband as well as a handsome one." Her hand continued its exploration across the flare of his hip and over the swell of his backside, where she stopped to knead his flesh. "And now you're mine."

Part of him wanted this sweet seduction to continue, to touch her as she'd touched him, to run his hands over her silky skin. Yet another part of him demanded to be fulfilled, to feel her flesh close around him, accept him, welcome him home. Heart surging and stumbling, he returned the kiss, forcing her backward until she lay sprawled out on their bed of leaves. "And you're mine," he whispered against the cleft of her collarbone.

She threaded her fingers through his hair, combing out the curls and waves, sliding her fingers to the ends of the strands, prolonging the sensation as long as possible. Braden closed his eyes and sighed deeply, wondering if he would ever again feel so contented.

Dancing Bird put a hand on the back of his head and pulled his head down. "Touch me," she whispered, "as I have touched you." She raised her arms over her head and plucked at fine tendrils of hair, then relaxed and lay vulnerable and open before him.

He'd never expected nor hoped for such blatant seduction. And to have the woman he so loved stretched out before him with no resistance and no shame was almost more than he could bear. He slid his eyes closed and struggled for control, feeling as though he would explode. When he opened his eyes, she stared up at him, her eyes dark and round.

"Are you ill?" she asked, an edge of fear in her voice.

"No, lass." He shook his head. "Yer always surprisin' me."

She sat up, leaves and sticks clinging to her hair. "I've displeased you?"

"Oh no, love. Not a'tall." He cupped one of her breasts in his hand, softly brushing the nipple with his thumb. "Nothin' about ye displeases me."

With a hand on each shoulder, she pushed him to his back and leaned over him, allowing her hair to brush lightly across his stomach. "You are the warrior. You will hunt the buffalo and defend our home. But tonight, I will be the warrior and make you mine."

Of all the fantasies he ever had, none could have compared to what his wife was doing to his body. With her hands and soft lips, she tortured him to the brink of disaster, finding spots on his body he'd never before considered particularly sensitive.

When she had nearly robbed him of his mind and his pride, she begged him to complete their union, and they made love with their horses cropping grass nearby and the voice of the river in their ears. And when the time came for the ultimate consummation of their bond, Braden hoped, with his last logical thought, that he would get her with child, a tiny life she could nurture and protect, a soul to replace those she hadn't been able to save.

Evening was well into night before Braden awoke in Dancing Bird's arms, his body curled against her, the soft flesh of her breasts pressed against his bare back. Alarmed at the chance they had taken falling asleep naked so close to the village, he sat bolt upright and looked around, panic replacing the blood in his veins.

"Walks Lightly moved the herd," Dancing Bird murmured sleepily. "No one will come here looking for their pony."

"How did you know what I was thinking?" He turned over and kissed the end of her nose.

She smiled and opened her eyes. "A good wife always knows what her husband is thinking."

"And who had the forethought to move the herd?"

She stretched, purposefully giving him another full length view of her body. Words she'd once uttered in fun, a threat to make him beg for her attentions, now rang dangerously true. "It was Walks Lightly's idea."

"I think I may have underestimated your sister. Apparently, ye aren't the only one with larceny in yer blood."

She sat up and braced herself on the palms of her hands. "Larceny?"

"It means sneakiness, willingness to steal things."

"Like horses?" she asked brightly.

"Yes, like stealing horses."

"I like to steal horses. I would have made a good warrior."

"I rest my case."

She scrambled to her knees and leaned toward him until he was leaning backward, braced on his hands. Her nose nearly touching his, she smiled.

"Are ye a devil as well as a horse thief?" he asked, already feeling the effects of her closeness.

"No, I am a woman in love with her husband. A woman who wants a baby."

Cold logic had returned with the deepening of the night. A baby now would impossibly complicate things. Even as his logical mind processed that thought, he smiled. Too late now.

Before he could react or formulate some speech about the advantages of postponing any more lovemaking until he had worked out the details of their marriage in the eyes of his law, she was on his lap, her ankles locked behind him.

"Dancing Bird," he whispered, a feeble effort at resistance as she laced her fingers into his hair and kissed him deep and hard.

Dawn was a pink promise in the east when he left her, and no leaving had ever ripped at his heart as this one did. Slow anger filled him as he swung into the saddle and looked down into her tear-filled eyes. They should be in their own soft bed, free to make love as many times as they pleased and leave their bed only when necessary. But now began their charade, and his resolve to keep their union a secret began to erode with every tear that streamed down her face.

"It will be hard not waking up with you beside me every morning." Her simple words encompassed everything swirling around in his head. Hard, indeed. Downright impossible.

He reached down and plucked a leaf from her hair, then tucked it into the pocket of his coat. No matter how many more times he kissed her or how many more times they made love, nothing would make their parting easy. And they had tested the theory several times since the moon witnessed the union of their hearts and bodies.

"I'll be back tonight to court you, as I arranged with your uncle."

More tears crowded into her eyes. "How can I stand so close to you and not touch you as a woman touches her husband?"

He'd wondered the same thing himself. How could he stand close to her and not touch her wonderful skin or want to see her as she'd been last night? How could he be satisfied with discussing village gossip and the day's events when he really wanted to return right here to this spot and spend another night making love to her?

All through the night, even during the times they'd lain face-to-face and talked, he hadn't been able to find the heart to tell her about the commission. Her people were content in this golden summer, hunting and living as they had for hundreds of years. How could he shatter that on the word of a people who hadn't yet kept their promises where the Sioux were concerned?

He leaned down from the saddle, his face close to hers. "We'll take the time Fate allows us and make the most of it. We'll be together soon. I promise." He kissed her and thought how chaste touching her lips now seemed. He instantly wanted more of her. Before he changed his mind, he gathered his reins and rode off into the morning.

Alarm chased away regret when he neared the dugout and saw Walsh's black horse tied to the corral fence. Knowing guilt was written all across his face, Braden dismounted, tied Brandy to the corral, and ducked inside the dugout.

Steven threw him a cursory glance, then returned his attention to a paper Walsh had spread out across the table.

James Walsh looked up as Braden entered. "Constable Flynn. Constable Gravel said he hoped you would ride in this morning. I've brought news that will affect your position here."

Braden slid into a chair, wincing silently at the soreness in his limbs.

Walsh leaned back in his chair, threaded his fingers together across the chest of his jacket, and looked at Braden. "I received a letter from Commissioner McLeod yesterday that related your conversation with him. He has assured me he will write the necessary letters, but I fear you will have a long wait, if our former communications with Ottawa are any example. In the meantime, at the risk of sounding unintentionally callous, your relationship with Dancing Bird may be just the thing that keeps the peace."

"Beggin' yer pardon, sir?" Braden said, wondering if his lack of sleep was telling on him.

Walsh leaned forward. "In June, General Miles was ordered to take the field against the remaining Sioux hostiles south of the border. I fully expect him to be efficient and expedient in that endeavor." Sarcasm dripped off his words. Walsh was well known for his disapproval of the United States' method of dealing with Indian troubles.

Pointing at the map spread out in front of them, he continued. "General Howard, God help him, has been pursuing Joseph of the Nez Percé since the middle of June, the deadline Washington gave them to be on their reservations. As with Sitting Bull's Sioux, Washington gave the Nez Percé an impossible deadline and expected them to round up scattered stock and possessions in an area flooded with spring rains. Needless to say, they did not make their deadline and General Howard is in pursuit—reluctantly, I might add."

"How does this affect us?" Steven asked, glancing again at Braden.

"The Nez Percé are moving north with an eye toward Sitting Bull for help."

Steven whistled low. "There's trouble aplenty now between the Blackfeet and the Sioux over the buffalo. This area won't feed many more."

"I want you"—Walsh looked at Braden—"to keep your ears and eyes open during your visits to Sitting Bull's village. Discourage them from meddling in the Nez Percé problem. I'm going there tonight for a chat with Sitting Bull, and I'd like both of you to accompany me. The messaging system within the Sioux tribe rivals any telegraph I've ever seen. I'm sure they already know all about this and, frankly, I'd like to know what they know."

Dancing Bird wove a drunken path through the sleepy, stirring village. From tipi to tipi, she skirted the traveled paths until she reached her sister's tipi. Wriggling under the cover, she shoved the bundled wedding dress into its place, noting that Walks Lightly and Standing Elk were still asleep, wrapped in each other's arms. A twinge of regret stung her as she withdrew and crept around her uncle's tipi, her stealth made harder by the fact the sides were rolled up and her mother slept facing the back.

She'd bathed briefly before leaving the willow grove, washing away the evidence of her lovemaking and taking care not to wet her hair lest her mother suspect her dishonesty. As she crept onto her sleeping robe, she held her breath as she heard her mother sigh, turn over, and begin making waking noises. Crunching her eyes closed, she waited.

Moving-Robe-Woman scrambled to her feet and moved toward the front of the tipi. Dancing Bird heard her pause over her for an interminable amount of time, then move on and begin breakfast preparations. After waiting a time, Dancing Bird rose and followed.

She moved into the practiced routine with ease. Her mother filled the buffalo paunch with water, and she dropped in the meat. Her mother shaped the cakes made from ground roots, and Dancing Bird filled another paunch in which to boil them. Throughout the preparations, her mother said nothing, and Dancing Bird felt an edge of regret for her angry words last night. She needed time to think, though, time to formulate some reason not to allow Big Dog to court her any longer, something her mother would accept.

Walks Lightly emerged from her tipi and cast a glance in Dancing Bird's direction.

"We need more water," Dancing Bird said, grabbing an empty bladder from its hanger outside the tipi.

"There are two others full," her mother said, but Dancing Bird hurried down toward the creek, knowing her sister would soon follow.

She didn't have long to wait. Walks Lightly hurried down the path and threw her arms around Dancing Bird when she met her and they were sure they were not seen.

"Are you all right?" Walks Lightly asked, holding Dancing Bird at arm's length and looking her over as if she expected to see a great difference in her.

"I am fine," Dancing Bird said.

Walks Lightly waited, her eyes dancing with mischief. "Tell me," she finally said, flopping to the ground and dragging Dancing Bird down with her.

They huddled in the bushes at the creek's edge as they'd done as children, conspirators in a tadpole hunt.

"It was wonderful," Dancing Bird said, gripping her sister's arm. "Just as you said."

"Was he gentle?" Walks Lightly frowned and again scanned Dancing Bird from head to toe.

"Yes, he was gentle. Many times." They hooted with laughter, then covered their mouths simultaneously.

"I have a secret," Walks Lightly said. "I haven't told Mother yet." She leaned closer. "I carry a child."

Dancing Bird's laughter stopped in her throat. "A baby?" Terrible stories played out in her mind, stories of tragic births where child and mother were lost. So many had happened on their flight from *Paha Sapa*. She pushed away the bad thoughts and refocused her attention on Walks Lightly's gleaming smile. "When?"

"In the spring, I think."

"Have you told Standing Elk?"

"No, I wanted to tell you first."

Tears sprang to Dancing Bird's eyes and she folded Walks Lightly in her arms. "I am happy for you."

"Do you remember when we used to sit by the creek just like this and catch fish and tadpoles?"

Dancing bird nodded.

"And you always fell in and Mother would be mad?"

"And you never did. She always compared me to you."

Walks Lightly's smile faded. "I'm sorry."

Dancing Bird flicked a leaf off into the water and watched it twirl in the current. "You cannot help you are like you are and I cannot help I am like I am. We are different. But now we are both women."

"Yes, we are. And we will always have each other." Walks Lightly threw a casual arm across Dancing Bird's shoulder, and together they watched the leaf float around a bend.

"I thought you both had gotten lost." Moving-Robe-Woman stood over them, a frown bunching the skin between her eyes.

"We were looking for tadpoles," Walks Lightly lied first.

Moving-Robe-Woman looked from one to the other. "You both are behaving strangely. If you were still children, I would look for bugs in my bed or sand in the water bladders." She turned and walked back up the creek bank.

"Do you remember when she used to smile and laugh?" Walks Lightly asked, tracing a pattern in the dirt with a stick.

"When Father was alive."

"And not since."

"No, not since."

"Did you know several men have offered for her as a second wife?"

Dancing Bird looked up. "No. Did Uncle not convince her to accept?"

"No. She wouldn't listen to him and sent the men away angry."

Dancing Bird picked up a stick of her own and traced her sister's drawings. "I think she should marry again." She glanced quickly at her sister's face. "Don't you?"

"I didn't . . . for a time." Walks Lightly looked up. "But now that I am married and you are married and Little Bear has died she will soon have no one. She should have a husband. But she says she will never be a second wife."

"Then perhaps we can find her a husband without a wife."

"Who?"

Dancing Bird threw down her stick, jarred from the solution that presented itself. Why hadn't she thought of this before? "Big Dog."

"Big Dog?" Her sister looked at her as if she'd lost her mind. "He is courting you."

"But he sneaks looks at her whenever she is around. I had never thought about it until now, I was so nervous around him. He is closer to her age than to mine. His wife has been dead a long time, and he has never taken another."

"Perhaps there is something wrong with him."

"Perhaps he does not want a young wife."

Walks Lightly snorted. "What man does not want a young wife so he can strut around like a prairie hen rooster and crow?"

"Maybe he has been waiting for Mother."

"Do you think so?"

Dancing Bird bunched her shoulders in anticipation of a wonderful adventure. "We can find out."

Walks Lightly dipped her discarded water bladder into the creek. "I have to get home and cook food. I will think about this."

Dancing Bird dipped her own water and stood, conscious of a slight soreness just settling in.

"Boil some willow bark and drink it," Walks Lightly said as she laced shut the top to her water vessel. "It will help the soreness." She smiled with twinkling eyes.

"I wonder if anyone will tell Braden the same thing."

"Did you tell Standing Elk?"

Walks Lightly grinned. "Only after I enjoyed watching him hobble about for an hour or so, stubbornly denying he was in pain."

They giggled again, admonished each other for being cruel, then set out for home, arms linked.

Fourteen

Low clouds hung over the prairie, harbingers of gloom trying to swallow the wide blueness of the sky and leave in its void an uncomfortable closeness. Lark song was muted and even the grasshoppers sang only in lone chirps instead of their usual harmony.

Bad weather was approaching, Braden knew, but he couldn't help attributing some of the eeriness crawling up his back to his inner turmoil. August held them all in her grasp. The end of summer was quickly approaching. Snow would fly even before the willows dropped the last of their leaves, and the situation with the Sioux was no more resolved than it had been when spring first flung wide her green mantle.

He'd covered these same steps this morning filled with joy and hope and soft memories of his new wife, but now, as he rode back to Sitting Bull's village three abreast with Walsh and Steven, he wrestled with growing hopelessness.

They passed through the outskirts of the village with little notice and pulled their ponies to a stop in front of Sitting Bull's great tipi. Dancing Bird stepped outside first and threw Braden a brief, sultry glance that stirred his blood, even from a distance.

"We'd like to speak with your uncle," Walsh said.

Dancing Bird nodded, ducked back inside, and quickly emerged with Sitting Bull at her side.

"We would like to sit in council with you," Walsh said. Dancing Bird murmured a translation. Sitting Bull nodded and crooked his fingers for them to follow him.

They ducked beneath the rolled tipi sides and sat on robes spread upon the floor. Weeks ago, the lodge had been bare of comforts and supplies, but now luxurious buffalo robes covered the floor and dried plants hung from the lodgepoles. Bows and arrows were tucked into the dew cloth and parfleches filled with pemmican and stored foods lay tucked against the outside wall. Canada had been good to the Sioux.

Dancing Bird hovered by the entrance as the men sat down. Sitting Bull quickly caught her eye and motioned her to his side by patting the robe next to him. She sat down and stared at the floor, an effort, Braden knew, not to give them away.

"Do you know of the problems of the Nez Percé?" Walsh asked, going straight to the point.

Dancing Bird translated, then listened to her uncle's words. "Yes, he does," she replied.

"Did you know that Joseph expects help from you and your people if they can reach the Medicine Line?"

Sitting Bull smiled slowly. "White Forehead has sharp ears." He waved away Dancing Bird's translation, and she smothered a smile. Apparently, his use of a translator depended on how mysterious he wanted to appear at any given time.

"Yes, I do have sharp ears," Walsh said, locking gazes with the chief.

Sitting Bull smiled. "I have heard the Nez Percé have

lost their home and are being chased like dogs, burying their women, children, and old as they run. I hear they are coming to the Land of the Great White Mother to find peaceful sleep, as we did."

"If they come, there will be less food, fewer buffalo for everyone."

"Would I turn away my brother if he was hungry?"

Walsh's jaw set underneath his tanned skin. "The White Mother will expect them to obey the same laws she set down for you and your brothers. You should send them that word by your messengers."

Again, Sitting Bull smiled slowly, respect in his eyes. "White Forehead is clever like the fox. I have already sent that word."

Walsh's full mustache twitched, hiding a small smile. "It would be better if they surrender before they cross the Medicine Line."

"White Forehead is a good soldier. He does what the White Mother asks, but I can see in your eyes that you do not believe those words."

Walsh held his gaze, even though his throat worked in a swallow. "I do what is best for everyone."

"That is the pain of a chief. He must consider everyone, and not the ones who need him most." Sitting Bull looked pointedly at Braden.

"Will you keep me informed of the Nez Percé's progress?"

Sitting Bull nodded.

"And if and when they cross the border, you will come and get Constable Flynn or Constable Gravel?"

"I will not have to ride far to find Constable Flynn." Sitting Bull grinned, and Braden felt his face flush.

He risked a glance at Dancing Bird. Her gaze flickered up to his face, then back down to the buffalo robe.

Walsh slanted him a brief glance. "Constable Flynn is here as a representative of the Great White Mother, also. He can help you if you need more of her words."

"Have the Long Lances found the men who killed my nephew?"

Walsh shook his head. "No," he answered honestly. "They have disappeared like a snake in the prairie grass. But we will find them. They cannot escape us."

The two men's eyes met and held for a time. "I believe you will find them," the chief said. "You have always kept your word."

"There is talk of men coming from the Long Knives to speak with you about your returning home. These men may come in the time of falling leaves. I will be here when they come, as will McLeod. I would like it if you would hear their words."

Braden watched Sitting Bull's face as Walsh plunged into the subject of the commission, but the chief's expression remained impassive. "I wish to hear no more of their words."

"They will not give up. They will send more men if you do not listen to these. They wish you to come to Fort Walsh to hear them."

Sitting Bull shook his head. "No. I will not hear them. I want no more words from the Long Knives. We are happy here in the White Mother's Land."

Walsh waited and let the moment of brief anger pass. "We will talk of this later," he said with his gentle tenacity. He stood, and Braden and Steven scrambled up behind him.

"Thank you for hearing us," Walsh said, nodding to

Dancing Bird. She nodded back, then averted her eyes again.

A fine rain was beginning as they stepped out of the tipi and into the gray day. Walsh paused by his horse's side and pulled on his long white gloves. "I'd like to take another look at the place Little Bear died while I'm here," he said, "and I'd like both of you to accompany me."

Yellowing grass bowed beneath the onslaught of wind, and in the west, dark clouds bunched on the horizon. When they reached the rolling landscape where Little Bear had been found, another premonition crawled up Braden's spine.

Walsh dismounted and squatted by the dark stain where the earth had soaked up Little Bear's spilled blood. Braden scanned the horizon, looking for some unknown danger. To the east, a herd of buffalo had clustered in the bottom of a coulee, driven there by the threat of storm. Their dark bodies milled uneasily, undulating like a cluster of dark ants.

A flash on the edge of a ridge caught Braden's eye. A lone rider, silhouetted against the growing clouds, rode slowly toward the herd. The sight was common enough; the buffalo were vulnerable there, driven together by their own fear, easy targets. Braden squinted. Something about the rider . . .

Then there was another movement to the right. Three more riders appeared, traveling a head-on course with the first. Braden's hand slid toward his rifle scabbard.

"What is it?" Steven's voice was crisp and alert.

Braden nodded. "There."

Steven turned in the saddle and Walsh stood. The first rider stopped and raised a weapon that caught the feeble light in a brief reflection. The discharge was delayed, then reverberated, bouncing off the hills. A buffalo plunged to the ground and the herd bolted. Another report followed close on the heels of the first. The first rider somersaulted backward off his black pony.

A black pony.

Braden whipped his rifle to his shoulder, aimed and shot toward the three. Their horses plunged and a breeze caught feathers and ruffled them to life.

"Are they Sioux?" Walsh asked as the three galloped over the ridge and out of sight.

"I don't know," Braden said, shoving his rifle into his scabbard and heeling Brandy into a gallop toward the fallen rider.

He knew even before he reached her. One arm crumpled underneath her, Dancing Bird lay in a slowly oozing pool of her own blood. Braden swung out of the saddle before Brandy stopped and went down on one knee at her side.

"Dancing Bird!" he said, his world spinning out of control. He turned her over, fear gripping him with cold, hard hands. A neat, red gash plowed a furrow on the soft golden skin of her shoulder, ripping her dress—a painful but not lethal wound.

"Dancing Bird," he said, gently nudging her, struggling to get a grip on his hammering heartbeat.

She murmured, blinked, then her eyes darted from one face to another of the three men who leaned over her. Her gaze settled on Braden. "What happened?"

"Someone shot you. What were you doing out here?"

Steven turned around, his rifle cradled in his arms, and scanned the horizon.

"The buffalo," she said, licking her lips. "They go together down in a coulee when a storm is coming."

"Are you still taking hides for your damned lodge?" As his heartbeat slowed, his anger grew. Damn it, she was his wife. She shouldn't be hunting buffalo. She should be safe at home in her own house. He placed his gloved hand over her wound and pressed to stop the flow of blood.

She furrowed her brows. "Yes, I was."

"That goddamned lodge will be the death of all of you."

Walsh threw him a quizzical glance, but Braden ignored him. What if he knew? So what, he thought recklessly.

"My mother needs a lodge."

"Your mother can come and live with—" Braden bit back his words as caution shoved aside anger and settled back in control.

"—Walks Lightly," he finished, swallowing down the words he really wanted to say.

Dancing Bird pushed herself up to a sitting position and flexed her shoulder. She stared down at her bloody and torn dress, then back up to Braden's face. "Who shot me?"

"I don't know. Three men to the east." He wanted to pull her into his arms and never release her. He wanted to stand and declare their union to the storm-washed heavens, then protect her for the rest of his days.

"Were they the same men who killed Little Bear?" Her question chased away the last of his anger, and his hands trembled as they helped her to her feet. Steven shoved a wad of cloth underneath the torn material of her dress—his only extra shirt, which he carried in his saddlebag. Braden flashed him a look of gratitude, and Steven raised his eyebrows behind Walsh's back.

"I don't know," he breathed, concentrating on the spot where their skin touched. "They wore feathers is all I know."

"I'm going to follow them," Steven declared, swinging into the saddle.

"Take her back to her village and explain," Walsh ordered. "I'll go with Constable Gravel."

Braden lifted Dancing Bird onto Brandy's back, then swung up behind her. Gathering the reins in his right hand, he held her against his chest. Intimately aware of her body against his, he pulled his attention away from their point of contact and constantly scanned the horizon. They were open targets if anyone chose to finish the job.

Their appearance at the edge of the village caused a stir, and Moving-Robe-Woman came running even before Braden could reach Sitting Bull's tipi. She reached up and pulled Dancing Bird into her arms, nearly collapsing beneath her weight.

"It's only a scratch, mother," Dancing Bird said, looking into her mother's terrified eyes and struggling to stand on her own.

"It is not a scratch. You were shot." Moving-Robe-Woman looped an arm under Dancing Bird's arms and started toward the rolled-up sides of the tipi.

"I can walk—" Dancing Bird began, but her knees buckled and her mother listed under her weight.

Braden was at her side in two steps and scooped her into his arms. He ducked inside the tipi and strode past startled family members eating their evening meal.

He laid Dancing Bird on a buffalo robe, and her

mother pushed him out of the way. Resigned to taking second place for the moment, he strode back outside and found Standing Elk waiting for him at Brandy's side.

"Is Dancing Bird wounded?" he asked, peering around Braden at the small crowd gathered inside the tipi.

"She was shot out where Little Bear was killed."

Standing Elk's eyes widened. "Who did this?"

Braden shook his head. "I don't know."

"You make guess."

"No. I can't. I didn't get a good look at them."

Standing Elk eyed him for a moment, then tilted his head back to stare up at the clouds racing past in the darkening sky. "We wander the land like the clouds wander the sky. We have no home. They will kill us one by one until there are no more Hunkpapa." He tipped his head forward to stare straight into Braden's eyes. "Unless we kill them first."

"We don't know who did this."

"I know. It is the Blackfoot. They do not want us here." Standing Elk shrugged. "I cannot blame them. We take away their buffalo, their game. But I cannot let them kill my people. I have a wife and soon a son."

"Walks Lightly is with child?"

Standing Elk's face lit up with pride. "Yes, when the new leaves come."

A niggling fear for Dancing Bird rose in Braden's thoughts, but he relegated the worry to the back of his mind for later consideration.

"A war with the Blackfoot would surely anger the White Mother and get ye sent back across the border. Ye don't want that, either, do ye?"

Standing straight and tall before him, Standing Elk looked every bit the noble savage Braden had envisioned from dime novels and newspaper articles before he left eastern Canada. Broad of chest and dark skinned, he was darkly handsome, and surely a fearsome enemy. But as he considered Braden's words, a look of sadness filled his eyes, heartbreak enough for an entire tribe of displaced people uprooted from their kingdom.

"No, I would not want that."

"Then let me handle the Blackfeet. They are Canadian citizens and subject to the law the Long Lances lay down."

Standing Elk considered his words with another look upward at the hovering storm clouds. "I will wait and trust you," he said after several moments.

Moving-Robe-Woman stepped outside the tipi and motioned to Braden. He followed her inside just as the sky opened and rain fell in sheets. He knelt at Dancing Bird's side while her relatives stumbled over his feet in an effort to roll down the tipi sides before everything in the lodge was soaked.

"How do you feel?" He touched her bandaged shoulder more for an excuse to feel her pulse jump under his fingers.

"I am fine. Mother bandaged it. It will be well soon." Her gaze flickered over the whole of his face like a warm caress.

"Why were you hunting alone?"

She looked away from him, and he was seized with the urge to cup her face in his hands and force her to look into his eyes.

"I need three more hides for my lodge."

"Why do you need a lodge now?" *Now that you're my wife,* he wanted to add, but couldn't. He had no home to offer her. Was she already doubting his abilities as a husband?

As if sensing his doubts, she turned her face back toward him. "I wish my mother to take another husband. She should have her own lodge to offer as her property."

What a leap of unselfishness that decision had taken. Braden wished he could hold her now and tell her so. But all he could do was nod and hope she read his eyes. " 'Twould be a good thing, that. I'll bring ye the hides."

"No, it is my responsibility."

He picked up her hand and held her fingers where no one could see. "Call it a wedding present," he said softly.

She smiled and threw a glance in the direction of her mother's vigilant scowl. "Mother wonders what is going on between us."

"Should we tell her?"

Dancing Bird smiled slyly, and her left hand moved to his knee and traveled up his thigh. "She would be surprised."

Braden caught her hand in his, their bodies hiding their joined hands. "If ye don't stop, ye'll be the one surprised, and I'll have to explain to yer mother." He turned and smiled at Moving-Robe-Woman. "And 'tis not a task I'd look forward to."

"When will you come again?" Dancing Bird asked when he turned back to her.

"Not for several days. I'm goin' to the Blackfoot village and see to this shootin' of yours."

Her fingers ceased their caress and gripped his thigh tightly. "No," she breathed, her eyes wide.

He loosened her fingers and held them enclosed in his hand. " 'Tis my job, wife," he whispered. " 'Tis what I do."

She swallowed and blinked away brief tears. "I know. Come to me when you return."

He squeezed her hand and pretended it was all of her. "Sure and it's a hasty trail I'll make back to ye."

Scattered sentries raised their guns and aimed down barrels that flashed in the morning sun. Braden drew Brandy to a stop and waited, resisting the urge to draw his Adams revolver. Slowly, one gun lowered, then the rest. A rider trotted his horse down the rolling hill and stopped in front of Braden.

"What do you want here?" he asked in the Blackfoot Braden had learned at Fort McLeod. Streaks of white paint smeared both cheeks, tapering onto his bare chest. He wore only a breechcloth and moccasins, and he propped the stock of the carbine rifle on his thigh with the nonchalance of a man used to handling a gun.

"I come lookin' for Dog," Braden answered in Blackfoot.

The brave grinned. "You are a Red Coat."

"Yes. Is Dog here?"

"I am Eagle Ribs. Why do you look for Dog?"

"I want to ask him some questions about the death of a young Sioux man."

Eagle Ribs narrowed his eyes. "The people of Sitting Bull?"

"Yes."

"We do not want them here in our land. They kill our buffalo, and our women and children go hungry."

Braden pushed back his helmet and crossed his hands over his saddle horn. " 'Tis a fine gift for story ye have, Eagle Ribs, but I'll wager yer women and children are never hungry—unless the Blackfeet have grown lazy."

Eagle Ribs frowned and slitted his eyes. "You are either a very brave man or a very foolish one."

"I'm neither, and the White Mother would be very angry if something were to happen to one of her Red Coats."

Eagle Ribs studied him a moment further, then reined his paint pony around. "Come, he is here," he threw back over his shoulder.

The reason for the security was soon evident. Pinioned through the skin of their chests, then tied to long strips of rawhide hung from a pole, several young men dangled in various stages of unconsciousness.

A sun dance, the Blackfoot ceremony to honor the sun, giver of all life.

As he rode past the self-torture, so sacred to those who performed it, Braden felt distrustful eyes follow him from the gathered crowd. A low lodge made of willow branches piled in geometric patterns sat in the center of the gathering—the Sun Dance lodge.

Eagle Ribs slipped off his horse's back and waited for Braden. Together they walked through the crowd to a colorful tipi pitched in the center of a circle of other painted tipis. Eagle Ribs poked his head inside, said Dog's name, then withdrew his head. "He comes," he said simply.

A blackened face emerged, followed by a blackened

body. A white half moon was painted on his breast and radiating white lines ran from his cheeks and chin to his forehead.

Dog frowned. "What do you want, Red Coat?"

"Where were you yesterday afternoon?"

Dog smiled, showing teeth made whiter by the black on his face. "My wife is the medicine woman at this Sun Dance. I was with her."

Braden ran through his mind what Jerry Potts, James McLeod's scout, had told them about the Sun Dance celebration. It was a sacred event. A participant, especially the husband of the chosen medicine woman, was unlikely to leave the celebration, which ran for days.

"A young Sioux man named Little Bear was killed a few days ago and another person shot yesterday where the Blackfoot and Sioux hunting territories join."

"I know nothing of this. Why did you ride here to ask me?"

"The Red Coats know the Blackfeet do not want the Sioux here. I saw ye there once, and ye ran when ye saw me."

Dog shrugged. "I do not remember. I ride many places. I have a family to feed, and sometimes I have to ride far to find buffalo."

Acknowledging he couldn't win a war of verbal exchanges, Braden shifted approaches. "If ye should hear of who did this, the Great White Mother would be very happy if ye would ride to the Red Coat fort and tell them what ye know."

When Dog didn't respond, Braden turned and swung into the saddle. Only one young man was left dangling from the central pole. He hung by puckered tents of skin just above his breasts. His knees had buckled and his arms hung limply at his side. One of the most sacred of ceremonies, the torture was based on answered prayers. A man prayed for health for a loved one or safety for himself. If his prayer was answered, he then offered bits of his flesh to the sun for her generosity. And as Braden reined Brandy around, he mulled the unlikely mix of such honesty coupled with murder.

"Red Coat!"

Braden stopped and turned in the saddle to look back over his shoulder.

Dog walked to his side and looked up. "I do not like the Sioux being here, but they are not my enemies. I did not kill Little Bear. You should go to the Long Knives who are camped in the Great White Mother's land for your answers."

Fifteen

Big Dog stood patiently in front of the tipi, a blanket folded neatly over his arm. Smoke from evening fires slithered through the village. From her hiding place, Dancing Bird watched the door to the lodge through the slit in her sister's tipi.

"Do you see anything yet?" Walks Lightly whispered loudly.

"Yes. He is there," Dancing Bird whispered back.

Moving-Robe-Woman opened the flap, saw who it was, then turned to go back inside. Suddenly, Sitting Bull emerged.

"Uncle's outside," Dancing Bird reported.

Sitting Bull spoke briefly with Big Dog. He disappeared into the lodge, then re-emerged holding Moving-Robe-Woman by the arm. He positioned her in front of Big Dog, took the blanket from his arm and draped it across the shoulders of both. She cast him a furious look which he received with a small smile. Then he went back inside his lodge.

"He's put the blanket over them."

Walks Lightly put down her bowl and scrambled to Dancing Bird's side. "Let me see," she said, pushing her sister away from the slit to peer through it.

"The two of you are going to be taken by evil spirits." Standing Elk's voice made them both jump and turn. He stood by the firepit, his hands on his hips, grinning.

Walks Lightly drew away from the slit slowly, as if uncertain what she should do. Standing Elk waved a hand in her direction. "Go on with your peeping. I will dip my own supper." Sighing, he sat down by the fire and scooped his supper out of the paunch.

"Is she staying there?" Dancing Bird asked as Walks Lightly returned her eyes to the slit.

"Yes, she's talking to him. And she's smiling!"

"Let me see." Dancing Bird took over the peephole. Indeed Moving-Robe-Woman was standing in the blanket with a man. And she *was* smiling. A tiny wave of jealousy passed through Dancing Bird, but she quickly pushed it away. Her father was walking the Spirit Path. He would not want Moving-Robe-Woman to live the rest of her life lonely and poor. He would have approved of the tiny lies Dancing Bird had told in the last few days to arrange this courting.

Abandoning her spying, Dancing Bird shuffled to the firepit and sat down on a robe across the fire from her brother-in-law. He cocked an eyebrow at her as she dipped her own supper from the paunch.

"Aren't you happy with your meddling?"

Dancing Bird threw him a frown and lifted a portion of delicate greens to her mouth. "Yes, I am happy."

"I hope you do not look more sad when you are unhappy. You will make the winds cry."

She glanced up and was tempted to stick out her tongue at him, but his dancing brown eyes made her laugh instead.

"He will return. Your husband is a good man," Standing Elk said as he bit off a chunk of buffalo meat.

Dancing Bird nearly choked and stopped in mid chew to throw a murderous look at her sister. Walks Lightly's eyes widened and she looked from her husband to Dancing Bird.

Standing Elk shrugged his shoulders. "Did you think I would not guess?"

"Did you tell him?" Dancing Bird hissed at her sister.

"No. You know I promised."

Standing Elk calmly continued with his meal, feigning disinterest. "A man can tell when a woman has given herself to a man."

Dancing Bird stared at him, and he grinned, tilting one corner of his mouth. "I was in the high grass that morning, when Braden Flynn left you at the river." He touched his stomach and jerked his head toward his wife. "She put too much buffalo fat in the stew the night before."

Horrified, Dancing Bird put her plate down by the firepit. If Standing Elk saw, who else knew?

Quickly, he dropped his teasing countenance and his face grew serious. "You are my sister. I knew you would not sleep with a man who was not your husband. You wore Walks Lightly's wedding dress. I saw his face as he left you. He loves you very much."

"The council of the Long Lances has to say if he can marry, and they take a long time to decide. I could not wait, and neither could he. I am still his wife, even if I did not come to his side on a pony and hear Uncle remind me of my duties." She babbled on, her words tumbling over each other.

Standing Elk reached a strong arm across the small

circle of rocks between them and encircled her wrist with his fingers. "It is all right, sister. I will not tell your secret. You are part of my family, and now so is he."

Dancing Bird drew in a breath of relief and wished away the pounding of her heart. "He will still come to court me, as he arranged with Uncle. We hope that someday soon I may marry him so that all can see."

Standing Elk held her arm for a moment longer, then released her and leaned back. "Besides, if I were to betray you, I would not dare close my eyes at night with your sister asleep in my arms for fear I would not wake up." He threw a teasing glance at Walks Lightly and she beamed back at him.

How long would it be before she would sit across her own firepit and gaze into her husband's eyes? As if in response to her thoughts, she heard the clomp of shod hoofbeats outside the lodges. She put down her meal and hurried outside as Braden pulled Brandy to a stop and swung down.

Standing Elk caught her arm. "Do not be so eager, sister, lest your secret be a poorly kept one," he whispered as he yanked her behind him.

A fine layer of dust covered Braden's usually pristine jacket, and he felt as weary as Brandy looked. "Can I speak with you?" he asked Standing Elk with a small glance at Dancing Bird.

Standing Elk moved to Braden's side, and they walked around behind the tipi.

"Have you seen any blue soldiers on the prairie when you hunt?" Braden asked.

Standing Elk frowned. "No. Why?"

"I have been to the Blackfeet and spoke with Dog. He says Long Knives killed Little Bear and that a small group of men have been crossing the border and trying to convince the Blackfeet to rise up against the Sioux for some time now."

Standing Elk stared at him, anger clouding his dark eyes. "Do you believe his words?"

"I think he's tellin' me the truth. I'm goin' to ride back along the trail to the border, and I'm askin' ye to come with me."

"We will leave in the morning," Standing Elk said, then cut his eyes toward the back wall of the tipi. "And I will scalp my wife and yours, too, if either of them follows us."

Rustling noises inside the tipi gave away the location of the eavesdroppers. Braden stared at Standing Elk and felt his heart drop all the way to his dusty boots.

Standing Elk grinned. "Dancing Bird is sly like the weasel, but she cannot keep her love for you out of her eyes." He touched Braden's arm. "You are welcome in my family and in my tipi. You will stay with us. I give my tipi to you and your wife for the night. I will take my wife and sleep in the soft grass under the stars." He raised his eyebrows, and Braden chuckled.

"Come, first you wash and then you eat." Standing Elk pulled him down the creek bank, deeper into the willow grove. As he stumbled along, Braden wondered if he'd be able to stay awake long enough to eat.

Standing Elk ripped off his breechcloth and slid into the deep pool. Braden sat down on the bank and pried off his boots, then peeled off his socks. As lithe as a river otter, Standing Elk swam and dived in the water, then crawled out on the opposite side and lay on his back, naked in a pool of dying sunlight.

Braden shed his clothes and waded in, sucking in his

breath when the cold water slid up his body. But soon the cold cleared his mind and revived his body, and his thoughts turned back to Standing Elk's offer—his wife all to himself for another whole night.

"Will the blue soldiers come and attack our village?" Standing Elk asked, an arm thrown across his eyes.

"No, they wouldn't be so bold, I'm thinkin'. They're out to stir up mischief is me opinion, cause more trouble between the Sioux and the White Mother."

"What will you do if you find these men?"

"I'll arrest them and take them back to Fort Walsh."

Standing Elk flipped over onto his side and pillowed his cheek with his palm. "I will help you arrest them and take them to the fort."

"Thank you. There is one other thing I would ask of ye. Would ye send a messenger to Constable Gravel to tell him where we've gone?"

Standing Elk nodded. "I will send someone in the morning."

Standing Elk stretched in the grass and Braden looked away. Another man so casually naked in front of him was unnerving, and yet Braden envied him his freedom. Standing Elk had been raised without an unending list of sins, and no hell yawned beneath him for every passing flight of fancy. They were children of the sun and the wind, governed by their hearts and instincts. Could he live such a life? Would he if Sitting Bull's band decided to return home and Dancing Bird chose to go with them?

He climbed out of the water and put his clothes back on, allowing the fabric to soak up the moisture still clinging to him. By the time he had buckled his belt,

Standing Elk had fastened his breechcloth securely around his waist and waited for him.

A small fire burned low in the firepit when they returned to the lodge. Layers of thick buffalo robes had been spread on the floor, and the sides of the tipi were rolled all the way down to the ground. Evening had given way to darkness, and night would serve as cover for their plan.

Dancing Bird picked up a bark slab filled with food and handed it to Braden. His fingers brushed hers as they transferred the meal, and his remaining fatigue dropped away.

"Come, wife," Standing Elk said, clasping her hand in his. "We will leave our tipi by your sister's way." He leaned down and lifted the back edge of the tipi cover a few inches.

Smothering a laugh with her hand, Walks Lightly wiggled out the hole. Standing Elk threw Braden a wink and followed her.

The world narrowed to Dancing Bird and the circle of light that softened her face.

"You should eat," she said, nodding toward the plate in his hand.

"Sure an' buffalo stew is not what I'm hungry for."

Her cheeks colored briefly before she moved a step closer. "You must have your strength, husband."

"Yes, ma'am," he replied, picking up a portion with his fingertips, all the while keeping his eyes on hers.

He ate the meal and tasted not a morsel. All he could taste was the memory of her salty skin and her sweet lips. And when he was finished, she lifted the bark out of his hands and dragged a kiss across his forehead. He grabbed for her, but she was too quick, easily sidestepping his grasp.

He'd have dragged her into his arms and made love to her on the spot if he'd had his way, but he sensed she had something in mind, so he lay back in the furs and locked his hands behind his head.

Sleep settled on him with gossamer wings and the firelight dimmed and wavered. Wisps of dreams floated through his head as his eyes drooped and grew too heavy to hold open. Small sounds marked where Dancing Bird moved around the tipi, and he surrendered and closed his eyes, listening to her closeness.

A small weight on his chest awoke him. Dancing Bird sat by his side, her fingers wrestling open his jacket.

"What are these?" she asked as he stirred. She held the gold crowns that adorned the points of his collar.

"They're crowns, to represent the Great White Mother."

"Crowns?" she asked, her hair sliding over one shoulder, reminding him of the first time he'd seen her.

"It's like a headdress. The White Mother wears one at ceremonies."

"Oh." She moved down the row of buttons, then pushed open his coat. He'd left off his shirt, and her fingers plowed little furrows through the hair on his chest. She leaned forward until her hair slithered across his chest and gooseflesh bloomed on his skin.

He sat up, propped on his hands, and she again scurried out of his reach and removed his boots.

"What is this?" Her finger traced a path up the outside of his leg, following the yellow stripe on his pants.

"It represents the Imperial British Army." He shivered and struggled to keep her from seeing.

"The Imperial Army?" she stumbled over the unfamiliar words.

"The White Mother's soldiers."

"And this?" Her fingers found his belt and slipped underneath.

"That"—he sat up and grabbed her hand—"holds me pants up."

He drew her to him and kissed her as she sprawled across his chest. "Yer a disobedient wife. And a cruel one, to tease yer tired husband."

She moved to make more contact with his body and grinned. "And you're a lying husband. I do not think you're as tired as you say."

He wrapped his arms around her and pinned her against his chest, leaving her hands free to roam through his hair. He kissed her and would have rolled her beneath him, except she again sprang away and scrambled to her knees. Then she took his hands and pulled him to his knees also.

She pulled his coat off his shoulders, slithering it down his arms until it dropped to the floor of the tipi. With quick fingers, she unfastened his belt, and he wriggled out of his pants. She regarded him with a hungry stare, tempered with no pretense nor shyness, the cold, calculating study of a predator. Not in all his imaginings, not in all the ribald stories he'd ever heard, had he dreamed he'd experience something so erotic with the woman he loved, the woman destined to bear his children.

Dancing Bird stood and dropped her dress. The gentle firelight brushed her skin with a golden glow, softening curves and deepening shadows. Unashamed, she offered herself for examination. He reached out and touched the red, puckered wound on her shoulder, feeling the rough edges of the scab beneath his fingers, reminding himself of her mortality before he bestowed her with the title of goddess. Reminding himself, too, of the fleeting nature of happiness.

He took one of her hands and urged her to her knees. There, face-to-face in the soft ocean of buffalo robes, he kissed her, entwining her fingers with his. He released her fingers and cupped the back of her head with one hand, pulling her hard against his mouth, and the rest of her followed. Warm flesh to warm flesh, she wrapped her arms around his neck and aligned her body with his.

He tumbled her into the soft nest of buffalo robes, entertaining the fleeting thought of how such a filthy, shaggy beast could produce such soft, luxuriant pelts upon which he could make love to his wife. But soon his thoughts were fully occupied with the woman in his arms.

She lost no time in letting him know her preferences, intimate knowledge learned in one night, and then she demonstrated that she remembered his.

She took him inside her, cradled him, caressed him with her soft body. As she took his life into the womb he'd unsealed, he briefly wondered if a man could die in such rapture without benefit of an ailing heart.

A cold wind swept out of the north, reminding Braden winter was near and summer would soon take her leave. Drawing his buffalo coat tighter around his neck, he squinted his eyes and surveyed the landscape before him.

The United States stretched to the south, the same hilly, windswept landscape he now sat upon, except for a magic, imaginary line drawn upon maps by men with inky fingers and a taste for dividing the earth into neat cubicles. The forty-ninth parallel, the Canada-United States border, had become known as the Medicine Line by the Canadian Indians because of its impact on their lives.

But that small black line on dusty maps defined the life of the American Sioux. On the Canadian side, they were free to pursue life as they had for centuries, roaming the plains to feed and supply their families. On the United States side, they would be forced to surrender their horses, their weapons, and their pride and live on scrabbled dirt and the white man's grudging generosity.

Standing Elk stared across the desolate land, and Braden wondered what was going through his mind. Was he remembering better days in their homeland, or was he merely grateful for each day that crawled by?

A sudden wind lifted Standing Elk's long dark hair and swirled it around the buffalo robe he held close around his shoulders. The picture he made—astride his horse, staring across into a life that had disappeared into the bowels of time—was an image Braden would always remember.

"There." Standing Elk raised his arm and pointed.

Braden followed his gesture. Tiny shadows moved along a rolling ridge barely on the Canadian side of the border. The majority of the riders appeared to be soldiers, United States cavalry, but trailing along closely behind were three riders on Indian ponies. Braden glanced at Standing Elk, and his face hardened.

Heeling Brandy, Braden urged her forward, and he and

Standing Elk galloped into an intercept course. Shadowing the convenient gullies and rises of the Cypress Hills, they emerged behind the group without notice.

The men wore the distinct dusty blue of United States cavalry. Their long sabers, for which the Sioux had named them Long Knives, rattled at their sides. The three additional riders were young warriors from Sitting Bull's village, including Little Calf, Little Bear's friend, all with their hands tied behind them.

Shock and confusion registered on the faces of the soldiers when Braden and Standing Elk rode out of a coulee and into their path.

Their hands flew to their weapons as they pulled their plunging horses to a stop. Braden quickly drew his Adams revolver and trained it on the rider at the head of the column, a man with cold, gray eyes.

"Constable," the man said with a nod, not a trace of alarm in his voice.

"Could I ask ye what yer doin' here and why ye have these lads?"

"He's a damned potato eater," a voice somewhere in the group said. Braden kept his gaze on the leader, ignoring the slight, knowing well the prejudice against his people in the United States.

"We're simply on patrol, Constable," the man said with a nonchalant shrug. "And if you're going to point that gun at me, I'd at least like a name to go with it."

"I'm Constable Flynn of the Northwest Mounted Police. Are ye aware yer on the Canadian side of the border?" Braden slowly lowered the pistol, but kept his hand on the trigger.

The man feigned surprise with a sweeping look around him. "Are we? Funny how everything looks alike here." He refocused his gaze on Braden. "I'm Lieutenant William Calder and honored to finally meet one of the famed Mounties. And I see you've brought a friend."

From the corner of his eye, Braden could see Standing Elk sat expressionless, the lieutenant's jibes failing to force him to drop his practiced mask of indifference.

Braden holstered his gun and shifted in the saddle. He glanced at the young Sioux men. They appeared unhurt, but scared. "Why do ye have these lads?" he repeated.

Calder glanced back at his prisoners. "We caught them trying to steal our horses."

"Yer camped here, then, in Canada."

"No," Calder quickly answered. "Just across the border."

"Ah, ye do know where the border is, then. Things just get a bit confused when the sun comes up."

Calder visibly bristled. "They rode across the border and into our camp and tried to make off with my entire remuda. We caught them with very little trouble and were bringing them home to turn them loose, as a matter of fact." He smiled and shrugged. "I'm sure we've all done foolish things in our youth."

One of the boys said something in Sioux to Standing Elk, and he barked a reply. The youth clamped shut his mouth and stared down at the ground.

"So ye weren't plannin' on killin' the lads and leavin' 'em for me to find?"

Calder feigned shock. "Murder these lads? Now that would be illegal, Constable, and would damage relations between your country and mine. I wouldn't want that to happen, especially since Canada has so graciously taken our garbage to her breast."

"And have ye made a habit of visiting us across the border in the last few weeks?"

"Why would you ask that, Constable?"

"I'm investigatin' a murder and I have a witness who says that some United States cavalry have been seen in the area Sittin' Bull's Sioux are occupyin'."

"A murder? Who was killed?"

"A young Sioux man named Little Bear."

"That ain't murder, that's pest control," another faceless voice in the group said.

"Ye can call it what ye will on yer side of the border, but here it's murder." Braden leveled his gaze on Calder. "Since ye've been enlightened to yer honest mistake and ye've no further business here, I'd suggest ye give these lads to me, turn around, and ride back the way ye came."

Calder folded his hands on his saddle horn. "Are you running me out of Canada, Constable?"

Braden paused, and Calder's eyes glittered in challenge. "Yes, Lieutenant, I am. I'll take no nonsense from the likes of ye."

Anger eclipsed the satisfaction in Calder's eyes. "You Mounties in your red coats and your arrogance are endangering the good folk who endeavor to settle these western lands by allowing these savages to run free to murder and maim as they please. The United States government has ordered that the Sioux report to their assigned reservations and yet you aid them in defying the government that will feed and clothe them."

"I don't remember hearin' 'em ask to be fed and clothed, Lieutenant. Seems to me they only asked to be left alone."

Calder's upper lip rippled in anger. "I'll not waste

good time arguing with a damned Indian lover. Take the bastards with you." He pointed at the boys. "But if I ever see them back across the border, I'll kill them."

One of Calder's men dismounted and untied the boys' hands. Standing Elk spoke and they docilely rode to his side and waited.

"I'll see you again," Calder threw over his shoulder as he turned his patrol around and trotted away.

Standing Elk and the boys exchanged words. "They are not hurt. They say the blue soldiers captured them while they were hunting buffalo. They say they rode many miles before reaching the blue soldier's camp."

"Think they're lyin'?"

Standing Elk glared at the boys, then asked them another question. They bowed their heads and spoke again for several minutes.

"They say they rode to the blue soldier's camp one night to try and steal horses, but ran away when the soldiers saw them. Then the soldiers came to the Sioux hunting grounds and captured them while they were hunting." Standing Elk turned to face Braden. "It has been very hard to keep the young men from crossing the border to fight the blue soldiers. This is not the first time some have tried it, but Sitting Bull has made strict rules now."

Braden shoved back his hat and scratched his forehead. The longer the Sioux stayed, the more volatile the situation grew and the more likely a confrontation became—a confrontation with either neighboring tribes or with cavalrymen bent on driving the Sioux back into their territory.

They turned their horses into the north wind and headed for home, the sheepish young men trailing behind, consoling each other for their foolishness. Autumn was quickly banishing summer, aging the once-young grass to a distinguished yellow and silencing the joyful insects. Soon cold and carefully monitored food would replace warmth and plenty.

And as nature prepared to pause and sleep, Braden felt the tendrils of dread creep back into his chest.

Sixteen

A lone rider topped the rise to the west, silhouetted against the deep blue sky. Braden dropped the fence rail he'd been shaping, straightened, and wiped the sweat from his brow. Squinting, he shaded his eyes with his hand. The unmistakable scarlet of the Northwest Mounted Police uniform stood out in stark contrast to the now-brown prairie grass.

September had arrived golden and warm. The days brought a relentless sun that cured the remaining grass to a golden yellow, and the cold, crisp nights brought clear, star-studded skies. There had been no more trouble between the Blackfeet and the Sioux, and still there was no word on his request to marry Dancing Bird. He rode the prairie by day and courted his wife by night, patiently standing underneath the blanket outside her lodge. Beneath the layer of gray wool, they talked of their future, touched, and wished for privacy.

The lone rider loped down the hillside, and as he drew closer, Braden recognized Walsh by his broad mustache. Something must be wrong, he thought, snatching his jacket off the fence post. Walsh had been by only a week or two ago to check on things.

Braden strode toward the dugout, buttoning his jacket

as he went. By the time Walsh drew to a stop by the door, Braden was back in uniform, his heart thudding. Walsh looked down at him, his face solemn, and Braden knew.

"They said no, didn't they?"

Walsh swung down from his horse's back, groaning, then braced both hands on his knees and bent over at the waist. He straightened and stretched his back. "They think the situation is too explosive to risk bringing in another source of irritation."

"How could my marrying Dancing Bird be considered an 'irritation'? They've accepted me into their midst. I've spent the night in their homes, eaten at their fires."

"You didn't really expect a different answer, did you?" Walsh asked.

Braden braced his hands on his hips as a thousand memories of Dancing Bird ran through his head. "No, I guess I didn't."

Steven emerged from the dugout, sleepily pulling on his jacket. He and Standing Elk had ridden all the way to the border yesterday, checking for signs of the American intruders, then ridden all night to return.

"Sir," he said with a nod as he stopped in front of Walsh.

"Ottawa has denied Constable Flynn permission to marry." Walsh answered Steven's unasked question.

Steven cut a sharp glance at Braden, silently urging him to confess to Walsh.

Walsh turned to Braden, expectation on his face. Did he suspect his secret? Of course he did.

"Sir, for all intents and purposes, Dancing Bird is already me wife and has been for two months."

Walsh's expression didn't waver. "All intents and purposes?"

"Yes, sir."

"Does that mean what I think it means?"

"I'm sure it does, sir."

Walsh pulled at his mustache. "I can't say I'm surprised, Constable, but I want to be clear on your intent here, so please forgive me my blunt language. Am I given to understand she is your wife and not your squaw?"

"No, sir. I mean, yes. She's me wife, sir." He looked into Walsh's face. "We pledged our own vows privately."

"I see." Walsh raised his eyebrows. "And does her family know?"

"Only her sister and her brother-in-law."

"What does her sister think of this?"

"Actually, sir, her sister helped arrange our . . . meeting."

"And what are your intentions from this point?"

They'd talked of that at great length in the past few weeks. He'd sworn to leave the police, and she'd refused to let him. He'd offered to barrage Ottawa with letters of objection, and she'd said it didn't matter. As far as she was concerned, no amount of words or agreements would ever make him more her husband than he was now. But he knew she longed for the union to be recognized among her people. And there was the possibility she had or could conceive a child.

"To her and to me, she is me wife, sir, even without the benefit of a Christian ceremony. We've kept our marriage a secret until now, but we would like to have her uncle perform the rites that will unite us in the eyes of her people."

Walsh stared at him a moment, then smiled slowly. "You are an admirable man, Constable Flynn. Lesser men would have wandered down a far less virtuous path. You will most likely not be the last mounted policeman to lose his heart to a native woman and be unable to secure Ottawa's permission for a legal and binding marriage. I can only hope others will follow your honorable lead."

Stunned by Walsh's flowing praise, Braden only nodded.

"Unfortunately, I have more bad news, I fear. The commission from Washington will arrive here on the twenty-ninth or the thirtieth of this month. General Terry has requested that Commissioner McLeod meet them where the road from Benton to Fort Walsh crosses the border."

"So they're really going to send Terry?" Steve shook his head. "A foolish mistake, I'd say."

"Indeed, a foolish choice. Sitting Bull will immediately balk at anything Terry says, and who can blame him," Walsh said with a tired shrug. "Would you listen to the man who'd driven your women and children to starvation and pursued you like animals?"

"What exactly is the commission's purpose, sir? To merely convince Sitting Bull to take his people back across the border? Or do they plan on bringing force with them?"

Walsh's eyes snapped with anger. "They'll bring no more troops with them than is necessary. Commissioner McLeod has already made that point clear. Once they cross into Canada, they will be escorted to Fort Walsh, which is where they would like the meeting to take place."

"Has anyone approached Sitting Bull with the suggestion that he go to Fort Walsh for this meeting?" Braden asked.

Walsh smiled. "That task, I fear, falls to me. I had planned to wait until I was sure the commission was on its way before I approached him—and any persuasion you might be able to add would be appreciated." Walsh looked at Braden.

Conflicting loyalties immediately raised their heads.

"You don't have a difficulty with that, do you, Constable?"

Braden met Walsh's gaze and knew the very heart of the problem was out on the table for discussion. "Sir, I have taken two sets of vows, and I don't intend to let one interfere with the other."

"To the extent that you can prevent it."

"Yes, sir. To the extent that I can prevent it."

Walsh stepped back and picked up his reins. "I sincerely hope you can keep that promise. When do you intend to participate in the marriage ceremony?"

Braden felt as if he were being pushed from behind by a stiff west wind. Life was moving along too fast, too quickly for him to think. The uncertainty of the meeting with the American commission loomed on his horizon like an angry storm cloud. Would Dancing Bird's people allow the marriage? Where would they live? What would they do if the Sioux went home?

"Before the commission arrives, I have to speak with her family."

Walsh put a foot in his stirrup and swung into the saddle. "I'd like to attend the ceremony, Constable, if you'd be so kind as to invite me. I'll be back by this way in a few days, and you can let me know then."

"Of course, sir," Braden replied as Walsh reined his horse around and rode away.

As he stood and looked after his commander, a warm wind buffeting his hair, he felt time and consequence flutter out of the blue September sky and perch heavily on his shoulder.

Dogs and children scattered in front of him as Braden rode into the village. As he passed the smiling faces that greeted him, he marveled at the difference from a few short months ago. Bodies had grown plump and ragged clothes had been mended. Scattered, tattered lodges had been replaced and multiplied. All in all, the settlement had taken on the appearance of a permanent, peaceful village.

A tiny bubble in time, destined to rupture.

And yet despite its peaceful façade, the village still bore evidence of its violent past. Many horses still wore the US Army brand on their hindquarters, and ragged scalps still hung from lodgepoles. Occasional pieces of blue cavalry uniforms were still worn by some warriors—all reminders that these were violent people living in uncertain times.

He swung down from Brandy's back just as Standing Elk hurried out of his lodge, stopped, and smiled broadly.

"Come," Standing Elk said, jerking two fingers. "There is hot food inside."

Braden followed him into his lodge, sweet memories of his night there with Dancing Bird rising up to tickle him with longing.

Walks Lightly looked up from her sewing and smiled

shyly. "You have come to see Dancing Bird, brother?" she asked.

"I came to talk to Sitting Bull," Braden said and the couple exchanged solemn glances.

"Is something wrong?"

Standing Elk pushed his food around. "There is trouble," he began and looked up.

"What kind of trouble?" A chill settled over Braden.

"A messenger came today. The Nez Percé have been driven from their land. They come this way and ask us to help them."

The sense of foreboding that had dogged Braden for months suddenly bloomed into full-blown dread.

"They are hungry and tired. The blue soldiers have made them leave their lodges behind. They wander with no food and no clothes. They look to the Great White Mother's Land for peaceful sleep as the Sioux did."

"What does Sitting Bull say?"

Standing Elk shrugged and stared pointedly into Braden's eyes. "How can we tell them no? How can we turn them away when we have food and warm lodges and they have none?"

How indeed? Braden thought. But the arrival of more hungry people would shorten the time they all had here.

"White Forehead will need to know this," Braden said, and Standing Elk nodded.

Standing Elk set down his plate. "I will take you to my uncle."

Sitting Bull sat cross-legged by his fire, patiently trimming feathers for arrows. Braden paused in the doorway and waited while Standing Elk squatted by his uncle's side and spoke softly.

Sitting Bull glanced up, nodded, then replied to

Standing Elk's words. As he waited, Braden glanced around the lodge and noticed that the number of sleeping robes had dwindled and the once-crowded dwelling was much more open. Family members had sewn their own lodges and moved out.

Dancing Bird hadn't greeted him outside. A little odd, he thought. She always seemed to know when he came to the village, even if his visit was unannounced.

Standing Elk motioned to him to come inside, and Braden ducked underneath the lodge flap and crossed the fur-strewn floor to sit down at Sitting Bull's side. The old chief kept his gaze on his work, giving Braden a few seconds to closely observe the most feared man on the prairies.

Tiny wrinkles crinkled his leathery skin at the corners of his eyes. Pronounced cheekbones defined a chiseled face. The weight of responsibility for an entire people was evident in the droop of his shoulders. A little past forty, by his own count of summers, Sitting Bull looked far older. Here, in this one tiny man, rested the exaggerated fear of an entire nation.

"What do you wish to say to my uncle?" Standing Elk asked.

Sitting Bull had a good grasp of English, but Braden was content to let Standing Elk translate. He wanted to be sure Sitting Bull understood every word he said.

"Tell him I have come to ask to take Dancing Bird as me wife."

Standing Elk grinned broadly and translated.

Sitting Bull didn't react, nor did he take his eyes off the arrow he slowly turned in his hands. After a pause, he spoke softly.

"He wants to know why you want her when no one else does," Standing Elk translated.

Braden thought for a moment, gathering up words to convince Sitting Bull of the depth of his love. "Tell him—" Words seemed so very inadequate. "Tell him I love her more than my own life, that I will keep her warm and happy and see that she is never hungry again. And when she bears me sons, I'll be at her side."

Sitting Bull looked up at him when Standing Elk relayed the words. Dark brown eyes, intelligent and calm, studied him for a few seconds. "She is stubborn woman," the chief said in halting English. "Bad wife."

Braden shook his head. "She will be a good wife to me."

Standing Elk began to murmur a translation, but Sitting Bull waved him away impatiently. "You love her? Make good lodge for her?"

"Yes." Braden nodded.

"You not make child and leave her behind?"

"No, never." Braden shook his head.

Sitting Bull studied him for a few more seconds, then smiled softly and pointed at Braden with two fingers. "I see your eyes. You are good man. Take her."

Braden started to rise, but a hand on his arm stopped him. He turned and looked back into Sitting Bull's face.

"When we go back. . . ." Sitting Bull paused, seemed to struggle for words, then turned to Standing Elk and spoke quickly.

Standing Elk's gaze flitted to Braden's face, then back to Sitting Bull's.

"He says when the Sioux go back to live on the white man's reservation, he wants your promise that you will keep Dancing Bird here with you in the White Mother's Land."

When, not *if.*

Braden looked into Sitting Bull's eyes and knew he meant exactly what he'd said. He was well aware their visit to Canada only delayed the inevitable. He was spinning his story to allow his people a last few precious months to live in the glorious way they'd lived for centuries as rulers of the grass-covered plains.

"Her home will always be here with me," Braden said around the lump that suddenly appeared in his throat. "Ask him if he will perform the ceremony." Braden looked over at Standing Elk.

Standing Elk asked and Sitting Bull replied.

"He says in two suns, under the willows by the creek where Walks Lightly and I were married."

Sitting Bull returned to his arrow making, signaling that the conversation was over. Braden rose and quietly left the lodge. Squinting as he stepped out into the light, he glanced around for Dancing Bird. Moving-Robe-Woman worked over a buffalo hide, her nimble hands rolling a hair-removing stick back and forth across the surface, accumulating a pile of hair at her feet.

Braden crooked a finger at Standing Elk and started toward her. Standing Elk caught his arm. "Uncle will tell her," he said.

"Among my people, 'tis my place to ask the permission of the mother."

She glanced up, surprised, as Braden squatted down at her side, planting his feet in the pile of hair. At one time, she must have looked much like her daughter, he surmised. Sleepless nights and worry were etched into the wrinkles that now haunted the corners of her eyes. Streaks of silver marred the blue-black of her hair.

"I wish to take Dancing Bird as me wife," he said.

Standing Elk repeated and Moving-Robe-Woman's eyes widened. She glanced between the two of them, then asked Standing Elk a question. He answered softly, and she returned her frightened gaze to Braden's face.

"She wants to know if you will beat Dancing Bird if she is disobedient."

Braden's heart twisted. Moved, he took Moving-Robe-Woman's hand in his. She stiffened and tried feebly to pull away, but Braden held on. "I would never beat her. Ever. She is a precious gift, and I will treat her as such."

She glanced up at Standing Elk as he translated, and when he finished he nodded. She returned her gaze to Braden's face and studied him for a time, then mumbled soft words and smiled shyly.

"She says she remembers gazing into the face of a man as handsome as you when she was a young woman. She thinks you are a kind man and asks that you be gentle with her daughter."

Standing Elk paused as Moving-Robe-Woman spoke again. "She says she remembers well her own wedding day and wishes the same happiness for you and Dancing Bird."

Windows to a mother's heart, her eyes scanned his face. These were no sudden words. Apparently, Moving-Robe-Woman had known all along what lay between him and Dancing Bird.

Braden squeezed her hand, then released her and stood. "I guess I should tell the bride."

Standing Elk smiled. "She is out there." He pointed toward where the pony herd grazed. "She is supposed to be here helping with this hide. And she has stolen my wife, too."

Braden saw her from the shadows of the now-bare willow thicket and stopped. Walks Lightly sat cross-legged on the ground, pulling tufts of grass and feeding them to Wind as the horse grazed beside her. Dancing Bird sat sideways on Wind's back, her feet dangling off one side. Then, with practiced nonchalance, she swiveled and lay down on the pony's back, stretching out full length, her arms dangling limply. A kind breeze ruffled their hair and made the tall grass dance. He committed the picture to his collection to be pulled out and enjoyed when hard times knocked on their door.

He stepped out into the sun, and Wind yanked up her head.

"Your mother says you have disobeyed her . . . again."

Dancing Bird shoved herself to a sitting position, the warmth of her smile reaching across the distance between them. "I told her I would work on the hide later, when the sun is not so warm and the sky not so blue."

Braden glanced up at the azure sky. He was inclined to agree with her. God never made a more perfect day.

Walks Lightly stood. "I will go and help Mother." She walked away toward the village, the long fringe on her dress swishing in the grass.

Braden waited until they were alone, then reached up and pulled Dancing Bird into his arms. She fell forward into his embrace, allowing her body to skim against his as she touched the ground and smiled slyly.

"I have asked your uncle to perform our wedding ceremony and he has agreed to do so in two suns."

Her smiled faded. "Your council said no."

"They think that the situation between your people and mine is too risky to allow our marriage."

Dancing Bird moved away a step or two and toyed with the seed heads of the waist-high grass, smiling. "White men love words and paper, many words and paper. They think when they write on paper what is in their heads, they can forget those words forever." She raised her head to look at him, love shining in her eyes. "Are they so foolish to think words would keep us apart?"

He would have taken her into his arms again, but she stopped him with a sudden frown. "You will not have the ceremony of your people."

" 'Tis not important." He stepped forward and she placed a hand on his chest.

"It is important to you." She tilted her head. "Will your heart know it is joined with mine without the words of your holy man?"

He caught her fingers in his hand and brought them to his lips. "Me heart has already been plucked by these sweet, nimble fingers. It doesn't need a holy man to explain things to it."

She looked up into his face. "Are you sure, Braden Flynn?"

"Aye, I'm sure," he whispered as he kissed away the rest of her objections.

Their wedding day was a gift, a pause in a relentless march toward winter. Frost had already gilded the grass and cold winds sent mothers scurrying to bundle their babies. But the morning of their wedding day dawned unseasonably warm, with a sky of unbelievable blue.

Celebrating villagers met Braden, Walsh, and Steven

at the outskirts of the village and offered good wishes and greetings with smiles and touches. They rode straight to the willow thicket, where narrow, delicate leaves lay on the ground in a thick mat. Sitting Bull stood beneath the bare branches, his hands folded in front of him, wearing the same long, sweeping headdress he'd worn for Walks Lightly's wedding.

"You are late, brother," Standing Elk said from his position at Sitting Bull's side."The sun is nearly overhead in the sky."

Before Braden could answer, a low murmur behind him made him turn around. Time froze, and he could almost believe that the pain and strife of the last few years had never happened.

She came toward him silhouetted against a clear, blue sky, the white of her dress and the cream of the eagle down in her hair blending perfectly. The swelling crowd around them vanished from his notice as she slid off Wind's back and into his arms.

She slipped her small hand into his hand and turned to face her uncle. Sitting Bull smiled down on her. "Today is a day I never thought would come," he began, and Standing Elk murmured the English.

"A Long Lance has tamed the heart of Dancing Bird, the mischief maker."

The crowd chuckled softly, and Sitting Bull shifted his gaze to Braden. "He and his people welcomed us when we came to them with no home and no food. We were like children to them, and now he is one of our children. He is a good man and speaks only the truth, like White Forehead." Sitting Bull turned an affectionate smile on Walsh, the only other white man, by Sitting Bull's own declaration, that he trusted.

"And now we give him our daughter, Dancing Bird. He will take her into his heart and into his home and stand at her side. Do you agree to do these things?"

"I do," Braden answered.

Sitting Bull swung his smile back to Dancing Bird. "And you, mischief maker, will you cook your husband's meals, care for his weapons and tend his wounds?"

"I will," Dancing Bird replied.

Sitting Bull's face sobered, and a sudden brisk breeze stirred the bare branches overhead as if in response to his change in mood.

"I asked Braden Flynn for a promise when he asked to marry my niece, and he gave me his word. I share that promise now with all of you." Sitting Bull looked over their heads to the crowd behind them.

"Today is bright and warm, but there are many hard days coming to our people." He swung his gaze back to Braden's face. "I asked Braden Flynn to promise me that if we return to our home to live on the white man's reservations that he will keep Dancing Bird by his side, safe here with him. He has promised me this, and he is an honorable man."

The old chief reached out and took Dancing Bird's hand in his. "Your father, Wolf, was like a brother to me when he married my sister, Moving-Robe-Woman. We hunted many buffalo and told many young men's lies together. He is walking the Spirit Trail, but I still feel him here." He touched his chest. "He would have liked this man you chose."

A tear left a shiny trail down Dancing Bird's cheek.

Sitting Bull placed her hand in Braden's. "You are now one. Today, you will begin to walk a new path."

Seventeen

The sharp odor of newly tanned leather was pungent and overwhelming as Braden and Dancing Bird stepped through the door of their new home and left behind the chill of the September day. Smoke from the small fire rose toward the smoke hole in a twisting, gray spiral. Tired and sated from their wedding feast, they ignored the thump, thump of drums and dancing feet and turned their attention to each other.

Moving-Robe-Woman and Walks Lightly had made them a gift of the new home, sewn from the hides Dancing Bird had risked so much to collect. For now, they would live in the village to keep Dancing Bird close to her family while she waited for Braden to return from his patrols. Someday, they would have a home of their own and land to surround it. But for now, a simple hide tipi was their palace.

Braden slid the pin through the loop of rawhide, securing the door from the inside. When he turned, Dancing Bird stood before him, her hands folded demurely in front of her. She smiled and cast her gaze downward in a display of submission he knew was insincere. What new game had she conjured in her sly mind?

All right, he'd go along with her little scheme. He

walked toward her. Without raising her eyes, she reached back, untied her dress, and let the buckskin garment slide to the floor.

Golden skin caught and enhanced the glow of firelight. Soft curves hinted at pleasures no longer unfamiliar, but even more enticing in their familiarity.

Her coyness abandoned, she stepped forward and quickly disrobed him, then was about to disassemble his belt when shouts and galloping hoofbeats rose above the drums. His senses leaping to alert, Braden kissed her fingers, swept his shirt from the floor, and hurried outside.

A lathered horse stood on wobbly legs, its head hanging nearly to the ground. An equally tired rider clung to the saddle. He was Indian, but dressed as no one they had seen before. Long ermine tails hung from his dark hair and layers of beaded necklaces looped around his neck.

"The Nez Percé have reached the Bear Paw Mountains," he said in breathless gasps. "Miles has attacked and surrounded the camp."

War shouts and shrill tremolos exploded. Sitting Bull pushed through the crowd, still wearing his ceremonial clothes. Word had come several weeks ago that the Nez Percé were fleeing American troops led by Colonel Miles, who had driven them nearly sixteen hundred miles. Rumors had flown that the persecuted Nez Percé, led by their Chief Joseph, would also ask for sanctuary in Canada, and Braden had kept Walsh informed of the potential of additional refugees.

"You have to come and fight with us, come and save my people from the blue soldiers. If they cannot defeat us, they will starve us," he pleaded desperately.

Sitting Bull cast a glance at Braden, then to Spotted Eagle, Sans Arc war chief. "We will have to sit in council." He turned to Standing Elk. "Bring the war chiefs to my lodge. Bring this man food and drink."

"Sitting Bull," Braden said, putting his hand on the old chief's arm.

Sitting Bull turned, looked down at Braden's hand gripping his arm, then raised his gaze to Braden's face. "I will speak only to my war chiefs. You have other responsibilities tonight."

"You cannot cross the border. You cannot make war on the blue soldiers." Braden removed his hand, a thousand desperate thoughts tumbling through his head. He could find no words to express them.

"We understand Long Lance Walsh's words. We will carefully consider our decision."

Then he ducked into his lodge as the exhausted rider was led away to sleep.

Braden returned to his bride and found her curled in a nest of robes, fast asleep. She slept naked, a fist tucked beneath her cheek.

As much as he wanted to wake her up and make love to her, he wanted to watch her more, to burn the peacefulness of her face into his memory. All too soon his greatest fears could come to life, and her people would be scattered like the dead willow leaves upon which they'd stood and pledged their lives to each other.

He touched her shoulder, and her skin was soft and warm. He smoothed his hand down her arm, across her hip, and across her stomach, wondering if a child slept there, cozy and safe in his dark world.

Dancing Bird stirred, turned onto her back and smiled

up at him with sleepy eyes. "Did you finally decide to come to your marriage bed, husband?"

She expected him to smile and reply with a cocked eyebrow and twinkling eyes, but instead he gazed down at her with such want and fear in his eyes that she pushed up to her elbows. "What's wrong?"

He dropped to his knees without an answer and stripped off his clothes. Then he gathered her to him and held her there in a desperate grip until she thought he would crush her ribs.

"Braden?" she said against his shoulder when he didn't move.

He pulled her away from him and kissed her with a ferocity she'd never seen in him. Frightened and excited, she returned the kiss, hoping her love would soothe whatever demons were pursuing him.

She expected endearments and teasing, as there'd been each time before when he loved her, and long passionate kisses. But tonight, their wedding night, he made love to her with such desperation that all she could do was hold on to him and allow herself to be swept up into his passion. Afterward, he fell asleep in her arms without an explanation, only murmured declarations of love made with an unsteady voice.

The future was a dark and uncertain place, the place she was certain gave birth to her husband's troubled dreams. Would the Nez Percé join them in exile and thereby shorten the time they all had here in a land of plenty? Would the white man's commission come and demand they return—or, worse, come with soldiers and weapons? Would the young Sioux warriors attack the blue soldiers that held Joseph and his people, as they were wont to do, and bring about the end of their lives as they knew them?

So many doubts. She looked down at Braden's face as he slept, his rough cheek pillowed on the hollow of her shoulder and knew whatever that dark and uncertain future might bring, she would be at his side.

Braden toed his boots further out of his stirrups and raised the rifle to his shoulder. Down the long barrel and across the beaded sight, the buffalo looked much smaller than the hulking beast it was. Braden squeezed the trigger. The report jarred his shoulder, and Brandy flinched and danced to the side.

"Good shot." Standing Elk winked and held his own U.S. Cavalry-issue rifle in the air. Braden had never worked up the courage to ask him where he'd gotten it. Some things were better left unknown.

With a pat to Brandy's neck, Braden gathered his reins and rode toward the heap of fur. The bull buffalo lay still, but Braden knew better than to trust his eyesight where the huge beast was concerned. A few feet away, he aimed and shot a second time, sending a bullet through the thick skull to assure certain death.

A chill wind rustled the dead grass and brought the scent of snow as Braden and Standing Elk butchered the beast and loaded the meat onto the travois. Dancing Bird would need meat for the winter in case he was snowed in on patrol and couldn't get home for weeks, as sometimes happened. They worked in silence for a time, with only the voice of the wind for company.

"What do you think the white men will have to say when they get here?" Standing Elk threw a hunk of meat onto the travois and straightened to stretch his back.

Braden did the same and wiped his hands down his blackened and greasy buckskins. "I'm thinkin' they'll say the same things they've said before. Try to convince Sitting Bull to surrender."

"Do you think they'll bring many blue soldiers with them?"

"No, they've assured Walsh they will not. Besides, Long Lance McLeod will meet them at the border to make sure."

"I think one day we will surrender to the blue soldiers and live on their reservations."

Braden looked up, surprised. There was no anger in his voice, no defeat, just a statement of fact. And when Braden looked into his eyes, he saw the same quiet acceptance, reminding him of Walsh's prophetic words.

"Why do ye think that?" Braden asked, knowing the answer and yet curious as to his reasoning.

Standing Elk smiled slowly. "We rode far to find this buffalo. Tomorrow we will ride farther. I can remember when the horizon was filled with them." He swept his arm toward the horizon. "Soon there will be no more food and the blue soldiers will win."

Braden could think of no denials or words of comfort. Very probably, Standing Elk was right. One day they would be forced back across the border, forced to accept the white man's charity.

"It is a fine day, and we have conquered the beast," Standing Elk said with exaggerated enthusiasm and a twinkle in his eye. "Let us celebrate. There will be fresh roast over the firepit tonight, brother."

Distant hoofbeats swung Braden's attention to the

west. A Mounted Police patrol topped the ridge, riding in his direction at a lope, their red and white pennons flying. When they arrived at his side, Walsh was in the lead, a deep furrow between his eyes.

"The commission is on the way. They should be here in about a week. McLeod's already left Fort McLeod. We've been ordered to bring Sitting Bull to Fort Walsh."

Before Braden could answer, another rider, this time from the south, thundered over a hill, long dark hair flying. Little Calf pulled his pony to a plunging stop and fired off a string of words to Standing Elk, who blanched.

"Miles has attacked the Nez Percé. Many are dead. They ask our help."

Caught between two worlds, Braden looked at first Walsh, then at Little Calf, and wondered how life could shift in another direction so quickly.

Walsh's patrol rode on toward the village and Braden and Standing Elk quickly finished loading the meat and soon followed. When they reached the village, it was astir with activity. Young warriors painted for war charged through the village, the tremolo cry of the women echoed against the sides of the lodges, and messengers came and went. A layer of fine dust, stirred to life by plunging hooves, crept through the village like a morning fog.

Leaving Standing Elk to care for the meat, Braden ducked inside the tipi for his uniform and found Dancing Bird standing in the middle of the lodge, her eyes large with fear.

Braden stepped inside and dropped the flap back into place, shutting out the confusion.

"It is true," she said. "The blue soldiers have attacked the Nez Percé, less than a day's ride from here."

Braden drew her into his arms and her heart hammered against his chest. "Will they come here next?" she asked, looking up into his face. The fear in her eyes was an old fear, born of horrible memories and a seemingly inescapable destiny.

"No, they will not come here. Long Lance Walsh and the rest of my company are here to see that they don't."

She stepped out of his embrace, picked up his uniform, and held it out to him. "Uncle has called a council of his war chiefs."

Braden quickly dressed, then paused with his hand on the tipi flap. She stood watching him, her face a convincing mask of calm, and he wondered how many times he would have to leave her like this, have to rely on her strength to propel him out the door to his sworn duty.

Braden pulled her into his arms and kissed her soundly. " 'Twill be all right, love," he whispered. "I'll be back before dark." And then he left her world and re-entered his, clad in a scarlet suit of armor.

Walsh's patrol stood in front of Sitting Bull's lodge. "Sitting Bull requested you be here," Walsh said as Braden strode up.

Braden followed Walsh inside the large lodge. A circle of powerful men surrounded the firepit. All were leaders who once commanded legions of followers, strategists as noteworthy as any Roman general, and men as respected among their people as members of the British Parliament.

Sitting Bull, his face solemn, waved to a place at his

side and Walsh and Braden sat down. Louis Levéille settled in directly behind them.

Sitting Bull stood, straightened with a soft groan, and stepped to the center of the circle. He drew in a breath and paused for effect. A true showman, Braden thought with a small smile.

"The Nez Percé have long been our enemies because they ally themselves with the Crow that steal our food and attack our villages," he began in a strong voice.

"But the Nez Percé are no longer strong warriors. They were driven from their lands, their homes, as we were, by the blue soldiers. Now they are weak and hungry and tired. All their numbers are surrounded by blue soldiers across the Medicine Line, less than a day's ride away. The blue soldiers have pursued them like dogs, burning their homes, killing their horses, destroying their food. They have come many miles hoping for our help."

He spread his hands, palms up. "Do we attack the blue soldiers and drive them away? Or do we let the Nez Percé fight their own fight?" He closed his hands and pulled his arms to his side. "That is what we must decide." His head bowed, he returned to his place in the circle.

No one spoke, and the crackle of the fire filled the lodge as it forced back the September cold. Here was their chance for sweet and well-deserved revenge.

Walsh offered no opinion and waited. Finally, Spotted Eagle stood and looked down at the men who surrounded him. "We have waited many moons for the blue soldiers to show us their soft underbelly. Now they are far from their forts and their people. If we strike now, we can kill them all, and the white chiefs will send no more soldiers. This is what I believe."

Louis murmured a translation, and Walsh's face remained impassive.

One by one, the men rose and spoke their hearts' beliefs. The afternoon stretched into night. Dancing Bird and Walks Lightly brought food and drink, distributing it among the men, their eyes downcast. Braden touched Dancing Bird's fingers as she handed him a gourd, and she smiled at him as she filled it with water.

The discussions for and against sawed back and forth. Miles's forces were a mere forty miles away, far from reinforcements or supplies. The Nez Percé were surrounded, neatly maneuvered into a position to starve to death in a matter of days. The Sioux were their only hope for survival, ready with men, horses, and food. Despite past differences, could they allow their brothers to simply starve?

The discussion continued as the night dragged on. Braden fought sleep as voices swirled around him. Once, he left the lodge when fatigue would not leave him alone. He stepped out into the crisp, silent night, a night very different from the sultry darknesses of summer which had been filled with voices and sounds. Now, a thousand silent stars twinkled overhead and the world held its breath while a half-globe moon ascended to her throne.

Braden looked at his dark tipi and wondered if Dancing Bird slept there, her arm pillowing her cheek, her face soft in sleep. He was tempted to go and investigate for himself, but duty called, and duty must come first. He filled his lungs with cold air, then exhaled in a misty cloud and went back into Sitting Bull's lodge.

The air inside the tipi had grown smokier and more tense as the discussion circulated round and round the circle of leaders. Stern faces hid fear just beneath the surface.

Braden slid back into his spot next to Walsh and his commander threw him a distracted glance, seemingly oblivious to the fatigue tormenting everyone else. As Braden's gaze flickered around the circle of men, he committed their images to his memory. He was part of what was possibly the last great council of the Sioux nation. Soon, too soon, their decisions would be made by men in stuffy offices with full stomachs.

Dawn neared, and still there was no consensus. Then, somewhere near the break of day, Walsh stiffly stood.

Voices ceased and faces turned toward him. "The man who crosses the boundary line from this camp is, from the moment he puts foot on United States soil, our enemy. Henceforth we shall be to him, if he returns, what he says United States soldiers are to him today—wolves seeking his blood."

Shock registered on upturned faces, and an uneasiness crawled up Braden's back. Sitting Bull looked Walsh directly in the eyes for several seconds and neither man broke the contact.

"I know you see yourselves in the Nez Percé, see the same injustices committed against them that were committed against you. You see a chance for revenge, to right the wrongs, at least in part, that you carry with you. But if you join with the Nez Percé, I can no longer protect you from the blue soldiers."

Sitting Bull glanced at Braden, watched him for a second, then brought his gaze back to Walsh.

"I came here today to ask you to come to Fort Walsh

and meet with the United States commission. They are already on the way and will be here in a few days."

A murmur slid around the room.

"How do we know this is not a white man's trick?" Spotted Eagle asked.

"I know it is not," Walsh said. "I give you my word."

"No, I will not speak with these white men. They bring no words I want to hear," Sitting Bull declared.

"They seek a solution to your exile."

Sitting Bull frowned at the unfamiliar word and looked to Louis for a translation. When Louis explained, Sitting Bull smiled. "This is our home now. Why should we go back to fight and starve?"

"You know the food will not hold out. The buffalo will disappear and your people will be hungry again."

Walsh's words seemed to make no impression.

"*Wakantanka* will provide. I will speak no more of this now," Sitting Bull said, effectively closing the subject. Then he stood and turned to the council, looking at every face in turn, a great sadness shadowing his eyes.

"We have talked of the Nez Percé until the sun is nearly here again. It is a sad day for our brothers, but I do not think we can help them. We must think of our own people first."

His words were received with little surprise, only silent acceptance of a sad truth.

"We cannot risk our home here in the White Mother's Land or break our promise to Long Lance Walsh. Our brothers, the Nez Percé, will have to fight this battle themselves."

The lodge was silent as he sat back down and folded his hands. No one rose to argue against him; no one made further comment. Then, as if on cue and one by one, the chiefs rose and quietly filed out.

A vengeful wind dragged itself across the hills and coulees, softly moaning its misery. With icy fingers, it lifted Dancing Bird's hair and ran those cold fingers down the warm skin of her neck.

In response, she pulled the thick buffalo robe tighter around her and smiled into the fur. No matter that the grass was brown and crushed. One day it would again be green and lush. No matter that the sun was weak and cold. One day it would again be hot and bright. Winter had come, and she would spend it growing a child.

She pulled her attention away from the rolling hills beyond her and concentrated on her stomach, hoping to feel a stir. He was in there, this tiny flicker of life. She felt sure of it. She'd missed her flow last month and now this one, and the mornings brought a queasiness that unsettled her stomach sometimes to the point of losing her breakfast.

She'd tried to hide her symptoms from Braden, wanting to be sure before she told him. But he'd often accompany her to the high grass beyond the tipi, rubbing her back and offering her water without a word. She was sure he already suspected, but he said nothing, allowing her the pleasure of telling him. And she loved him all the more for his consideration.

She shaded her eyes with a hand to her forehead. If she'd figured the days correctly, Braden should be riding home in this direction, and she'd ridden out to meet him. They would ride the few miles to the village together, and maybe she'd decide to tell him his son slumbered within her.

Movement on the horizon caught her attention. Mounted figures rode in a straight line down a slope and disappeared one by one into a dense coulee. Dancing Bird quickly assessed the unfamiliar territory. Numerous coulees slashed across the landscape, furrowing the ground into dip and height, providing ample cover for a party of mounted men. Frantically, she glanced around for cover and found she was completely exposed from all directions. She yanked up her reins and turned toward home, kicking Wind into a gallop, cursing her carelessness.

She'd only gone a short distance when pounding hooves drew up beside her. A blue-clad arm reached out and caught the rope of Wind's halter and drew them both to a stop.

The Long Knife watched her with calm, gray eyes. Under other circumstances she'd have called him handsome.

"And who might you be, Miss?" he asked. "Is she Nez Percé," he threw over his shoulder to the men just riding up behind him.

"Naw," said a soldier as he spit a stream of brown onto the ground. "She's one of Sittin' Bull's. They's about twenty miles north of here, up by Pinto Buttes."

"Why are you so far away from home?" he asked as he held her with those cold, clear eyes.

She couldn't tell him she had hoped to intercept Braden on his way home from patrol, of at least scaring up some game to surprise him with for supper. "I was hunting," she said finally.

"She ain't huntin'. The Sioux don't let their squaws

hunt. She's got somethin' to do with them Nez Percé, I'd bet this here pouch of tobaccy on it," said the man with the streak of brown juice running down his chin.

"I'm Colonel Gray with the United States cavalry. Are you bringing food to the Nez Percé? He reached over and gripped her arm. "Where is White Bird?"

The Nez Percé, surrounded only a few miles from where she sat. The gravity of her situation dawned, and she felt the color leave her face. "I know no White Bird. I am hunting game."

"Ain't no Sioux gonna let his squaw ride this fer from home. Besides, she speaks English too damn good."

Colonel Gray continued to watch her. "Then where is your gun?"

She'd brought no weapon, only her slingshot and a small handful of rocks for rabbits and birds. She reached for the pouch at her side and heard the metallic click of the gun. When she turned, the tobacco juice-streaked soldier was leveling a rifle at her.

"Sergeant Dolton, put down your gun," the colonel barked.

"Nits make lice," he said as he slowly lowered the weapon, a gleam in his dull eyes. "I'll bet she's making lice right now. She's got the look of one that's been popped and often."

"That's enough, Sergeant." Colonel Gray turned back to Dancing Bird. "We know White Bird and his band of escapees are headed here to Canada to join with Sitting Bull's people. From where I sit, Miss, it sure looks like you're waiting to lead them to safety."

Her mouth went dry and her stomach roiled. "Escapees?"

Gray frowned slightly. "A Nez Percé chief named

White Bird escaped with a large party of followers last night. We think Sitting Bull promised them refuge if they could get across the border."

As the first flush of fear dissipated, Dancing Bird narrowed her eyes. "And where is the border, Colonel?

For a second, Gray broke the steady gaze that held her and uncertainty passed through his eyes. "Back about five miles or so," he said.

She'd listened at the edge of the council lodge and eavesdropped on every other conversation she could in the last few days, and she'd gathered that the Nez Percé's only chance was to cross the magical Medicine Line into the White Mother's Land. If indeed there was a band of Nez Percé making their way toward her village, they were desperate and tired. The soldiers before her were just as desperate to intercept them.

"You are on the White Mother's Land now."

"Yes."

Warming to the game of wits, Dancing Bird shifted in her saddle. "Did your white chief not tell you you were not to come to our land?"

"There's no 'our' to this. This is not your land, nor is it mine. We are both trespassers here. My duty is to capture White Bird and return him by any means possible. Chief Joseph has already surrendered his weapons."

The colonel turned and crooked two fingers to a young soldier behind him. "And perhaps with you as our prisoner, we can lure Sitting Bull to us and have killed two birds with one stone." He smiled slyly. "So to speak."

Eighteen

On the valley floor below, sun-bleached tipis dotted the winding path of the White Mud Creek. From his perch atop a windswept butte, Braden surveyed the temporary kingdom and wondered if history would remember that the Sioux nation spent their last glorious days camped among the clustered willows. A brisk, cold wind tickled his lungs as he inhaled, and he wished for the warmth of home and Dancing Bird's arms.

Squinting against the overcast sky, he picked out his tipi, its cover still dark and painted with bright yellow suns. The scent of snow brought to him on another puff of breeze reminded him that the day was growing late and she would be waiting with supper and kisses.

As he turned Brandy around and rode down the incline, he measured one waiting delight against the other. After three days of eating pemmican, he couldn't decide which part of him he wanted to satisfy first.

Grim faces greeted him as he rode into the village. Eyes were quickly averted from his. His alarm began to grow. Down at the end of camp, he saw Walsh's horse, along with Steven's and the escort from Fort Walsh, all waiting in front of Sitting Bull's lodge. So

Walsh had not yet been successful in convincing Sitting Bull to meet with Terry's commission.

According to his mental calculations, the commissioner should be nearing Fort Walsh, with Commissioner McLeod in attendance. It would be an embarrassment for both Terry and McLeod if Sitting Bull held firm to his stubbornness.

Brandy stopped at her customary place in front of their lodge and nudged at the matted hay left from days before. Odd, Braden thought. Dancing Bird knew he'd be back today, and she usually had hay waiting for Brandy. He swung down, wincing as his feet hit the ground and his thigh muscles groaned in protest. No tantalizing smell wafted from the lodge. No Dancing Bird flung open the lodge flap and flew into his arms.

He dropped the reins to the ground and opened the tipi. The inside was dark and cold and smelled of old grease and dampness.

Perhaps she was at Walks Lightly's. Perhaps she'd lost count of the days and forgotten he was returning today. He walked the short distance to his sister-in-law's home and rapped on the lodgepole. Walks Lightly shoved open the tent flap and looked out, tear tracks staining her cheeks.

"What's happened?" Braden asked, fighting the rising panic.

"She rode away two days ago to meet you near the Medicine Line. She never came back."

Swallowing down the fear that threatened to disable his mind, Braden tried to think. "Has anyone been to look for her?"

Walks Lightly nodded numbly. "Standing Elk and several other men went yesterday. They found nothing."

He turned away and headed toward his own lodge. Surely there had to be some clue there. Maybe she had left him something, anything to tell him where she might be. Had she gone hunting, gone to someplace new? She wanted to give her mother a new tipi cover for her impending marriage to Big Dog. Perhaps she had gone after buffalo, despite his warnings to her. After all, when had Dancing Bird ever listened to anyone's advice except her own?

Walks Lightly's hand on his arm stopped him. When he turned, her eyes were large and sorrowful. "She wanted to tell you herself. . . ."

"Tell me what?"

Walks Lightly paused, seemingly searching for the words. "She carries a child."

Until that moment, Braden would never have imagined a man could feel so many emotions at the same time.

Joy. Love. Anger. Loss. Hope. They all vied for command of his heart and his mind. Instead, he pushed them all aside and opted for the one thing that had seen him through some of the most difficult days of his life—clear, logical reasoning.

Walks Lightly let him go, and he walked the short distance to home. Once inside the dark interior, he was shut in with his fears. Their sleeping robes lay folded neatly along the edge of the lodge. Fresh firewood lay beside the firepit, and the fire had been banked to preserve the precious coals that had long since burned out. Her essence was here, everywhere, swirling around him. Every parfleche, every bundled herb, every swirled pattern in the dirt floor made by her hands and a grass broom, all held her touch.

Possibilities poured through his mind . . . so many possibilities. She could be hurt or dead. Lost? Never.

Or captured?

The Terry commission? But its accompanying entourage supposedly had been left south of the border. Or perhaps the troops surrounding Joseph and the Nez Percé?

A cold wave of knowledge washed over him. The marauding cavalrymen. The Nez Percé only forty miles or so away. The perfect opportunity to lure the Sioux into vulnerability with more than their surrounded brethren. A ready-made excuse to cry foul, ride across the border and herd them all south. Then they'd report to Washington that the Sioux had come to the aid of Joseph and his followers, crossing the border and thereby placing themselves at the mercy of the US cavalry. Taking the opportunity like good soldiers, Howard's forces would take them all captive and effectively pull the thorn from the sides of both the United States and Canada.

He squatted and picked up her beading, neatly tucked inside a fold of leather. An uneven pattern of blue and red beads meandered across the chest of a buckskin shirt, the quality of workmanship sure to bring a scolding from Moving-Robe-Woman when she saw it. A surprise for him, no doubt.

He picked up the shirt and spread it across his bent knee, and another bit of work caught his eye. Soft white buckskin had been cut into a tiny garment. Eagle down adorned the neck, and he wondered when and what she had traded to get such a valued item. Quick, hot tears blurred his vision and a lump in his throat strangled his breathing. Was he again to have happiness yanked from beneath him? How many times was a man to have his heart pierced without dying?

He blinked back the tears, folded the sewing carefully, and replaced it in its leather cover exactly as she'd left it. When he brought her home, she'd never guess he knew her secret.

When he brought her home, he repeated to himself.

A commotion outside brought him to his feet. He stepped out of the lodge into a swirl of men and horses.

"Sitting Bull has agreed to speak to the commission," Walsh said at his elbow. "They're moving the whole village west toward the fort. Sitting Bull and his war chiefs will leave immediately, accompanied by myself, you, and the escort from Fort Walsh."

Braden turned toward his commander, and Walsh beamed his pleasure. But Walsh's smile quickly faded. "What is it, Constable?"

"Dancing Bird is gone."

"Gone? What do you mean gone?"

"Her sister says she rode toward the border three days ago, hoping to intercept me when I returned home from patrol."

Walsh glanced at the activity milling around them. Women folded tipi covers and uprooted lodgepoles, placing all carefully on waiting travois. Warriors, stripped to the waist and painted for war, led remudas of horses through the village. Amid the dust, a child cried for its mother and a pack of dogs fought over an unearthed bone.

He returned his gaze to Braden's face. "I can give you five days. Then I need you at Fort Walsh. You've been instrumental in winning the confidence of the

Sioux, and I need you there when the negotiations start."

"Yes, sir." Braden turned and saw Walks Lightly loading his and Dancing Bird's belongings on a waiting travois. He stepped forward to offer a hand, but Standing Elk moved into his path.

"We will move the lodge. When you return with her, her home will be as she left it, Standing Elk said, a hand on Braden's chest.

Seeing that he was outvoted, Braden nodded, robbed of his voice by the compassion from people he'd once been sent to watch and police, people who were now his closest relatives.

He gathered Brandy's reins, and she danced sideways as he swung into the saddle. Moving-Robe-Woman placed a hand on his thigh, and he looked down into her worried eyes. "She will follow the river," she said, in halting English "Her father taught her this way."

Braden nodded and heeled Brandy into a gallop for the edge of the village. Two lathered horses galloped past him, exhausted riders clinging to their necks.

"The blue soldiers come!" The cry went up and the methodical dismantling of the village flew into chaos. Sentries had sighted a large party of people moving toward the village. Men wrestled their weapons from loaded travois. Women made the tremolo of battle while they stripped down their homes and planted crying children onto the backs of fat ponies. And amid the confusion, Walsh stood, explaining to all who would listen that the blue soldiers would not dare come north of the border.

With a heavy heart, Braden reined around a plunging Brandy and returned to Walsh's side.

"You said they would not come to the White Mother's Land," Sitting Bull said, anger furrowing his forehead. "You said they would not come here." The old chief watched the confusion swirling around him, wincing from the frightened cries of the women and the wailing of the children.

"It is not the blue soldiers," Walsh reassured. "I will ride out and make sure," he offered.

Sitting Bull pondered a moment, then nodded.

Braden waited while Walsh caught his horse. Then they rode to the south, accompanied by two hundred Sioux warriors. They didn't ride far before they encountered the force that had caused the panic. Nez Percé war chief White Bird led an exhausted army of wounded men, women, and children staggering north.

Children with broken arms and legs clung to the backs of grievously wounded mothers steadily trudging north where they anticipated comfort and safety. One woman astride a limping mare bore a chest wound that drenched the front of her dress with dark blood, and yet she held in her arms a small boy whose broken bone protruded from his leg.

Warriors with gaping, oozing wounds barely stayed astride their battle-scarred horses. Without emotion or expression, they all streamed past Walsh and literally fell into the arms of the waiting Sioux warriors. Walsh's face paled as he watched the carnage parade past.

"How can men sleep who inflict such suffering?" he muttered beneath his breath.

His heart in his throat, Braden studied each face as it passed, hoping—and then not—to recognize Dancing Bird in the stream of humanity.

The Mounted Police escort dismounted and began to

drag wounded men and women off horses as human touch and compassion filled the gap between languages. Some of the Nez Percé spoke a little English, and those individuals encouraged the others to place themselves in the hands offering solace.

His scarlet coat made more so by the blood that streamed down it, Braden carried women and children to a coulee nearby that hosted a modest smattering of trees. The extra shirt in his saddlebags went for bandages, as did his only other set of underwear.

A child, barely seven or eight, whose chest was a mass of tortured flesh, clung to Braden's jacket, his tiny fingers worrying the bright, gold crown on his collar. Braden looked into the dark eyes that would likely soon be closed forever, unfastened the glittering emblem, and folded it into the boy's hand. He was rewarded with a small smile. Then he made the lad comfortable, packed the wound as best he could, and held the child until his inquisitive fingers stilled and the gold crown dropped into the dead grass.

Braden gently laid the boy in the grass and moved to take another broken body into his arms.

By nightfall, the bloody stream of wounded Nez Percé, Sioux, and police had limped back to the Sioux village, where fires and hot meals awaited. Staring their own feared fate in the eyes, the Sioux women had re-erected the lodges and offered comfort to those set upon by the blue soldiers. Only then could Braden turn his attention back to his missing wife.

He'd asked every person conscious enough to understand about Dancing Bird, using her name and description. Always, heads shook in the negative. He wearily gathered up Brandy's reins where he'd dropped them by the side of his lodge. A hand on his arm made him turn. A tiny woman stood at his elbow. A deep slash crossed her forehead, the white flash of bone showing beneath the brown ooze of a healing poultice applied there.

"Your woman, Dancing Bird?" she asked, raising her eyebrows.

The words barely penetrated his tired thoughts at first. Then her name sang through him. "Yes, she is my wife."

The little woman smiled and blinked bright brown eyes. "She is there with the blue soldiers. I saw. She ride black and white pony. I know words of black shirts. I hear them make talk. They hope Sioux will come, so they take." She clenched her fist until her knuckles whitened.

"Is she well?" Braden took her fragile shoulders in his hands.

The little woman nodded. "She well." And then she chuckled. "Your woman have sharp tongue."

" 'Tis me wife, all right. Where is she?"

"She with blue soldiers that hold Joseph. His daughter here. She tell." She pointed to a group of Nez Percé huddled around a large fire in the center of the village.

The little woman led him by the hand to a dark, sedate woman sitting alone, holding a buffalo robe around her shoulders. She raised her head when the woman spoke.

"She is one day past Medicine Line, at Bear Paw Mountain," she said in a calm voice. "Soon soldiers take my people to reservation. You find her. They will make no difference between Nez Percé and Sioux. All

'Injuns' to them." She spoke the nickname with sarcasm and hatred.

With a quick thank you, Braden hurried to Brandy's side and swung into the saddle. Without stopping to get supplies or change clothes, he rode south, accompanied only by the light of a cold, watchful moon.

The silhouette of Bear Paw Mountain loomed dark against a moon-brightened sky. The open prairie offered little cover, but Braden managed to slither along on his belly close enough to observe the sentries that guarded the pitiful cluster of people. From what he could make out by the light of dancing fires, those who had remained behind had wounds as bad as those who had escaped. Again pushing down his fear for Dancing Bird, Braden concentrated on crawling closer in the dew-dampened grass.

The guard surrounding Joseph and his people was heavy, every sentry watchful and alert . . . except for two. On the far side of the encampment, two men in cavalry blue sat on barrels and dealt a hand of cards. Braden inched in their direction.

"This shit they call tobaccy ain't good fer nothin' 'cept makin' a body puke," a voice said, soon after accompanied by the sound of a heartfelt spit. The closest man wiped his mouth on the back of his coat sleeve, then leaned over and spit again.

"You gonna deal them cards, Tom?" a second voice asked. Stiff paper slapped rhythmically on the barrel head. Both men picked up their hands and quietly studied them.

Braden wiggled closer, freezing when one of the men stood and looked out into the dark in his direction.

"This damn place gives me the creeps," the voice identified as 'Tom' commented. "It's too close to that bastard Sittin' Bull fer my likin'."

From his point on a slight rise of ground, Braden could survey the prisoners illuminated by the leaping fire they huddled around. There were so many. How would he ever find Dancing Bird . . . if she was here?

He glanced down at his blood-soaked sleeve. And especially in a bright scarlet jacket. He looked back at the prisoners. Which would work best? Walk in as a representative of Her Majesty's government or sneak in, take his wife, and sneak out? He was only one man, far from his forces, and on the wrong side of the border, where he had no authority at all. He opted for sneakiness.

Wriggling back from the edge of the knoll, he made his way back to Brandy. Deep in his saddlebags were the buckskin pants he'd used the last time he and Standing Elk butchered a buffalo. He'd pulled them out earlier today and considered using them as bandages, but they were too stiff with blood. Now they were perfect.

He stripped off his uniform jacket and pants and donned only the buckskin pants. Blood had already soaked through his coat and stained his shirtless chest. With a little dirt rubbed onto his face and arms and a little into his hair, now grown long and badly needing a cut, he might pass as a Nez Percé, as long as they didn't get too close a look at his red hair. With that thought, he rubbed in a little more dirt.

Retracing his path, he returned to his vantage point. The two sentries seemed engrossed in their game of cards. He scanned the crowd of captives, looking for a spot where he could get inside the circle. A lone woman sat with her back to the fire. Something about the way she held her head and folded her hands made Braden's heart leap into double time. She turned her profile toward him, a profile he'd last seen in the dim firelight of their home.

Dancing Bird.

Quickly he scanned the area around her. She sat barely within the circle of light, as if she were working her way to darkness and freedom. As he watched, she glanced over her shoulder to the two card players.

Immediately to her right was what appeared to be a stream. Grass choked a shadowy area, and the tinny tinkle of flowing water rose from the quiet evening, but the patch was barely long enough to conceal a man or a woman. Once disturbed, the grass was sure to wave and attract attention.

In the darkness behind him, Brandy whickered softly, calling to him as she often did in camp at night. The two men stopped and looked in his direction. Cursing his luck, he lay pressed to the ground. Dancing Bird looked up and into the darkness. In a few seconds, the card players had returned to their game, but Dancing Bird continued to stare in his direction.

She suddenly stood, dropped the buffalo robe, and walked a few feet toward the edge of the light. Hoisting her dress up above her hips, she squatted and began to urinate. Braden smiled to the dark. Indelicate but functional, he thought, watching her stare at the ground. She instantly had the attention of the two men. But what did she have in mind?

Finished, she rose and, keeping her dress raised,

moved another step or two toward the tall grass as if she had other business to attend to.

"Hey. Come back here," one of the men said. She stopped, stared innocently in his direction, and frowned.

"Come back here." Tom motioned with his hand.

She pointed to the grass and put a hand to her stomach.

"Let her be," the other man said, slapping a card on the table. "Deal me one card. We won't lose nothin' if'n she gets away. Where's she gonna go?"

Tom watched Dancing Bird for a few more seconds as she moved into the edge of the grass and squatted again. He laid his cards on the barrel and rose with a grin.

"Well, I'm gonna take me a peek anyways."

"C'mon and finish the game. Ain't no use a-stirrin' trouble where there ain't none."

Tom moved toward Dancing Bird, and Braden's heart hammered. The other man's attention was on his partner as he tried once more to convince the man to finish the game. He could take one of them, but he couldn't handle two.

Suddenly, Dancing Bird rose and bolted into the darkness.

"Hey!" Tom cried and started after her.

"Shut up, you damn fool," the other man hissed. "My ass is sorer than a dog's butt full of porcupine quills. You wanna have to ride all night lookin' fer one Injun squaw? Like I said, where's she gonna go? We'll find her come light. Ain't nobody gonna miss her."

Tom gazed out into the night for a few more seconds, then reluctantly returned to his seat.

Braden never heard her coming, only felt her arms as they slipped around him and rolled him to his back.

"How did you know I was here?" he whispered between her showers of kisses.

"I heard Brandy. I knew you were here, and I was afraid you would be hurt."

He enfolded her in his arms. "Ye took an awful chance, ye did." Then he rolled to his stomach to watch the camp again. "This was too easy."

"They let me go," she said quietly. "There are so many, Braden. So many sick and wounded. They have traveled many miles for many days. The soldiers are tired and so are the Nez Percé. I knew if I could get to the edge of the light, they would not follow." She paused and let the silence of the cold night punctuate her words. "I wish I could have brought some of the children with me."

Braden pulled her to her feet and lifted her onto Brandy's back. Then he leaped up behind her and rode north as quickly as he dared. When he judged they were out of earshot, he urged Brandy into a gallop, and they rode until he knew they were on Canadian soil. Then they spent the night inside a dugout area washed into a steep bank, sleeping an exhausted sleep in each other's arms.

By morning, the temperature had dropped, and Braden changed back into his uniform. Wrapping the blood stained buckskins around Dancing Bird's shoulders, Braden stuffed her behind him, blocking the wind from her as they rode.

They rode through the day, stopping only once to drink and eat some of pemmican. The sun was low in a cold, wintry sky when they sighted the first glimmer of campfires. A crowd surged forward to meet them as they rode into the village. Before they could reach Sitting Bull's lodge, Walks Lightly had dragged her sister off Brandy's back and had her firmly wrapped in her arms. Moving-Robe-Woman stood to the side, her heart in her eyes, but reserved in her public affections for her daughter.

"Long Lance Walsh and Sitting Bull have gone to Fort Walsh to meet the council," Standing Elk said as Braden swung down. "He asked that I tell you this when you came."

Braden squatted to stretch his legs, then straightened and raised his arms over his head. "General Terry's Commission will have to wait one more day."

"We moved your lodge," Walks Lightly was saying as Dancing Bird opened the tipi flap and stepped inside. "I put your things where they were before."

Dancing Bird glanced around. No one would know the village had just moved a day's ride west. Everything looked the same as the day she'd left, except the floor of the lodge was now thick with brown grass instead of bare dirt.

"You did not tell him?" She swung her gaze to Walks Lightly.

"No, I did not. That is for you to tell your husband."

Dancing Bird would have sworn she saw a hint of guilt pass through her sister's eyes, but Walks Lightly blinked, and her face took on an expression of serenity, probably enhanced by her own rounded belly.

Braden opened the tipi flap and darkened the interior with his shadow. Walks Lightly grinned at her sister and mouthed, 'Tell him,' before she backed toward the opening. Braden stepped inside and smiled at his sister-in-law as she ducked under his arm and disappeared into the orange glow of sunset.

A small fire burned softly in the firepit. A supper brought by Walks Lightly warmed in a paunch filled with steaming water. But food was on neither of their minds. Braden stepped toward her, shedding his jacket and dropping the stained garment to the floor.

"I will clean that," Dancing Bird offered and bent to retrieve the coat.

Braden grabbed her wrist, pulled her closer, and locked his arms at the small of her back. "Later," he said against her lips.

Nineteen

Braden caught the hem of her dress and stripped the heavy buckskin over her head. By the golden firelight, he allowed his gaze to travel over her beautiful body, lingering only briefly on the suspicious rounding of her belly. Whether in reality or born of his secret knowledge, she seemed to carry a glow with her, an invisible shield bestowed upon her to protect the tiny life within.

He buried his face in the soft skin of her neck and inhaled the scent of her he'd learned to love. Smoke and wind and horse all combined to create the perfume of Dancing Bird, an aroma so heady desire immediately uncoiled within him.

Laughing, Dancing Bird pushed him away. "You are an eager husband," she said, holding him from her by his shoulders. "Especially for one wearing so many clothes," she said in a sultry voice that ran up and down his spine with tiny galloping feet.

Her fingers slipped inside the waistband of his trousers and quickly manipulated the buttons open. Then she encouraged the buff-colored garment all the way to the floor, squatted down, and removed his boots with an occasional sassy look up at him.

When she stood again, he was at her mercy, a quivering pile of raging desire, clad only in a baggy set of winter underwear. With fingers trained by demons, she teased each tiny white button from its carefully embroidered hole, exposing more of him with each success. When he stood before her, as naked as she, only then did he know true intimidation.

She sauntered around him, her gaze hot upon his skin, but he was eager and willing to play along with her game. She passed out of his sight behind him, and he flinched as she touched him between his shoulder blades. One finger trailed down his spine and stopped at the small of his back. She laughed softly, but remained behind him out of sight, tormenting him with the absence of her touch.

Then her arms slid around him, encasing him in her embrace, pressing her bare skin against his back. The softness of her cheek fit into the hollow between his shoulders, and the swell of her breasts followed perfectly the curve of his spine. With only the occasional pop of an ember to disturb the silence, they stood skin to skin, and marveled at the everyday miracle that their bodies could mold in such perfect symmetry.

"I thought I had lost you," Braden murmured, revisited by the horror of believing she was gone.

She slid around him until she stood in front of him, still in his arms. "And I was afraid you would charge into the camp like a warrior and be killed."

"And so ye devised yer own escape and didn't need me a'tall."

"I knew you were there, watching. I'm not sure I would have had the courage if I had not known that."

"Sure ye would have. But go on lettin' me think I had a part in it."

He picked her up into his arms and kicked at a sleeping robe. Obligingly, the robe unrolled and Braden laid Dancing Bird down on the soft, brown fur. She watched with wide, dark eyes as he touched her skin, cupped her breasts, and smoothed his palm across the rise of her stomach, amazed that life could be there, silently slumbering beneath the smooth, velvety skin.

"He will learn your touch."

His hand stilled and he raised his face to look into hers, his eyes soft and unsurprised. "And what if 'tis a daughter?"

"Then she will worship you and follow at your heels." Dancing Bird frowned. "You knew, didn't you? How?"

"A man knows the body of the woman he loves," he said, sliding his hand lower. Her stomach muscles tensed in anticipation. He smiled slyly and smoothed his hand down her thigh, avoiding the area she most wished he'd touch.

"How did you know?" she asked again.

Braden smiled. "I found the shirt you are making me as a surprise and with it the baby's dress."

"Walks Lightly told you, didn't she?"

He leaned over her, brushing his skin against hers, and kissed her lightly. "She told me just before I left to find you. She thought I should know."

Dancing Bird reached for him, but he leaned just out of her reach and grinned. "Now who's eager?"

But when she reached for him a second time, smoothing her hand up the sensitive inside of his arm to the tender place above the elbow, his expression sobered.

Easily, she enticed him to lie down beside her on his stomach and give her access to his broad back. She straddled his hips and kneaded his knotted muscles, feeling the ridges and dips of his rib cage roll beneath her fingers.

His face buried in his arms, he made muffled noises of pleasure as she bunched and caressed the tightness from his body. Suddenly, he rolled over beneath her. When she tried to scramble away, he caught her hips in his hands and held her above him. Desire darkened his eyes to the amazing deep, stormy blue she loved, and her heart pounded, yearning for him and anticipating his next move.

His broad, gentle hands guided her body to his, but the boldness of his actions made her resist for an instant.

"Do ye think we'll hurt the babe?" he asked, sensing her reluctance. The want in his eyes mellowed into soft concern.

Slowly, she shook her head. She knew nothing about babies, but surely nature would protect this tiny bit of life, tuck it safely away from harm.

She leaned down and kissed him, restoring the storminess to his eyes and the tremble to his hands as he joined his body to hers in a sweet union.

"I want you to sit in the council."

Dancing Bird's hand paused halfway to her mouth, bits of tantalizing stew dangling from her fingers. "What, Uncle?"

Sitting Bull shoved his food around absently on the birch slab plate. "I want you to sit at my side in the council with the Americans."

Braden met his wife's amazed gaze across the family

fire, and Moving-Robe-Woman's face blanched. Walsh and Sitting Bull had decided on a small party to meet the Terry Commission at Fort Walsh—Sitting Bull, his war chiefs, and a few others whose opinion the old chief valued. To have a woman in council would be an offense to the visiting parties.

"Why?"

Her uncle's eyes searched her face, a tired smile riding the leathery ridges. "It is easier to kill an enemy when you cannot see his eyes, when he is only an enemy and not a man."

Dancing Bird slowly put down her plate and narrowed her eyes. "You want to insult them and use me to do it."

A collective gasp went around the firepit as Dancing Bird and her uncle locked gazes.

"The white man does not see us as people, only as enemies to be conquered. They put on their blue coats and their long knives to ride over our villages and chase away our horses. I want them to know we are just like them, with wives and families."

"I will sit by your side if I can speak to the council," Dancing Bird said. "Would they be impressed by a woman who says nothing for her people?"

Sitting Bull's mouth tipped up in a small smile and a twinkle of humor grew in his eyes. "And what would you say, little one?"

What would she say when faced with the people who murdered her father, who contributed to the death of her brother? What would she tell the men who drove them from their home and forced them to seek peace and shelter on the other side of a line in the dirt, a line known and respected only by the white men? What knowledge could she bring to the meeting that the powerful war chiefs could not?

A soft fluttering teased her insides, making her catch her breath and put a hand to her abdomen. She met Braden's eyes across the lodge. The men could talk of glory and honor and pride all they wanted. Only she could tell them about conceiving and carrying life, about haunting worries that teased away sleep on dark, silent nights. Only she could impress on them the women's concerns with keeping their men alive long enough to get them with child so that their people might multiply and prosper.

She glanced away from Braden's face and back to her uncle's. "I will tell them about the children and how it feels to see them hungry and frightened. I will tell them of the women who lost husbands and children they loved and how it feels to slash our wrists in mourning."

Sitting Bull glanced at Braden, who raised his eyebrows and shrugged his shoulders. Returning his gaze to Dancing Bird, her uncle smiled softly. "Then you shall speak."

Red and white pennons fluttered against a brilliant blue October sky. Headdresses, almost never worn, waved in a cold breeze, and Dancing Bird looked with pride upon her people. Arrayed as she remembered from childhood, with eagle feathers and bright war paint, they rode their ponies with war lances upright. Fort Walsh spread out in the valley before them, its whitewashed log stockade gleaming in the morning sun.

She craned her neck to catch a glimpse of Braden riding ahead of them, a member of Walsh's escort. His horse's tack gleaming and his scarlet uniform resplendent, the sight of him made her heart swell with pride. As she watched his broad back and how easily he adjusted to Brandy's gait, she suddenly wanted him with an intensity that blurred her thoughts. She was ever amazed at how much pleasure his body could give hers, and how he could then don the scarlet uniform and stand with his commander as a single line of defense for her people.

Commissioner McLeod's escort had joined theirs a few days ago and swelled their numbers to a small parade. A tall, dark man, James McLeod watched life with few words and unparalleled common sense. Dancing Bird immediately liked him and knew why his reputation for fairness and slow anger had quickly spread among the Blackfeet.

The column abruptly halted. Up ahead, her uncle was in serious conversation with Walsh, Braden, and McLeod. He shook his head, setting the feathers on his headdress to waving. Dancing Bird glanced at the fort, where the wide front gate had swung open and a river of people had poured out, scarlet coats dotting their numbers.

Again her uncle shook his head and turned his pony away from the fort. What had happened that he had changed his mind about this meeting? Her heart pounding, Dancing Bird followed the column as it swung right, glancing around her, expecting blue soldiers to come sweeping down upon them.

Braden circled back and slid into place beside her. She looked up at him and saw no fear in his eyes. "Your uncle refuses to go into the fort. He said he'd never been inside a white man's fort and he wasn't going to start now."

Dancing Bird laughed with relief and felt some of the tension drain from her shoulders.

They established camp a short distance from the fort, setting Sitting Bull's huge lodge apart from the others, a solitary reminder of the responsibility he now bore. Moving-Robe-Woman had accompanied them, and she and Dancing Bird put up their lodge. Braden had withdrawn to the fort, where he would spend the night with the troop. The loneliness of their secret union settled into his place in their sleeping robes and curled around her like evening fog as she lay down to sleep. But sleep was elusive, chased away by threads of doubts that wound themselves through her mind.

Before, alone in their cocoon of happiness, far away from the white man's world, their marriage seemed real and binding. But here, exposed to the strangeness of the white man's world, their differences became glaring realities, and small doubts crept in to torment her.

Would he acknowledge her as his wife? Would she stand by his side here among his people, or would she be relegated to the shadows of this meeting, a guilty secret that would endanger the fragile peace?

She flipped over on her side, and the baby stirred in protest. Tiny flutterings feathered against her insides, reminding her she was no longer alone and every decision was made for two. He was part of her and part of Braden, part Sioux and part Irish. Braden would never leave them, never desert the family now begun. Hugging that faith close to her, Dancing Bird concentrated on the tiny stirrings within her and remembered with a smile the numerous possibilities for her tiny companion's conception.

Voices echoed in the officer's mess hall and a cold wind swept down to nip at exposed ears and fingertips. Dancing Bird glanced at her uncle as he stood nervously outside the low, long building, waiting for Walsh's signal to enter. They were within the solid, whitewashed stockade Sitting Bull vowed he'd never enter.

Sitting Bull's long raven braids lay over his shoulders, and he wore a wolf-skin cap. Large white dots cavorted across his black shirt, bought from a trader. A blanket was draped around his middle. His leggings peeped from underneath, the soft buckskin spilling onto his new, richly beaded moccasins.

Walsh opened the door a crack and raised a red-sleeved hand. Sitting Bull leaned close to Dancing Bird. "Do not speak until I tell you."

She frowned up at him, a slight anger growing in her.

"Please?" he said with a smile.

She'd no doubt he had some plan, some carefully orchestrated purpose for her words. "Yes, Uncle."

Two small tables faced the doorway of the crowded room. The members of the commission were easily recognizable by their bright blue uniforms. Two men wearing brown sat at the end of the table, heads dipped, quickly scribbling on pads of paper.

McLeod and Walsh sat at the second table, the Mounted Police officers standing behind them, hands folded, the feathered plumes of their helmets moving in the slight breeze. As she stepped into the room, Dancing

Bird glanced at Braden and he acknowledged her with a slow wink.

She sat down on spread robes between her uncle and Spotted Eagle. Every eye swung toward Spotted Eagle as he tilted his chiseled chin forward and expanded his naked chest. A belt of rifle cartridges jingled across one shoulder, and a single eagle's father knotted his hair back. From his waist down, he wore a silky, splendid buffalo robe wrapped about him. Aware of the attention now fixed upon him, he fingered his war weapon—a stout staff several feet long ending in three long knife blades projected at right angles to the shaft. With a smile lurking in his eyes, he looked down at Dancing Bird and winked at her, too.

A pair of interpreters positioned themselves strategically between the commission and the Sioux.

"I wish the tables be moved," Sitting Bull said in Sioux, and the translator pivoted and relayed the information to General Terry. He nodded, and the furniture was rearranged with much scraping and shuffling until General Terry and Sitting Bull sat directly across the room from each other.

General Terry arose from his chair, combing his fingers through his long, pointed beard. He was well over six feet tall and imposing, and yet as he began to address his interpreter, he did so in a soft, genteel voice.

"We are sent to you as a commission by the president of the United States at the request of the government of the Dominion of Canada to meet you here today. The president has instructed us to say to you that he desires to make a lasting peace with you and your people. He desires that all hostilities should cease and that all shall live together in harmony."

Sitting Bull listened, his face unreadable. Terry went on to outline the conditions of surrender. The Sioux would be granted pardons for all unlawful acts. They were the only band of Indians who had not surrendered. Of the bands that had given up their freedom, none had been punished or harmed. They would be granted the same consideration. Food and clothing would be supplied in return for the surrender of their horses and arms. Cattle would be given to them to raise and butcher for food. Under no conditions would they be allowed to keep any weapons or ammunition.

As Terry spoke, it was evident that he absolutely believed the words he uttered. His faith in the president's sincerity was complete and unwavering. Sitting Bull listened unperturbed, exhibiting an occasional sneer—whether in sarcasm or disbelief, Dancing Bird could not determine.

During Terry's discourse, Spotted Eagle turned and winked at the line of Mounted Police officers at several points, causing titters of laughter among the Sioux.

When Terry finished, Sitting Bull rose, threw off his blanket, and stepped into the open space between the Sioux and the commission. With a sweeping motion of his arm, he encompassed the entire room and claimed everyone's attention.

"For sixty-four years you have persecuted my people," he said to Terry through the interpreter. "I was forced to leave our country, and I took refuge here. I learned to shoot and ride as a young man on this side of the border, and for that reason I have come back. I was raised close to and today shake hands with these people."

He crossed the room and shook hands with first

McLeod and then Walsh. Whirling back toward the commission, he continued his dramatic address. "We did not give you our land; you took it from us. You see how I stand with these people? This is how I shall live with them."

He approached Terry, and the general looked up at him, his face calm and without rancor.

"You think I am a fool, but you are a greater fool than I am. This house is a medicine house, and you have come to tell us lies. We do not want to hear them. Now go back and say no more. Take your lies with you. I will stay with these people."

Several of the war chiefs rose and spoke in kind. They, too, refused the commission's offer, refused the kind and conciliatory words Terry offered, and belittled the Americans' magnanimous offers of a peaceful return home.

When each chief had spoken in turn, Sitting Bull rose again. He stopped in front of Dancing Bird and held out his hand to her. Hesitantly, she placed her fingers in his and stood, throwing Braden a quick glance.

Braden, standing with his arms crossed over his chest, pushed away from the wall and let his hands drift down to his sides.

Terry and the members of the commission leaned their heads together. Their interpreter came to lean over the table and confer with them. When finally they leaned back, Dancing Bird stepped into the center of the floor.

She was facing the man who had directly caused the death of so many of the people she loved. By his hand, their entire tribe had fled across a thousand miles, strewing property and dead in their wake. Now, looking into his eyes, her only weapon with which to stab him as her words, and she must choose them carefully.

Terry steepled his fingers and rested his folded hands against his mouth. "What does she wish to say?" he asked the interpreter.

"I speak the white man's words," she said to him, and he quirked an eyebrow.

"All right. What do you wish to say?" he repeated softly.

He didn't appear the black-hearted villain she'd imagined him, so she shifted her approach. Instead of scathing words meant to shock him, she searched for words to make him understand.

"I wish to make you understand that the Sioux are more than the men you face in battle. We are warriors, yes, but we are women and children and the old. Many, many died on our way here."

"A war fought on homelands always results in the death of innocents."

"We do not make war on your women and children."

Terry shifted in his chair and cast a glance down the table to his companions.

"You have left them safe at home and bring your soldiers into our lands to burn and destroy our homes. You drive us out as you would drive out a nest of snakes."

Again, Terry shifted and raised his eyebrows. "What is your name?"

"Dancing Bird."

"And I have been told you are Sitting Bull's niece."

"Yes—"

"And my wife."

Braden stepped forward from the line of Mounted Police and moved to Dancing Bird's side. "She is my wife."

James McLeod batted not an eye, but Walsh looked at his feet and shook his head.

"This woman is your squaw?" Terry asked, shock and disdain in his voice.

"No, sir. She is my wife."

"You were married under British law?"

"No sir. I was denied permission to marry her under British law by our government in Ottawa. Therefore, we were married under Sioux law."

"So she *is* your squaw."

At that moment, Dancing Bird realized that the council was futile. Terry and his officers did not and would not understand the Sioux and would make no effort to understand them. He regarded them as less than people, their customs and laws less than binding and honorable. And he now lumped Braden in that number. In his estimation, no white man could truly love a Sioux woman, so she must be a whore and he a fool. Anger heated her cheeks.

"Is there anything else you would like to say?" Terry asked, looking straight at Dancing Bird.

"I speak for the Sioux women who are not here. Their arms are empty tonight because you and your men will not give them time to breed."

The interpreter's eyes widened and his neck turned red. When he related the information, a titter of comment went around the room. The men of the commission looked first embarrassed, then amused at her bold comments.

Terry shifted his gaze to Sitting Bull, now standing beside the couple. "Do you refuse my offer?"

"I told you what I meant. That should be enough," Sitting Bull snapped.

"I think we can have nothing more to say, Colonel," Terry said to McLeod.

The war chiefs rose and followed Sitting Bull as he stalked past the Americans and embraced the offered handshakes of the Mounted Police. As many times before, he expressed his affection and trust for McLeod and Walsh. Then the Sioux leaders quietly filed out of the mess hall and into the soft September afternoon.

"Taste it. It's apple pie," Braden whispered, his breath swirling the fine hairs above her ear.

Dancing Bird glanced around the table of red-suited men, who were laughing and talking, completely ignoring the two of them. The members of the commission had beaten a hasty retreat back across the border with McLeod and his men escorting them. The men of Fort Walsh had insisted the Sioux eat the evening meal with them and had carted out their cache of delicacies for the occasion.

Dancing Bird stuck out her tongue and touched it to the fork full Braden held in front of her face.

"Hmmm. It's good," she said, then snapped the rest of it off Braden's fork.

Another voice chuckled behind her. She swiveled around as Walsh sat in the empty chair at her side. His elbows resting on his knees, Walsh looked tired and in need of a good night's sleep. "General Terry will remember this meeting for a long time. You two created quite a stir."

"I spoke the truth," Dancing Bird said. "And so did my husband."

Walsh looked up over her head, meeting Braden's eyes, she imagined. "Yes, you did. And you did well. Terry needed to hear the truth, and that's what he got."

"What do ye think'll happen now?" Braden asked from behind her, his hands playing with the top of her shoulder.

Walsh shook his head. "I don't know. But let's think no more of General Terry and his men. Tonight we are celebrating." The joy in his voice was undermined by the sadness that flickered briefly through his eyes. He took Dancing Bird's hands and encased them in his. "I would like you to know that I, and these men around you, understand and accept that you are Braden's wife. General Terry's remarks came from ignorance and not malice toward you. And despite that ignorance, I believe he is an honorable man. The Long Knives will make no more trips across the Medicine Line, I feel sure."

Dancing Bird smiled at him. "Thank you. You are always welcome in our tipi."

Walsh patted her hands. "We will live the days as they come and enjoy what each sunrise brings."

"You sound like my uncle."

"We are two old warhorses, he and I. He, too, understands that life is to be lived in minutes, not days." He slid back his chair. "If you will excuse me," he said, nodding, and then disappeared to the other end of the room, where a group of Mounties and Sioux war chiefs were gathered.

"Let's go," Braden said, and scraped back his chair.

Dancing Bird rose and followed him out into the crisp, still night. They walked through the gates of the fort and out onto the flat plain that surrounded the stockade. In a velvety black sky, stars winked and flirted with pitiful earthbound beings.

Braden's arm tightened on her shoulders as he pulled her snugly against his hip. What will we name the baby? he asked.

Dancing Bird stopped and looked up at him. "Someone will have a dream or a vision and know his name."

"Oh."

"How do your people name a baby?"

"The mother and father decide. They usually name the babe after someone they hold dear."

"Oh."

They moved forward again, their steps taking them toward the Sioux encampment. Suddenly Braden pulled her to a stop and dropped to his knees in front of her. He put his arms around her hips and pressed his ear to her stomach.

"Someone will see," she hissed, glancing wildly about them.

"Let 'em," he said. "I'm listening to my son."

Dancing Bird pulled off his helmet and ran her hands through his hair, reveling in the way the waves tickled her fingers. "You're a silly man."

His hands, clasped behind her waist, slipped lower and cupped the flesh of her backside, pulling her against him.

"Am I still a silly man?" he whispered against her stomach, his breath warm even through the leather.

"Hmmm," she acknowledged. "I think I must take you home before you embarrass yourself."

He stood, purposely sliding his body up the length

of hers, heating her with the friction between them. "Or perhaps I will make love to you here, beneath the stars."

He took her in his arms, and she leaned back to see his face. "Promise me you will never leave us."

The teasing left his face and his eyes darkened. "I will never leave you."

"Even if my people go?"

"Then I will go with you."

"And if I want to stay?"

"Then we will stay and make a home here."

She smiled and again ran her hands through his red curls. "Take me home husband, before *I* embarrass *you.*"

Epilogue

As Inspector James Walsh and Sitting Bull feared, the once plentiful buffalo began to dwindle in numbers in 1878 after a mild winter and numerous prairie fires. With the shrinking source of food came more mouths to feed.

On September 5, 1877, Crazy Horse was killed in a guardhouse scuffle. Bearing his remains with them, two thousand Northern Sioux simply walked away from their reservation and streamed toward Canada and James Walsh's unerring compassion and logic.

By the spring of 1878, the Sioux numbered nearly six thousand on British soil, and they began to straddle the "Medicine Line," often venturing into US territory to hunt buffalo wherever they could find them.

With the formality of the Terry Commission out of the way, the United States began to press their true stand on the Sioux—convince Canada to accept them as citizens. But Canada—and Walsh—held fast to their promises. By spring of 1879, Washington officials were beginning to consider a plan by Nelson A. Miles to "advance north to the British line, drive back Sitting Bull and Co. And if necessary follow them across the border."

In January of 1879, Sitting Bull, along with Nez

ABOUT THE AUTHOR

Kathryn Fox started writing when she found herself devising alternate plot lines for *Cinderella* and *Sleeping Beauty* videos while at home with three toddlers.

She holds a bachelor's degree in Horticultural Science and has worked as a research technician, secretary, and wedding dress seamstress. When she's not writing, she works as the Nematode Assay Laboratory Supervisor for the North Carolina Department of Agriculture and Consumer Services.

She lives in eastern North Carolina with her husband of twenty-three years, three sons, one cat, three dogs, one cockatiel, one hamster and a house rabbit. You can contact her by e-mail: Ribbons@aol.com.

Look for the final novel
in this series
THE THIRD DAUGHTER
a December, 2001 Ballad romance.

When Northwest Mounted Policeman Steven Gravel stumbles across a thriving cattle ranch in thinly settled Alberta Territory, he thinks he has solved a major problem: a supply of beef for newly established Fort McLeod. But what he finds is trouble times three in the form of the Dawson sisters. Emily wants a husband. Thirteen-year-old Libby wants someone on which to practice her budding feminine wiles. Willow wants an independent life, her own ranch, and Steven Gravel gone. But beneath Willow's rejection of Steven's affections lies a dark secret that has gripped her with such fear of intimacy that she is willing to turn Steven away rather than facing it. And, so to Steven falls the task of softening Willow's heart and teaching her how to love.

his people as intimately as I was able to do. John Peter Turner's work, *The Northwest Mounted Police: 1873-1893*, provided day-by-day accounts of our knights in scarlet, complete with journal entries from Commissioner James McLeod and Major James Walsh disclosing their private thoughts on the Sitting Bull situation.

While Braden is the hero of this work, Major Walsh was a real-life hero, then and now. Throughout the turmoil that revolved around the Sioux exodus from the United States and ensuing four years of exile in Canada, he kept his compassion, common sense, and humanity in tact. He became Sitting Bull's friend and protector, admittedly by the chief the only white man he ever had or ever would trust.

AUTHOR'S NOTES

Fate sometimes smiles on the historical author and places an actual historical event directly in the path of her characters. Such was the case with *The Second Vow.*

So here I confess to "messing" with history a bit. While the meeting of the Terry Commission took place as portrayed, the woman who testified was the wife of a Sioux named The-Bear-That-Scatters. Her comments were not nearly so cloaked as Dancing Bird's. Embarrassed at being the center of attention, she murmured softly to General Terry that he and his troops would not give her time to breed and then sat down. I just couldn't resist expounding on her statements and herewith beg the forgiveness of any who might be offended by my tampering.

Sitting Bull learned some English, but not to the extent portrayed in this book. I granted him command of the English tongue to make his relationship with Braden more intimate, instead of constantly having to include a translator in their scenes together, and to allow you, the reader, to hear his words from his own lips.

My undying gratitude goes out to Robert M. Utley for his wonderful book, *The Lance and the Shield,* without which I could not have portrayed Sitting Bull and

Percé Chief White Bird, sought to enlist the aid of the United States Crows in rebuffing the increasing US presence at the border. The overture was soundly rejected and prompted a Crow raid on Sitting Bull's village that cost the Sioux a hundred head of irreplaceable horses. Humiliated to fury, Sitting Bull invited all warriors to come to his lodge to plot a war of revenge. Word reached James Walsh, who rode through deep snows to intercede in this crisis.

Sitting Bull and his chiefs surrendered to Major David H. Brotherton, commander of Fort Buford, on July 20, 1881, at 11:00 in the morning. Hunger had again returned to the Sioux remaining in Canada. Many had given up and surrendered to United States forces. Large numbers of buffalo never again returned to the Canadian hunting grounds after that last summer of plenty in 1877.